D1564423

Robber's Roost

GUYANNE BOOTH

BROWN BOOKS PUBLISHING
DALLAS, TEXAS

Robber's Roost

Manufactured in the United States of America

For information, please contact:
Brown Books Publishing Group
16200 North Dallas Parkway, Suite 170
Dallas, Texas 75248
www.brownbooks.com
972-381-0009
A New Era in Publishing™

ISBN-13: 978-1-934812-02-0
ISBN-10: 1-934812-02-1
LCCN: 2008921132
1 2 3 4 5 6 7 8 9 10

Dedication

Dedicated to my late husband, Clint Booth, with gratitude for his patient attention and his continuing faith in the outcome of this story and to our grandchildren, Lisa Turner Anastasi and her husband Tim Anastasi, Beau and Clint Justice, and Duke Norris.

"In the prison of his days teach the free man how to praise."

WYSTAN HUGH AUDEN

Acknowledgments

I acknowledge first and foremost my daughter, Katharine Booth Goodson, whose screenplay, *Robber's Roost*, inspired me to write a more detailed account of her fabulous and witty characters. I thank her for giving me poetic license in the enhancement of her people. I also acknowledge my eldest daughter, Elisabeth Booth Turner, for being my first fan and editor. For critiquing and encouragement, I am most grateful to Dr. Thomas Howard, with whom I studied creative writing during five summers at Laity Lodge in Leaky, Texas. All my love and appreciation to all my supportive listeners over the years; Carol, Jane, and Jim, Carolyn in South Texas, my sister Emmy in Burnet, Texas, Carol, and Frances in Colorado, Claudia and St. Andrews in Little Rock, Arkansas, the five Birthday girls, the Inclings, Ben and Sybil, Jane and Gary; to Sharon, my personal editor and business manager; for the hospitable people and quiet environs at the Stagecoach Inn and Fletchers Bookstore in Salado, Texas, Jim and Janet Morris and their house in Durango, Colorado, Cynthia England and the Austin Street Retreat in Fredericksburg, Texas; and to all those who kept me sane during this adventure; my Vicar and spiritual director, Fr. Rick

Philputt and his wife, Nancy; Donna, Lorraine, Frances, Cedric, Adrian, Bill, Kendra, Linda, Pat, Artis, Nadine, Philippa, and Leah; and to Pringle Patrick for her architectural sketches. I thank my youngest daughter, Caroline Booth Norris, for her final edits, and my sons-in-law, Don Turner, David Goodson, and Matthew Norris, for their support in financial and business decisions and the time they allowed their wives to spend holding my hand and keeping me on task. Lastly, I am so very grateful to Brown Books, my publishers, for showing me what to do with all this marvelous mess.

The Family Tree

Descendants of Zita

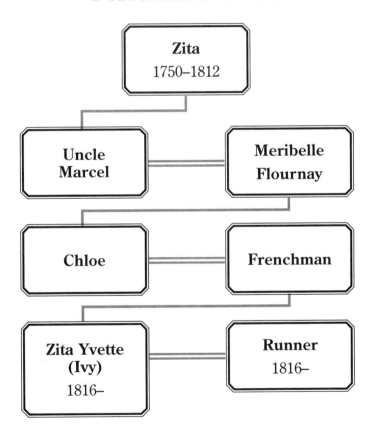

Zita
1750–1812

Uncle Marcel

Meribelle Flournay

Chloe

Frenchman

Zita Yvette (Ivy)
1816–

Runner
1816–

Blakemore Slaves

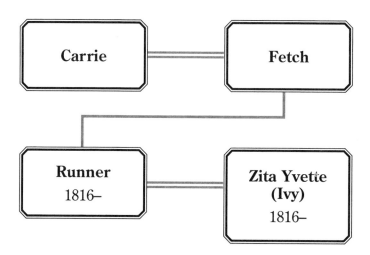

Descendants of William Blakemore

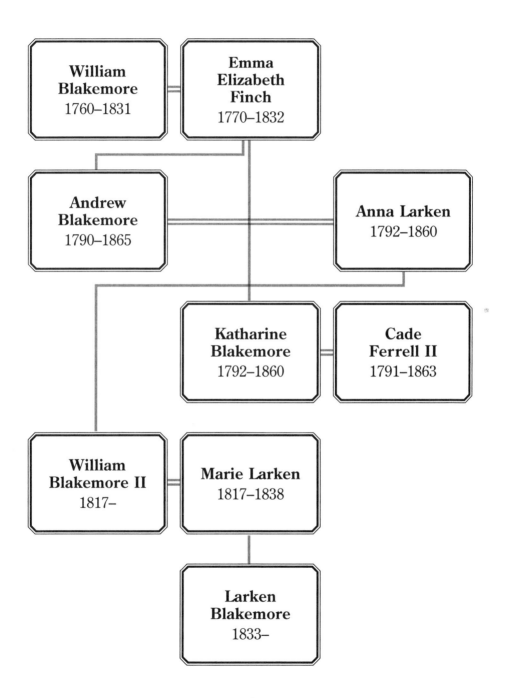

Descendants of Francis Ferrell

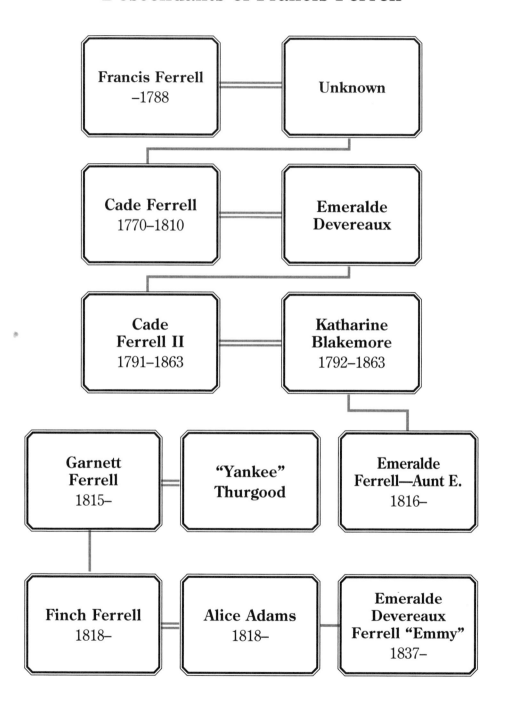

Chapter One

Canst thou draw out Leviathan with a hook . . . which thou lettest down? His teeth are terrible . . . His scales are his pride . . . Out of his nostrils goeth smoke . . . His breath kindleth coals, and a flame goeth out of his mouth . . . His heart is as firm as a stone; yea, as hard as a piece of . . . millstone.

THE BOOK OF JOB

Larken Blakemore's fingers itched as he watched the woman's heaving bosom rise and fall on either side of a large cabochon ruby pendant that nestled in her cleavage. Suddenly, in the midst of her prattle, she clutched at the mountainous flesh and the ruby disappeared.

"I miss him, Larken. Sometimes I feel my heart breaking." Larken pulled her into his strong chest. As he peered down, searching for the ruby, he whispered into her ear. "I have mystical powers; I believe in the laying-on of hands."

Wide-eyed, she stiffened, losing her breath. "I heard that about you!"

Larken looked past his latest flirtation through the blue-smoked haze of the casino, toward the craps table where his cousin Emmy held fast. Larken's focus on acquiring the woman's ruby and her inheritance was interrupted momentarily.

His beloved cousin was named Emeralde Devereaux Ferrell to compliment a long line of headstrong women, but Larken, at the age of five had christened her his own Emmy. Larken's grandfather and Emmy's grandmother had been brother and sister. *I wonder if our grandparents fought and loved as much as we two.* Larken mused to himself as he watched the fire in Emmy's eyes rise.

As usual, Emmy was in charge. Her victim this time was a plump and lustful old geezer. He was a frequent patron of the casino with plenty of money and little gambling sense. Like most men he was totally captivated by Emmy. Larken was distracted by Emmy's excessively seductive behavior, and he wavered between disgust and fascination. He glanced beside him at the cabochon ruby pendant, but then looked up and caught Emmy's eye. He always did. It was quick and unnoticed, like a liaison between lovers or a signal between thieves.

Quickly returning his attention to the woman, Larken patted her hand, soothing her. "Stop worrying about all that money your Daddy left you. You just let ole Larken take care of it for you. I am going into the bar, darlin', and I'll be right back with a little toddy to ease your grief."

Larken crossed the room for a closer look at Emmy in action. He thought, *We're a pair, Cousin, inseparable and unmanageable.*

Emmy's sugar daddy held out the dice to her and wheezed in a lewd tone, "I'm about to come out, Honey. What'll it be?"

With eyes held fast to Larken's, Emmy slithered her shapely arms around sugar daddy's neck, nibbled his ear, and breathlessly panted, "Seven."

Larken's heart beat wildly as his eyes coolly held Emmy's stare. Under full auburn lashes her green eyes blinked once, then twice, to break the spell. Now, her sugar daddy was totally enamored, his bald head gleaming with the sweat of anticipation. "If I roll a seven, I'll give you half my winnings."

Emmy, her mouth seductively close to his ear, murmured, "Then, sir, you best double your bet."

Larken leaned against a marble column, lighting a cigar. *Just how far will you go, Cousin? Holy heaven, she's beautiful and hateful. I guess I better check on Aunt E., Runner, and Ivy. We are truly a merry band.* Larken looked back to where he had left the woman and swore to himself when he saw she and the large cabochon ruby pendant were no longer waiting there for him. *And I was about to make a real kill.* Aloud he cursed, "Damn you, Emmy."

Emmy stood by her victim fluffing her skirts, smoothing her shimmering green gown, and mopping her dampened auburn curls. She dried off the perspiration from her victim's bald head with her lace handkerchief. Then, cool as a breeze, she seized the dice from his hand, popped them into her mouth, then sweetly smiled and lifted his fingers to her lips to retake them. He doubled the bet and rolled the dice, then wheezed and clasped his heart. The crowd that had gathered shouted, "Seven!"

The sugar daddy counted his winnings. He took hold of Emmy with one hand, extending her half of the money with the other. She took his money and slipped from his weakened hold on her. Emmy winked and, tossing her red curls, announced over her shoulder, "I'll be back to wet your dice right soon."

The crowd gasped and applauded. He whispered hoarsely and pled, "But Honey . . ."

Larken was disgusted by his fascination with this high drama and rather piqued with Emmy for the whole episode. He hoped he might still have his way with the woman and went looking for the cabochon ruby pendant.

Emmy slipped quickly out of the casino in the main drawing room of the house and down the long, wide hall. When she reached the door to the library, she paused for a moment to stash the recently earned winnings into the bodice of her gown and then very slowly and quietly turned the brass lion's head knob to open the massive oak door. She did not want to disturb the card game in progress within. She wanted to check on her Aunt E.

Aunt E., never having had children, embraced Emmy and Larken as her own. They reciprocated with clear adoration. Aunt E., like her niece, Emmy, had been named for the matriarch, Emeralde Devereaux, but was dubbed "Aunt E." by Larken, her much younger second cousin, as soon as he could talk. After the early death of Larken's mother, Marie, Aunt E. welcomed the baby Larken and his distraught, grieving father, Billy, into her home in New Orleans.

When the threat of war loomed, Emmy's parents, Alice and Finch, sent her to New Orleans. Emmy relished her bond with Aunt E. They shared more than a name.

Emmy's namesake, an elegant lady, sat poised at the table and straight in the elaborately carved high-back chair, one of the few remaining family pieces of fine furniture left in the old house now turned casino. Emeralde Ferrell's taffeta gown of peach and ecru fell in ruffles from her lovely slender throat. One stocking foot was revealed, extended, its silk slipper turned aside as her tiny aristocratic foot caressed the ankle of the gentleman to her left. Two other women were also seated at the table; one was E.'s partner and the other woman, the man's wife, sat to her right. All were deep in concentration.

This was Emmy's favorite room in the house on Rue de Toulouse. The old New Orleans home had been handed down through three generations to Aunt E., who had sold it to its present owner.

The first owner in the family, Francis Ferrell, was a mysterious man whose past was unknown to anyone in New Orleans. The rumor persisted for many years, though the fact was never substantiated, that Francis Ferrell was indeed a pirate. When he did sail into New Orleans to see his young son, Cade, he always brought books to fill this library, books from all over the world. Francis Ferrell furnished and outfitted the house with elaborate and exotic interiors, giving all the more credence to the rumors of his piracy.

Emmy knew of her great, great grandfather's dubious reputation and relished the mystery it gave her heritage and this home she knew so well. She settled on a rung of the library ladder, quietly awaiting the conclusion of the rubber of bridge. She sighed as she inhaled the rich odor of the mahogany floor-to-ceiling bookshelves. The shelves had housed all those books until her aunt had sold the house on Rue de Toulouse to pay rising taxes and afford E. and her companions traveling money. The present owner promptly converted the property into a casino and hotel, much to the delight of E., Larken, and Emmy. With no need for the books in either venture, he encouraged E. to remove the books from the shelves that had housed them for generations. The shelves now stood empty: tall and stately, they seemed gaunt and violated. Emmy's mother, Alice, had taken control of the valued books, lovingly and possessively taking guardianship over the precious words and leather spines. Emmy expected those books would be part of her inheritance one day. She quietly hugged herself at the grandiose thought. *The money will be lovely, too.*

Emmy surveyed the room and noted that the only furniture left in the library was a card table intricately inlaid with various woods and four elaborately carved chairs. Most of the antiques had been moved to Fairlake Farm, where her parents and her other aunt, Garnet, and Larken's father, Billy, now lived. The library ceiling was frescoed with murals of fat, golden, pastel cherubs and lions and lambs cavorting in Elysian meadows. The gas lit chandelier's prisms twinkled and lighted the faces of the foursome playing bridge. Fairlake Farm was comfortable and nice, but never as majestic as this.

The jeweled fingers of the ladies reflected the light as each one pensively and carefully selected a card. A gentle humid breeze stirred the lace curtains of the floor-to-ceiling windows, but brought little relief from the heat of this late spring evening.

Emmy looked with admiration at her aunt, thinking

her still such a girl at fifty-one, her henna-dusted hair belying any hint of gray, her mouth and cheeks naturally pink. Aunt E. could still make any man her servant. Emmy noticed a slight bulge in Aunt E.'s jaw. *She's sneaking a chew*, Emmy thought, amused at her aunt's audacity. Sure enough, cradled in E.'s lap was a small Dresden spittoon.

"You trumped your own wife!" shouted the woman on E.'s right. The bridge players arose abruptly, toppling a glass of red wine onto the table and cards.

The flustered gentleman apologized, "I . . . I didn't mean to," never taking his eyes off E., who was leaving the three for the door where Emmy stood smiling. The gentleman followed behind E., whispering, "I felt your little nudge."

As E. stuffed her winnings into the silk purse hanging from her wrist, she replied, "I'm known for my little nudge." Aunt and niece quietly slipped through the oak door and returned to the casino.

The two women spied Larken in a discreet corner. Having reclaimed the attentions of the woman, Larken sat, gently wooing the cabochon ruby. The piano and string ensemble laboriously played a series of Strauss waltzes, totally failing to be heard above the shrill, raucous voices, as now more guests had arrived after late suppers. Larken's familiar laughter could be heard above the noise as the woman with the cabochon ruby squealed with delight at

Larken's suggestive remarks. His tall frame was balanced on one leg with the other leg swinging to and fro over the back of a gilded casino chair.

Emmy clinched her teeth. "He's still with that woman, Aunt E. He's a handsome brute, my cousin Larken, and hardheaded and single-minded enough to own that ruby pendant by morning!"

Nearby, the large poker table was crowded with players, and the kibitzers hovered behind them. A beautiful Negro woman, Zita Yvette, who was called Ivy, mingled, pausing now and then to make some casual remark to one of the players. Her perfect white teeth flashed a brilliant smile in harmony with the dazzling rhinestones on her ears and throat. She wore a stunning lavender satin gown, perfectly suited to her tall, elegant bearing and dusky complexion. Almost unnoticed, she nodded her head a bit and gave a sweet reassuring smile to her husband, Runner, the only black man seated at the table.

Emmy and E. sauntered over to watch the kill. "The rest of us are amateurs, Aunt E.; Ivy is aces up. That lavender satin she found in Paris is divine."

The gray-haired black man was impeccably dressed in formal attire. He never looked up but, in a quiet, hoarse voice edged with humility, announced, "I raise you fifty."

His opponent responded, "I see it. Call."

"What's he got, Aunt E.? Can you see?" Emmy asked anxiously.

Aunt E. craned her neck for a better look. "He's got two jacks and three tens."

"And Runner?"

"He's raking in the money with four kings and an ace."

At the table the indignant loser's face flushed, and he grumbled, "You're one lucky ni . . ."

"You bet I am," Runner interrupted him as he stood up, tall and grinning. With a deferential tilt to his head, he remarked, "Once you been a black man with luck, you'd never want to be a white man again, luck or no."

Runner crossed to E. and Emmy. Aunt E. extended her hand to congratulate him and whispered to Ivy, "Nice job."

Aunt E. and Ivy were born on the same night in the same house. Their relationship could not have been closer had they been sisters. In fact, E. never could remember enjoying or loving her own sister as much as she loved Ivy. Runner was born on the adjoining Blakemore plantation earlier the same day. Bless his Mama's soul, she went to heaven before E. and Ivy had come into this world. The three grew up as inseparable playmates and, though there were people around them who did not understand the unusual relationship between Negro and White, E., Ivy, and Runner just laughed at their ignorance. Not one of them would enjoy something until they had shared it with the other two.

Still holding E.'s hand, Runner responded behind closed teeth, "Got all I could without getting shot. How'd you do, E.?"

"All right, but I have a jealous wife with a two-foot hat pin after me."

"And you, Emmy?"

Emmy giggled, then discreetly covering her mouth, boasted, "A hundred and forty-six dollars but, if I spit on that man's dice again, I'm afraid I'll be forced to bear his children."

Runner scanned the casino and the ladies' eyes followed his. He frowned. "Where's Larken?"

In the corner where Larken and the woman had been earlier, the casino chair had been overturned. Emmy took a frustrated stance, legs apart and hands on hips. Her green eyes flashed as she snarled, "He'd do better with her if he'd get his hands out of that woman's dress and into her pocketbook."

Ivy excused herself to Runner. He squeezed her hand and said, "Don't be too long, my Darlin'. Never could celebrate without you right by me." Ivy wrinkled her nose at him and then turned to cross the lobby of the hotel. She stepped outside onto the street, hoping it might be a bit cooler. A light rain had fallen earlier in the evening but the air was still muggy. However, it seemed better than the stifling smoke-filled casino. Her new slippers pinched her toes, so she returned to the lobby and settled into a secluded chair behind a palm plant, facing the backside of the winding oak staircase, to remove her shoes and massage her feet. From this vantage point she could see through the banisters to the front desk. The hotel clerk emerged from an office behind the reception desk. Thinking himself alone, he lifted what looked like a telegram to the light. Ivy, in stocking feet, quietly crossed over to him to chat. The startled clerk, recognizing Ivy as one of Larken's intimate circle, thrust forth the envelope, sheepishly announcing that the telegram was for Mr. Blakemore. Taking the envelope out of his hand, Ivy smiled at him reassuringly and went back to sit behind the stairs and read the message.

She was so preoccupied with the urgent news and the need to find Larken that she failed to see a man enter the lobby. Ivy had squatted down to retrieve her slippers from under the chair when she heard a rasping, sneering voice demand of the timid clerk, "You got a man here name of Larken Blakemore?" Sensing trouble, Ivy quickly stuffed the telegram in her decolletage and crouched back behind the palm branches.

The timid clerk nodded his head. "He's one of our most preferred customers; in fact, his family once owned this place."

Though Ivy could not see the man's face, she noted that he wore traveling clothes. A long slicker hung from his muscular, bulging shoulders down to his muddy gray boots. His backside and chilling voice were familiar to Ivy and revived old ancestral instincts in her: the primitive mixture of superstition and wise, cat-like caution inherited from her Island forebears. The atmosphere of irredeemable evil and imminent danger prompted her into action.

Ivy knew she must warn Larken and she needed time. The telegram could wait until later.

The ominous voice continued, "Then you must prefer your customers to walk on their bills." Defiant now, having a favored guest insulted, the clerk answered, "Mr. Blakemore would never walk on a bill. His family . . ."

The intruder, now snarling in rage, grabbed the clerk by his coat lapels and, pulling him forward, spit into his face. "His family stopped payin' his way over a year ago. He's wanted in every state. It's a fancy price on Blakemore and I want it!"

Now, Ivy remembered: The enemy was Bates! Forgetting her slippers, she crept forward stealthily and reached for matches from a nearby table.

As Bates leaned over the desk with both hands still clutching the ashen-faced clerk, Ivy lit the hem of his slicker in three places and, praying for time to warn the others, fled into the casino.

Emmy and Runner had been looking for Ivy; Runner never let his wife out of his sight for long. He opened the side door of the casino, and he and Emmy peered into the hall.

Ivy ran toward them, her skirts held high above her knees, shouting, "Bates is here!"

Runner grabbed Ivy by the hand and the two sprinted down the hall toward the back of the house.

He yelled to Emmy, "I'll get a wagon. You get Larken and E."

Emmy screamed back, "Meet us behind the kitchen."

Emmy was relatively sure that Larken and the woman with the cabochon ruby were in one of the downstairs private rooms. Hurriedly passing through the casino, she grabbed Aunt E.'s arm and jerked her away from one of the gaming tables. The two of them burst into a card room, abruptly interrupting the privacy of Larken and the woman. Larken, irritated, waved them away as Emmy, now more angry than frightened, shouted, "Cousin dear, Uncle Bates is here!"

Larken sprang to his feet, dumping the woman from his lap. With a gentlemanly apology, he helped her recover her composure, and then bolted from the room to find the others.

Thinking Larken was close behind them, Emmy and E. ran out the kitchen door into the alley. Larken's apology to the woman had cost him precious time; when he finally entered the kitchen, Bates was waiting. His rough hand grabbed the ruffles of Larken's blouse and Larken felt the cold metal of the revolver against his neck, aimed toward his brain.

Bates smelled nauseating, his sweat reeking with the excitement of a hunter who has cornered his prey. His soggy, burned slicker added to the stench. He breathed on Larken the stink of liquor and rotted teeth. The black hairs of his flaring nostrils protruded.

Larken was more repulsed than afraid. Bates wanted money. He would not shoot him, at least not yet. Larken typically avoided conflict of any kind. He preferred a cool mind and a quick slight-of-hand over firearms and fists. He said to his nervous captor, "It's always a pleasure to see you, Bates."

This calm, gentlemanly approach had always worked before and it seemed to again, for Bates, the adversary, was trembling and his voice squeaked. "There's a bounty on your head, Blakemore. I want it and the money you owe me."

Larken sensed an odd advantage in this most unusual

situation and goaded Bates further. "So, this visit isn't purely social. I'm wounded."

Bates, shaking with anger, hissed, "You will be if I shoot your smart-ass mouth off."

"Bates, I don't know about any bounty, but as to the question of owing you money—I won that card game fair and square and you know it." Grinning broadly, Larken continued, "I'm pretty good, aren't I?"

Larken grinned as, out of the corner of his eye, he spied Runner slipping in through the pantry door. Runner squatted in the corner, out of Bates' sight, ready to spring.

Suddenly the kitchen door flung open and startled all three. The cabochon ruby woman entered whining, "Larken, weren't you even going to say goodbye?"

Runner sprang full force onto an astonished Bates, knocking the revolver from his hand. With a blow to Bates' head, Runner flung him unconscious into the arms of the woman, who flopped to the floor still cradling the out-cold Bates. Runner and Larken stood gawking as the woman's enormous bosoms heaved and the ruby pendant winked.

Larken sauntered over to the sink and picked up a green onion. He bit off the bulb and tossed the green stems over his shoulder. Laughing heartily, he bid the woman adieu. "Bye bye, Darling."

Runner ran ahead to steady the nervous horses and to

reassure E., Ivy, and Emmy in the wagon. Larken, not far behind, leapt into the wagon ordering, "Emmy, grab my trousers and help me up."

Emmy, still mightily peeved with Larken, slapped at him, hollering, "I'd sooner suck a rattlesnake's face!"

Runner took the reins and the horses lunged forward. He reached out and grabbed Larken's trousers and heaved him into the wagon seat. The wagon turned abruptly to the right and Runner quickly steadied the horses and headed for a back road. Aunt E. shouted over the racket of the wheels on the road, "I'm sick of trying to outrun Bates. Where to this time?"

Finally remembering the telegram, Ivy pulled it from her decolletage and handed it to Larken. "From my bosom to the bosom of our family."

After many blocks Runner slowed the horses to a complete stop under a gas lamp on a deserted street. In the silence of the stilled wagon wheels and the quietness of the city in the dark hours of morning, Larken read the telegram.

"I'll take the reins from here, Runner. We're headed home. Poor Aunt Garnet finally died. Hot damn! We look good in black. Where there's a funeral, there's a Will!"

Chapter Two

Where ignorance is bliss, tis folly to be wise.

THOMAS GRAY

Larken raced the wagon along at full speed toward the lakefront to catch the last steamboat across Lake Pontchartrain. He would have just enough time to wire his father, Billy, of their expected arrival late the following afternoon; Billy could send Fetch, Runner's father, with a wagon to meet them at the dock. Larken briefly thought, with a pang of guilt, of how long it had been since he last saw his father. Quickly, though, his mind returned to the problem of the menacing Bates. The rat had smelled blood and would be in hot pursuit.

They boarded the steamboat quickly and found seats on the deck to catch the evening breezes. As the boat glided away from the dock, Emmy played nervously with the fingertips of her gloves. Being reunited with her father,

Finch, would be heartwarming. As a child she always knew she could go to her father with any thought or emotion and he would support her. On the other hand Emmy's mother, Alice, hardly approved of Emmy whatever the situation. Emmy never doubted her mother's love, but she knew she did not measure up to the high ideals of womanhood that Alice held for herself.

As soon as Larken was confident that Bates had not followed them to the boat, he moved from the railing to sit by Emmy on a deck box. He broke into Emmy's reverie. "Where would you like to travel next? With Aunt Garnet's money how far do you think we can get?"

Emmy giggled. "Larken, you're being premature. Don't you think we should mourn first before we make travel plans? Although, I have heard the silks in the Far East are divine."

Aunt E. smiled slightly at Emmy and Larken, but rode most of the way in silent mourning. E. had not realized what the passing of her sister would mean to her. She and her sister, Garnet, had not been friends. Their meetings were usually by accident. Their paths crossed at funerals and family gatherings, their greetings toward each other cordial and reserved. Garnet and her sister-in-law, Alice, were more like sisters, with mutual interests and matched dispositions. Both Garnet and Alice disapproved of Aunt

E.'s chosen way of living.

Aunt E. sighed to herself. *I really admired Garnet, though she never appreciated me. She sided with Alice's dislike of my style of life. Both women have always been jealous over the affection of Emmy and Larken for me. Garnet could run the farm with economy but she didn't know how to enjoy life; very sad. Oh, Garnet, why didn't you join our fun rather than envy it.* Looking around the coach at Runner and Ivy and Emmy and Larken she thought, *The years of Runner and Ivy helping me raise those two, more my children than had I given birth to them, were my happiest times.*

Garnet and Alice had formed a united front in the last years. Garnet had sold the family plantations when her health had begun to fail. She moved to Fairlake Farm to live with Alice, Finch, and Billy. It was from there that she held the purse strings tightly over her brother, Finch, and her sister, E. Alice was a most capable ally in all financial affairs, and Garnet admired and thoroughly trusted her sister-in-law. Their first cousin, Billy, who had lived with them since the death of his wife, Marie, went along with the women. He was grateful for their kindness to him and their indulgence of his irresponsible son, Larken. Finch had long ago turned all of the business matters over to his wife and sister. Since Garnet had no children of her own, it was assumed that Emmy, Alice and Finch's daughter, and Larken, Billy's son, would inherit what was left of her assets.

Though Larken and Emmy respectfully grieved over Garnet's death, the thought of inherited money occupied their conversation through the rest of the trip across Lake Pontchartrain.

E. looked out over the dark waters and listened to the rhythmic chugging of the steam engine as she pondered their return home after six years. *Those two are truly mine in spirit, and, in fact, this will not be an easy homecoming.*

Sitting between Runner and E., Ivy dozed throughout the journey, thoughtful and pensive. She knew the stories of the Blakemores and the Ferrells as well as she knew her own family stories. Their lives were entwined all the way back to the Battle of New Orleans. Some said the first Mr. Ferrell was a pirate. Ivy smiled. *He'd sure be proud of this group then.*

Ivy's earliest memories were playing with E. on the wooden kitchen floor under the watchful eye of Chloe, Ivy's mother. Garnet was older, by only a year or so when E. and Ivy were born. In the early years, E. and Ivy looked up to Garnet, and Garnet treated them with disdain. For some years E. and Ivy worked to gain Garnet's approval but their efforts were futile. As they grew older, Garnet's disapproval simply grew more pronounced.

Ivy sighed, remembering the first time she saw Runner. Runner lived at the Blakemore Plantation. In time, Runner, well-named, became the messenger between the two plantations. Though he was the child of slaves, he was treated with the utmost respect and affection by the two girls. Ivy thought he was the most handsome person in the whole world, even if he was only five or six at the time.

Runner had all the news and he was their leader. If any of the grownups minded, they didn't interfere. E. taught Ivy and Runner, as she was taught by her tutor, to read and write. She loaned them all the books from the family library and shared every detail of her experiences and knowledge with them.

Ivy recalled one chilly afternoon all three were stretched out before a warm fire in the library at the Ferrell plantation. They lay on their stomachs with black legs and white legs askew and pored over a Paris fashion magazine E. found in her mother's bedroom.

"Just look at the pictures: the silks, the lace, the taffetas," exclaimed E. "We'll go there one day, I promise. Together we'll go and see it all."

"Look there," said Runner, "a saloon and card-playing!"

As they were growing up, Ivy and Runner often accompanied E. to the Rue de Toulouse house in New Orleans. She took them with her to the historic sites and recalled with them the history of the now large city. They visited the gardens and the market and the wharfs; sneaked in and out of the grand salons; and peered into the enclosed patios of the sophisticated houses of ill repute.

E. Ferrell became the belle of New Orleans and the whole of Louisiana. She never tired of hosting parties or of encouraging the attentions of many suitors, since she had no intention of settling on just one beau.

The boat began to slow down with many lurches and chugs, bringing all five of the travelers back to the reality before them. Only Runner looked anxiously out over the railing scanning the small crowd on the pier for the dark, lined face of his beloved father, Fetch. Fetch's beard had grown creamy white over the years, but the smile was still broad and warming to Runner as their eyes met. The boat docked, and Runner jumped down from the gangplank to embrace Fetch. Then Fetch reached forward to greet his daughter-in-law, Ivy, with an immediate hug.

Larken helped Aunt E. down the gangplank. "Oh Fetch, you are a sight for sore, old eyes."

Fetch chuckled and hugged E. "Miss E., if you're old then I am ancient. Let's not talk about age! You will always be a sight for these old eyes. We best be goin'. They've all been waitin' since we got your wire yesterday. They had to go and bury Miss Garnet this mornin'; she wouldn't keep in this heat."

Fetch looked around for luggage, but saw none. He just shrugged his shoulders. Over the years he had gotten used to this fivesome's quirky ways. At least it would be faster loading up the wagon.

Runner rode up front with Fetch. Father and son had been in ceaseless conversation since they left the boat dock. Fetch continuously wiped the tears from his eyes, brought on by raucous laughter and long-winded tales from his son. Their affection was obvious as they patted and slapped each other's knees and backs.

Fetch gave the reins to Runner and turned around in the wagon to face the others. His cotton-gray head was beaded with perspiration and his black cheeks still wet with tears. He shaded his eyes from the morning sun just rising in the East.

"Yes, sir, they're waitin'. The judge, he be stayin' for supper. There's lots of food. Lots of folks brung it. Chloe's waitin' fer ya, Ivy. She'll have your ol' grandpappy settin' under his tree waitin' fer y'all. It'll do him some kind'a good to see your faces agin."

E. squeezed Ivy's hand and she asked, "How old is

Uncle Marcel, Fetch?"

"He'd be hundred and five and some more. Still eats good ifin' you mash it up; got fer-off seein' eyes and his thinkin' better than mine."

This last comment brought more slaps, pats, and tears. "It's your Ma, Ivy, keeps him goin'. Chloe's God's gift. You know fer sure." Old Fetch heaved and sobbed, turning around with bowed head. Runner patted his father's back as the horses, who surely knew the way, kept up their lively pace.

It was with guarded expectations and some feigned remorse that the five drove into the Fairlake Farm lane in the early afternoon. They crossed the bridge over the small lake that gave the farm its name. The man-made lake was set within a clearing of timber trees bordering on three sides. A half-dozen mud ducks floated on the surface, and a long-legged frog leaped and splashed among the lily pads.

Fetch veered the wagon to the right onto the encircling road that led around the large front lawn to the wide porch steps of the house. Ancient Uncle Marcel sat on a bench in the center of a copse of tall crepe myrtle trees. The long, skinny tree trunks glistened white in the last rays of sunlight, and Marcel's spindly crossed legs resembled their dark budding branches. As Marcel gestured and pointed with his cane toward the approaching wagon, Chloe ran for the road, and Fetch slowed the wagon for a barefoot Ivy to alight and meet her Ma halfway.

Fetch kept the horses still for a moment as all watched the emotional reunion of the three generations. Leaving Ivy, Chloe, and Uncle Marcel to themselves, they slowly rounded the curve to the first open view of the house. To the right of the front verandah was an enormous oak tree meant for climbing. Its lowest branch was easily reached from a wooden bench encircling the trunk. Large bunches of gray moss hung down from the upper branches in wispy tendrils that blew slightly in the gentle twilight breeze. The sun was sinking over the top of the timber trees. The oil lamps and candles flickered through the windows of the parlor and dining room.

The Fairlake farmhouse was a white, two-story, wood-shingled house with a verandah fronted by six plain columns. These supported the upstairs porch and ran halfway toward the back of the house. There were four large windows on the verandah below, matched by four windows on the porch above. Faded green shutters propped on their supporter posts slanted out from the windows. They could easily be lowered and fastened shut during the hurricane season. The architecture was more comfortable and hospitable than grand.

Alice, Finch, and Billy stood waiting on the front porch.

E., Larken, and Emmy climbed out of the wagon slowly, hesitating as they brushed dust from their clothes. Fetch and Runner took the horses on around the road to the stable at the rear of the property. The three on the porch approached the weary travelers and the six greeted each other in low tones of respect for the recently departed, amid the early evening chorus of katydids.

When Alice saw the three dressed in rumpled formal attire, she briefly embraced her daughter, Emmy, and scolded, "Mourning clothes are in order. I see you have no baggage."

Ivy and Chloe crossed the lawn, keeping a slow pace with Uncle Marcel. Alice called past the others to Ivy, "See to the proper attire for all of you before supper."

As Ivy came up the porch steps she muttered a respectful, "Yes Ma'am."

Noticing Ivy's dirty bare toes, Alice ordered, "And do something about your feet!"

Chapter Three

A perfect woman nobly plann'd
To warm, to comfort, and command;
And yet a Spirit still and bright
With something of angelic light.

W<small>ILLIAM</small> W<small>ORDSWORTH</small>

Emmy and E. sat straight and somber on the ebony horsehair settee. Larken stood behind them, alert and wary. "Colonel" Alice had assembled them in the parlor after a late and indigestible supper. The food had been wholesome and the travelers ravenously hungry, but the cool reception and Billy and Finch's nervous chatter had them all on edge. Judge Brink had stayed overnight after Garnet's funeral, awaiting their arrival. He was petulant and not the least bit socially accommodating. Alice had insisted that, due to the late hour, the judge stay the night and not try to make the trip back to Ponchatoula until morning.

E. felt emotionally uncomfortable wearing her late sister's mourning ensemble, and Larken was physically miserable in his father's second-best black suit. The trousers were too short in the stride, and the coat sleeves grabbed him under the arms. Larken's eyes were fixed on the locked liquor cabinet, and his thoughts were focused on where Alice might keep the key. Emmy wore an old, faded, black dress of her mother's. Ivy and Runner hovered in the shadows outside the parlor door, and Billy and Finch stood behind Alice's chair fidgeting.

Funeral easels cluttered the room, permeating it with the pungent, stifling aroma of wilting tuberoses and snapdragons. It was hot, stuffy, and close. Judge Brink sweated profusely as he droned on with the preliminaries of Garnet's will. He stood with authority in front of the red oak mantle, reading by the dim lamp on the desk to his left. The judge paused several times to wipe his fogged glasses and mop his drenched forehead. He cleared his throat and read to himself a bit more of the contents of the Will before continuing.

Wide-eyed, he turned to look directly toward the settee at E. Once again, he cleared his throat and slowly and deliberately read aloud. "Sister Emeralde, you are and have always been dear to me." The judge hesitated and E., having heard, savored these words from her sister. Whether or not the sentiment was true, she would give Garnet the benefit of her doubts.

Judge Brink uttered the next word, "but," long and loud. He stared at E., Emmy, and Larken, demanding their fixed attention. The judge continued. "Emeralde Ferrell you've thrown your lot in with Larken and Emmy. So goes your bequest. Emmy and Larken, you must marry to receive or even know of your inheritance, darling children. It is time for you to grow up. This fact, and not my money, will be the making of you. Signed, Garnet Ferrell Thurgood, Fairlake Farm, Tangipahoa Parish, Louisiana, in the year of our Lord, 1867."

The three stiffened and their jaws dropped. Ivy and Runner's gasps could be heard from the hall.

Little more was said. Emmy and Aunt E. were too stunned to protest and Larken had disappeared from the room. Ivy and Runner tidied the parlor as Alice, Finch, and Billy repeatedly thanked Judge Brink and ushered him off to bed.

As Emmy and E., still stung by the revelations of the Will, supported each other as they walked toward the stairs, Emmy motioned to Runner. "You and Ivy find Larken and meet us in my bedroom in an hour."

When Runner returned to the parlor to help Ivy, she was smiling and humming. Puzzled, he returned a faint smile and asked, "What are you so happy about?"

Now almost radiant, she took his hands in hers. "God's

mysterious working, that's what. You know, Runner, there's a balm in Gilead."

"Lord, woman, you have gone and lost it; none of us is normal, what we've been through." He kissed Ivy and turned to look around. "This room's a mess. There always was too much furniture jammed in here. Could we take these awful dead flowers and rest them?"

Ivy sighed. "Better wait for orders on that one. Chloe'll tell us tomorrow. Where did Larken go?"

Runner pulled a few limp stems from one of the easels and stuffed them into his pocket to throw in the trash. "Probably out there smoking a cigar. Let's go on up, Honey, and see to E. and Emmy. Larken'll find us directly."

Ivy and Runner tiptoed up the straight, steep staircase to the second-floor landing. They paused to catch their breaths, their candles casting shadows in the wide upstairs hall. A murmur of voices fluttered from the room across the hall from Emmy's room, Alice and Finch's bedroom. On the landing directly in front of them was Billy's room, the smallest, dark and quiet. The other back corner bedrooms and the hallways that led to them were silent. Ivy and Runner crept to the door of Emmy's bedroom directly across from her parents'. The wide upstairs hall and the thick bedroom doors offered a degree of privacy. Runner turned the doorknob to Emmy's room back and forth, signaling. Immediately Emmy opened the door just enough for Ivy and Runner to slip inside.

Aunt E. sat on Emmy's bed, resting her back against one of the tall, carved posts. She stared into space, furiously fanning for air with one of the paper funeral-parlor fans. Runner quietly settled into a small, green boudoir chair, after removing its teddy bear occupant. He straddled the bear on his crossed leg and closed his eyes. Ivy perched on the little French desk and, absentmindedly, began to swing her legs. Emmy climbed onto her bed, exhausted, and fell back among the many pillows.

No one spoke. The lace curtains stirred at the tall open windows on either side of Emmy's bed as a faint breeze attempted to break through the humid night air. Emmy sighed. She was so tired and numbed from the shock of the contents of Garnet's Will.

The mantle clock ticked. Its gentle, steady beat always gave Emmy comfort. The shepherd and shepherdess still flanked its dial. She smiled at the remembrance of them. As a child, they had been to her like confidants with whom she shared her secrets. Emmy recalled their first meeting. Her great-grandparents, the Blakemores, brought the clock to E. from one of their trips to England. Aunt E. gave the clock to Emmy on her sixth birthday. It had been packaged in a beautiful Chinese-silk hatbox, covered with bright red and green dragons. The shepherd wore yellow and the shepherdess green. Their broad brim hats and crooks were brown and their faces rosy and kind. Alice had papered her daughter's room to match the clock.

Emmy began her childhood ritual. She counted the brown-eyed daisies that ran up and down the yellow- and green-striped wallpaper; her eyelids grew heavy and she dozed. Something startled her and she sat up abruptly. "Where's Larken? Mother's up to something!"

<hr/>

Across the hall, Alice and Finch were cloistered in their bedroom, sitting in their accustomed lounging chairs, enjoying their usual nightcap. Finch refilled his glass and leaned forward to better hear Alice's low, cautious remarks. Alice sputtered as she spoke. "Those three will put their heads together and be up to something."

"Oh, come on, Al," argued Finch, for the port had given him a bit more courage. "They'll be reasonable; Billy and I feel . . ."

Alice interrupted, slightly raising her voice. "There's the whole problem. You and Billy wait for the good in them to out. It hasn't. It won't. It just won't until we force their hands. Garnet has done her part. Now is the time to strike. You and Billy must talk to them. Their finances are a mess, and their many creditors are not going to wait. For our sakes, they need Garnet's money. If they have it now, they'll squander it. They have to change their ways or we're all in for it. You go to bed, Finch, I'll keep watch. I can't sleep; I need to think."

This conversation made Finch tired. He got along with Alice in every way until they discussed his sister, Emeralde, or their daughter, Emmy. *Anyway, Alice is probably right,* he said to himself as he yawned and stretched and climbed into their bed, still half dressed. As Alice paced, the clock on the mantle chimed midnight. Finch cherished this clock, a beautiful rubbed-mahogany wood with carved wooden doves in flight. It had belonged to his great-grandfather Ferrell and had once stood on the mantle in the Rue de Toulouse house. Finch began to drowsily count the wine and pink roses that ran in stripes up and down the blue wallpaper; soon he was snoring.

In another upstairs bedroom, Billy Blakemore stared into the darkness. He wanted the best for his son, and he readily admitted that he and Aunt E. had spoiled Larken. He was easy to spoil, with his charming, happy-go-lucky ways. But there was a serious, sensitive side to the young man. Larken and Emmy could be happy as husband and wife. They were much alike and had been devoted to each other as children, but the last few years they bickered incessantly. He wondered why.

When they were little, Larken had transferred his love to Emmy after his mother, Marie, died. *Oh, Marie,* Billy spoke aloud into the darkness, *will the ache of your absence never leave me?*

Billy Blakemore got up and lit a lamp so Larken could see his way. When at Fairlake Farm, Larken always slept in the other twin bed in the room with his father. In a weary voice, Billy said aloud to himself, *I don't want to talk tonight. Morning will be better.* He returned to his bed and finally went to sleep, dreaming of his beloved Marie.

As the shepherd clock in Emmy's room struck twelve, Larken swung both legs over the windowsill. He carried a decanter of sherry, and four glass stems stuck out of his pockets.

"Greetings and grand salutations, little black sheep. Forgive my cavalier reference to color but we are, all of us, little black sheep, for we have not been good little girls and boys. We have been eating of the fruits of the devil."

The four were now most assuredly roused from their silent deliberations. Runner popped up to help Larken with his welcome libations; E. and Ivy muffled their giggles and Emmy scowled. "Shut up. What took you so long!"

As Larken poured each one a glass of sherry, he

explained his whereabouts for the last hour. "Stern 'Colonel' Alice, keeper of the keys to the kingdom, is also the keeper of the keys to the liquor cabinet. Brand new lock, took forever to pick it."

Emmy gulped her first glass of sherry and extended her glass to Runner for a refill. She cautioned herself to sip the next one, for most assuredly she needed a cool, calm head. She was amused at Larken—the rascal—and that was the problem. She had never known life without him, and with him she was thoroughly entertained and constantly irritated. Emmy was physically attracted to him, as were all women, and she was jealous of his flirtations. Their common bond was their mutual greed and their devil-may-care attitude.

Larken looked at Emmy as if reading her mind; she abruptly avoided his eyes and turned a cold shoulder. To address the situation at hand, she decided to come to the point immediately. "What kind of money did Aunt Garnet have, Aunt E.?"

E. slid off of the high bed until her feet hit the floor. She began to pace as she thoughtfully responded. "All I know is she married a rich Yankee with a heart condition."

Runner sputtered with a hiccup and a sardonic retort. "Question here isn't how much. Unless you two marry, it's nothing."

Larken passed around the sherry decanter and then, retrieving it, climbed onto the bed. Sitting cross-legged, he leaned toward Emmy and breathlessly whispered, "We could marry, get the money, and then divorce. I'll give you grounds."

Emmy gasped and slapped him away. "You'll give me what! No! Then I'm known as the pitiful divorcee who couldn't keep her husband at home." She pondered a moment. "You could die, and then there'd be no stigma for me."

Aunt E. reached for Runner's and Ivy's hands to steady herself. "I'm too tired to think. Come on, Ivy, Runner."

As the three passed quietly into the long hall, they failed to notice the furtive dark form crouched in the corner shadows—"Colonel" Alice keeping watch.

Emmy was so angry with Larken that she forgot to sip her sherry and drained her glass. She thrust it forward to him for yet another refill. Larken tipped the decanter to his lips. Emmy glared at him in disgust. He grinned at her sheepishly as he reached inside his inner coat pocket and produced a flask. He sat back against the bedpost and removed the cork with his teeth.

In earnest, he asked Emmy, "You have the money you, Aunt E., and Runner took the other night at the casino. What's that tally?"

Stifling a yawn, Emmy pondered. "Not quite three hundred."

Larken grimaced. "How far can we go on three hundred dollars?"

Emmy glared at Larken. "Where are we welcome?"

From drink and frustration, Larken raised his voice. "Nowhere! We've scammed them all: Boston, New York, hell, all the north, the southeast, the south. What's out west?"

Emmy slid down further in the bed and, stretching her legs and yawning, she sleepily answered, "Dirt and Indians."

Larken slapped his thigh. "San Francisco. There's bound to be action out there, a safe place where Bates wouldn't even think to look."

Emmy sat up and unashamedly pulled her dress over her head with a muffled, "All our friends in New Orleans know about Fairlake Farms. They could send him here without realizing they are putting us in danger."

The faint breeze was totally stilled and the curtains hung limp. The humid heat and sherry and their vexation had them both perspiring. Larken, who had earlier removed his coat, now removed his shirt.

Emmy continued, "We couldn't pay for passage for one on a ship, let alone all of us."

Larken reached over and pulled Emmy's big toe. "We could go over land."

She kicked his hand away and moved her foot. "Like apple farmers? Stop it, Larken."

He reached again for her foot. "Just a thought."

By now both Emmy and Larken were lying in the dark, he stretched out at the foot of the bed and she among the pillows. Emmy whispered, "Why didn't you ever marry?"

Larken hesitated. "Never needed to, I guess."

Emmy hissed, "Needed to? You're vile."

"I'm not vile, Emmy. I'm worthless, just like you. And we're vain."

Rolling out of the bed, she tiptoed to the bedroom door and listened. As she returned to her bed, Emmy paused before her dresser mirror and lit a candle. "We *are not* vain. Anyway, I'm not." She peered at her reflection and straightened her hair; she blew out the candle and climbed into bed.

Larken began to laugh and Emmy giggled. "You're lower than a toad's butt."

Larken kicked her. "You *are* a toad's butt."

As her eyelids closed, Emmy muttered, "You really are a waste of time."

Larken crawled up on the pillow beside her without

complaint from Emmy, who was asleep. Before he passed out, Larken spoke aloud into the night. *And so, dear cousin, are you. We are two of a kind, which is a lousy poker hand, but it is never lonely.*

———

As the clock chimed two, Emmy's bedroom door slowly opened and Alice, like a phantom, approached the bed of the sleeping cousins. When she was satisfied, she left and, quietly shutting the door, crossed the hall to retire to her own quarters. Alice sat in her accustomed chair by the bed, and to the rhythm of Finch's snores, she spoke into the darkness. "I am loath to discover that those qualities you possess which I despise, I share also. Sleep well, cousins, for 'Colonel' Alice has a big, big day planned for you."

Chapter Four

And this maiden she lived with no other thought
Than to love and be loved by me.

EDGAR ALLEN POE

The familiar rustle of her mother's skirt woke Emmy. Her head and neck ached, lolled as they were over the side of her bed. Her mouth was open and she drooled. She wiped her lips dry with the bed sheet and opened one eye to see the tapping toe of Alice's shoe and hear her impatient breathing. Without lifting her head, Emmy hoarsely greeted the still-tapping toe with a weak, "Good morning, Mother."

The shoe retreated beneath the hem of the skirt but the body of her mother didn't budge, and Alice coolly responded. "Good morning, Emmy. Is he dead or just unconscious?"

"Who?" Emmy frowned, still half asleep and puzzled.

Alice lifted Emmy's head and rolled her over. Pointing with a bony finger, she replied with obvious disgust, "Cousin Larken."

One of Emmy's feet was lodged under Larken's lifeless form, and she kicked at him as she innocently protested Alice's silent but obvious insinuation. "He's not dead. I think we must have had a bit too much sherry. I guess we just fell asleep like when we were children."

Alice gathered the sherry decanter and the glasses and started from the room. At the door she paused and, with her back to Emmy, firmly ordered, "You are children no longer. Collect yourselves. Your fathers will have to speak to you."

Emmy was furious with her mother's line of thinking, and she was angry with Larken for his indiscretion. Crying with frustration, and groaning, she frantically leaned over Larken and tried to shake him awake.

"Wake up, this is it! Larken, please! Mother says the fathers want to speak to us."

Larken opened his eyes with a shudder. "I'm so tired. What did we drink? What time is it?" He looked at his disheveled cousin with a faint smile and pushed the red curls back from her face.

Emmy sat back abruptly, blushing at the unintended intimacy. "I don't know, just get up."

Emmy paced back and forth, blowing her nose and

dragging Alice's faded black dress on the floor behind her. The thought of wearing the awful garment yet another day added to her irritation.

Larken sat on the side of the bed rubbing his face. "I have a fuzzy chin. I'm going to shave."

Emmy grabbed his sleeve. "You can't shave, they want us now. Just go fuzzy. How do I look?"

Larken stood facing Emmy, buttoning his shirt and fixing his tie. He spoke gently to her. "Put your dress on. Your face is gray. Smooth your hair."

Emmy reached for his tie. "Your tie's all twisted around." As Larken glanced into the dresser mirror, Emmy pulled him back to her. "No, let me fix it."

The two fell into their familiar childhood routine. Larken licked his hands and smoothed Emmy's hair back from her temples and thumped her cheeks for color. Emmy licked her fingers and settled Larken's wayward cowlick. He took her by the hand and led her to the bed, where they sat side by side, nervously awaiting their summons. "You're not so gray now, Emmy. Bite your lips."

She obeyed and leaned her head against his shoulder. "Larken, you're slumping."

He straightened. "I know I'm slumping; my head aches. I'd love a tonic."

Emmy replied with pathetic resignation. "Don't even

say it. If we had some . . ."

Alice entered the room carrying a tray with two glasses. "Oh no, Mama, not one of your herbal remedies."

Alice thrust the glasses into their hands. "Drink," she ordered. "The day we buried Finch's parents, I remarked to Finch how terribly alive they both looked. How I wish I could say the same of you two now. Drink it all." They did. Alice retrieved the tray and glasses and led the way for Larken and Emmy to follow.

"Alice, what do Billy and Finch want?" Larken's voice croaked from rapid swallowing of the vile-tasting tonic, but his headache had miraculously disappeared.

Alice called back over her shoulder, "You'll see." A wicked smirk had replaced her former somber expression.

———

Alice Ferrell had not slept that night. Providence had placed the future survival of them all into her most capable hands. She was not the least bit tired; actually, she was alert in the predawn hours and ready to carry out the heaven-sent plan. Alice tingled from the excitement. For years she had worried about Larken and Emmy and cared more deeply about their well-being than she had ever allowed known. She had managed to cover her concern with the busy preoccupation of ordering and directing.

Garnet had shared her concern. Garnet would be so happy with the turn of events that had followed so fortuitously the ingenious conditions of her will. Alice knew, given the copious amount of sherry Larken and Emmy had drunk, that she had plenty of time to assemble her household and put her plan into operation.

At first light, Alice had roused Finch and suggested that he dress hurriedly on the pretext of the hospitality due their guest, Judge Brink. She explained that they must breakfast early so the judge could get home to Ponchatoula. Alice knocked at Judge Brink's door. In answer to a sleepy response, she advised the judge that breakfast would be served within the hour, adding that this was for his benefit.

The door to Billy's room was ajar and Alice tapped lightly as she entered. Billy sat in a chair staring at Larken's empty, untouched bed. Seeing Alice, he hung his head in shame.

Alice knelt down beside him and whispered, "Dear Billy, take heart, for I have observed all and only good will come of what I know. Trust me as you always have before. Breakfast will be served within the hour."

Alice entered the bustling kitchen shouting one order after another. She stopped momentarily to pat Uncle Marcel's hand as he sat in the corner rocker dozing. Alice advised Chloe and Ivy to prepare breakfast for four and set the table in the library for Finch, Billy, the Judge, and herself. Next, they were to replenish the dining room table with all of yesterday's casseroles, entrees, salads, and desserts. They were, by no means, to enter the library until she rang. At that time, they were to quickly remove the breakfast dishes and not return until she called them. Ivy and Chloe stared stupefied, and even Uncle Marcel, now startled awake, cupped his ear and gawked.

Alice clapped her hands, breaking the silence. "Let's get busy. This is a most important day." As she poured herself a cup of coffee, she asked Chloe, "Where are Fetch and Runner?"

Chloe was washing the fresh hen eggs, and she motioned with her elbow toward the parlor. "In there movin' easels and dead flowers."

"Ivy, go now, and stop them. Tell them to put everything back and leave it all as is." After this final order, Alice headed for the library to drink her coffee and await the next event.

"What's going on?" questioned Runner. "Why does she want to torture those poor dead flowers?"

"Hush, Runner, keep your voice down," Ivy whispered. "'Colonel' Alice is up to something and she's setting the stage."

"What's all the hush-hush about?" Aunt E. entered the kitchen and, as they poured her a cup of coffee, Runner and Ivy filled E. in on the strange early morning orders from Alice.

"It looks to me like you've been left out of the breakfast gathering in the library, E. Sit down here next to me." Runner stood and seated Aunt E.

"Well," E. sighed, "my being left out is nothing new."

"From my point of view, you're safer here and," Runner added with a grin, "a whole lot more appreciated."

Runner, Ivy, Chloe, and even old Fetch scurried in and out of the library according to Alice's explicit orders. They tried their best to pick up on something to report to E., but no conversation of any importance took place in the serving of breakfast and its removal. "I will say," offered Runner, "Miss Alice looks mighty pleased with herself."

One final cup of coffee was poured, and Alice stood and posed authoritatively beneath the elegant gold-framed portrait of William Blakemore's father. This was a dramatic move on her part, for both Billy and Finch revered their lineage. Alice addressed her first remarks to Judge Brink as she offered him a discreetly small tumbler of blackberry cordial.

"We are a family in great need of your expertise and your discretion. We implore you to bear with us for a while longer. Events took place last night, under this most hallowed and honorable roof, which require the attention of a man of your moral and legal standing." Billy was chagrined. Finch poured them both a glass of the cordial.

Alice continued, "We are all fully aware of the rather unusual relationship that has existed for some time between our daughter, Emmy, and her cousin, Larken Blakemore. This peculiar behavior has been encouraged by Miss Emeralde Ferrell, my dear husband's somewhat eccentric sister. It is also true that Emmy and Larken were betrothed by their fathers at the time of Emmy's birth, which in a way complicates matters further. I ask you, Judge Brink, to perform an honorable marriage between these two precious, ah, children of ours this very day, and thus redeem their souls."

Finch poured the judge another glassful and remarked to Billy in passing, "My Alice is one helluva woman."

By now Judge Brink was smiling sweetly and, though a little unsteady on his feet, stood to give his brief answer. "If they are willing."

"They will be," Alice assured them all and, as the men shook hands, she left the library to summon her two totally unaware innocents.

When Alice had deposited Emmy and Larken with their fathers, she assisted Judge Brink into the garden, where she continued to praise and magnify his character and importance. The moral issues that Billy and Finch extolled left Emmy and Larken dumbfounded, and their excuses and denials fell on deaf ears. The possibility of their inherited wealth outweighed their indignation, however; they finally submitted and agreed.

When Runner saw Alice in the garden with the judge, at Aunt E.'s urging, he eavesdropped at the library door to hear what Finch and Billy were saying to Emmy and Larken. He darted into the kitchen, almost hysterical with the news. "Our Larken and Emmy are gonna get married!"

Emmy wandered out of the house in a state of shock with mixed emotions. She slumped down on the oak tree bench, cupping her chin in her hands in disbelief. Larken followed Emmy and quietly sat beside her, not disturbing her or speaking. From the windows of the house, several eyes watched them, for at last they seemed to be in agreeable conversation. Those eyes exchanged many a knowing look and, as the importance of the decision made set in on their hearts, tears of joy ran down black and white cheeks alike.

What the adoring eyes next observed left most of the lookers baffled. Only Aunt E., Ivy, and Runner understood. Emmy jumped up and ran, and Larken followed and tackled her. They rolled over in the grass, Emmy punching and kicking and flailing her arms. Alice stood on the front porch with a perplexed Judge Brink. With her hands on her hips, Alice shouted, "Come on in, children. It's time to begin."

Chapter Five

The bride hath paced into the hall
Red as a rose is she;
Nodding their heads before her goes
The Merry Minstrelsy.

SAMUEL TAYLOR COLERIDGE

Emmy, pensive and glum, stood beside a slightly subdued Larken. She wore her mother's wedding gown of white silk, taffeta, and lace. Though the bride was exquisitely adorned, her grim countenance and clinched jaw shattered the nerves of an inebriated Judge Brink, who stammered and slurred the opening words of the solemn wedding vows.

A violent spring storm rolled in and eclipsed the noon hour. The wind gusts and torrential rain necessitated the lowering of the window louvers, and many candles were lit to brighten the darkened parlor.

Emmy's thoughts surged within her like the wildness of the weather. *Could a man love me who treats me like a sparring cousin or an imbecile sister? Greed is our compan-*

ion, Larken, not love.

Larken took Emmy's hand on command. She did not resist and blushed at his touch. Her heart thumped within her breast and unwanted tears slipped from her lashes onto her cheeks. Larken's hands were strong, masculine, and handsome. As always, he wore his mother's gold wedding band on his little finger. The ring shone in the candlelight and crushed Emmy's fingers. Larken's grip hurt her.

Judge Brink repeated, "Do you take Larken? Emmy, answer."

"Yes, I suppose I do."

Larken's scowl reflected the darkness of his thoughts. *Alice is a ghoul. These dead flowers are a statement of her control on earth and Garnet's from the grave. What better reason can a man have to marry than to inherit and save his eternal ass? Emmy, you are so beautiful; why can't you be lovable?*

A bewildered Billy stood beside his son, and, at Larken's insistence, to which Alice finally acquiesced, a bemused Runner stood directly behind Larken. A radiant Aunt E. stood beside Emmy, lovingly clutching her brother Finch's hand. No matter the circumstances, this was Aunt E.'s happy day. Ivy bent over behind Emmy, carefully arranging the folds of the wedding dress and correcting an upturned hem. She signaled Runner with a nod, which he interpreted immediately; Runner reached forward and gently tapped Larken on the shoulder.

Judge Brink had to repeat the question. "Do you, Larken, take Emmy?"

Larken's reply was terse. "Yes."

A weary Judge Brink brought the whole episode to a close, raising his voice above a final clap of thunder. "Then by the power vested in me by the great State of Louisiana, I pronounce that you are man and wife. What God hath joined together let no man put asunder. You may kiss your bride, sir."

Larken turned to Emmy and, noting her dirty look, sarcastically replied, "Maybe another time. How much do I owe you?"

The judge whispered, "Five dollars."

Emmy glared at Larken. "Make him give you cash." Larken felt around in his pockets and came up empty-handed. Billy handed him the money. Emmy rolled her eyes and laughed out loud hysterically, while Alice clapped her hands.

Emmy crossed the wide hall with her head held high, trying to regain her composure. She paused in the corner of the dining room, where Uncle Marcel and his rocker had been moved for the festivities. Emmy held Marcel's thin little hand sadly, while he babbled and cried his well-wishes. Fetch and Chloe offered their congratulations, handing Emmy a luncheon plate and glass of wine. She took the wine but waved the food away. She half-heartedly thanked them, then stood by the dining room table and absentmindedly picked at the food laid out for buffet.

Larken came up beside her. She stiffened in his presence. "Well, Larken, we did it, even if in name only."

Larken shrugged his broad shoulders. "Don't worry. I promise to keep this marriage in name but not in my bed."

For once in their lives, E. and Alice entered the dining room arm in arm. They seemed well pleased and, smiling broadly, Aunt E. embraced Emmy and Larken. "When you all said 'You did,' Runner and Ivy and I said we did too. It was all lovely, especially the flowers, just as though they'd been pressed in the family Bible for the past thirty years."

At E.'s sarcastic mention of the dead funeral flowers, Emmy laughed. Larken thrust a bite of ham into her laughing mouth and remarked, "More ham. Is there nothing Aunt Alice can't think of to do to a pig! Here, a wedding gift."

"Or payment for a job well done?" Emmy retorted with her mouth full of ham.

Ivy set the dishes she was removing from the table on the sideboard and quickly laid a firm hand on Emmy's arm. She had heard the rising anger in Emmy's remark.

Larken would not let the matter lie. "Job well done? We just agreed there would be none of that."

Emmy pulled away from Ivy and stood close to her new husband, looking up into Larken's face. "You're disgusting."

Aunt E., sensing trouble, moved between the newly-weds. "Oh my! Your first quarrel as man and wife."

Fetch and Runner raised the window louvers and a cool, refreshing, northeasterly breeze blew the lace curtains. The storm had blown through. The brilliant sunshine blinded their eyes, its warmth easing the tension. Runner placed a strong arm around his friend, and Larken responded to E. "I'm reasonably sure it won't be our last. Wonder when we find out what our fortune is for this done deed."

Judge Brink was jovial as he said his good-byes. The cleared weather and the praise of his performance reckoned his happy departure. When the judge was out of sight, Alice reentered the house and, poking her head into the dining room, summoned everyone into the parlor.

"Said the spider to the fly: stand tall, it's money time, boys and girls." Larken said as he led the way.

"This settee-sitting is getting monotonous," quipped E. to Ivy and Runner, who stood behind her as she settled herself between Emmy and Larken, hoping to keep a little peace.

Billy sat across from them flanked by Alice and Finch. It seemed Billy was to do the honors, since he nervously patted a sealed envelope in his lap. He cleared his throat and, in his kind and gentle voice, addressed Emmy and Larken.

"Larken, as my only son, and Emmy, as Finch and Alice's only daughter, it is no secret that we hoped you two would marry. It was obviously Garnet's wish as well."

Billy's hands shook as he opened the sealed envelope and read, "Congratulations on your marriage. I have left to my sister, Emeralde Ferrell and to Mr. and Mrs. Larken Blakemore the sum of two hundred dollars. And there is a little surprise package for each of you. God help you all. Garnet."

Finch crossed the room and timidly handed each of the three a package. E., Emmy, and Larken sat mute and motionless. Ivy and Runner hovered protectively, moaning in disbelief. Alice silently signaled Billy and Finch to follow her into the hall. She whispered, "We need to leave imme-diately to avoid the temper fit that is most likely to ensue. Besides, we need to go to town—now. We will buy a trous-seau for the bride and necessities for the rest of them."

Emmy looked past Aunt E.'s stunned face to Larken. "I married you for two hundred dollars? Or is it one third of two hundred dollars?" Holding up the envelope in her hand and ripping the end off she sputtered, "and what's this?"

Aunt E. spoke blankly, "We are . . ."

Emmy sifted through the papers in her envelope and interrupted in a whisper, "We can't be."

All three had ripped open their packages, and papers lay in their laps and strewn on the carpet. Ivy and Runner left the stunned trio long enough to gather glasses and a decanter of sherry. Larken looked at Runner in horror and, downing his sherry in one gulp, turned to Emmy. "A warrant! Look at this! They've already taken legal action. What's in yours?"

Emmy stared in a state of shock. "Bills! Flocks of unpaid bills! And a warrant! Doesn't that mean I am wanted?"

E. fanned herself with the empty envelope. "Two hundred dollars from Garnet does not begin to cover these bills. How many months has it been?"

Larken stood up and papers fluttered to the carpet. "None of this has been paid in months, maybe years. I guess they have every right to demand their money or come after us. There's maybe fifteen thousand dollars worth of unpaid bills here. It could be more." He looked to Runner for support, but Runner was momentarily in shock.

Larken began to pace. "We'd better get on a train and fast! If Bates wants his money, he can't kill us. Then he'd never get it. If he is trying to collect on a bounty, he has to bring us in alive."

E. fanned furiously. "Somehow that doesn't reassure me. We'd better get on that train tomorrow. Madisonville is the closest depot."

Emmy stood up and brushed the sorry evidence from her lap to the floor. She stretched out her glass to Runner for a refill and dramatically proclaimed, "I'm a felon. I used to be such a nice girl. And I've married a felon!"

Larken turned on Emmy. "I'm not giddy about this either. You think I've lived my life hoping to be a felon?"

Emmy began to pace alongside Larken. "You've lived your life being as worthless as pantaloons to a prostitute. My heart is beating so fast. Please, God, let me die before that train leaves tomorrow!"

Larken raised his eyes to heaven. "Listen to her, God; she means it. For my sake, let her have this one request!"

Emmy sank to the floor, the beautiful wedding dress billowing around her. "That's right, wish me dead. Then you could be wanted for murder too."

Larken squatted before her. "Being hung at sunrise would beat the hell out of going through life, let alone God knows how many miles, with a shrieking shrew!"

Emmy pounded Larken's chest. "A shrew? I didn't get us into this!"

Larken, now vexed to the marrow, grabbed Emmy by her wrists. "No? Every damn bill in these boxes was incurred for the pleasure and comfort of all five of us. Yes, Mrs. Blakemore, all of us."

Emmy strained to release his grip. "Shut up! Don't you

call me that!"

Larken released Emmy and sat cross-legged on the floor. He reached for one of the scattered papers and read aloud, "Boston Arms, bar tab, bill for a new dress for that party."

Emmy nodded. "That dress was for your birthday."

Larken lowered his voice. "Well, I never received that dress."

Emmy picked up one of the papers from Larken's batch. "Two cashmere coats, Larken? Two? You must have looked pretty thick."

Larken scrambled the pile of debts and pulled one out at random. "Here's a topper, baby. Nine hundred and fifty dollars for an emerald bracelet and earbobs?"

Emmy smiled sweetly at Larken. "What did you expect? You only gave me the choker. It looks cheap not to have the set."

Larken was now on all fours. He lunged at Emmy and growled, "Choker, that's what I should do, choke her. God, go ahead with her heart attack before I choke her!"

E., Runner, and Ivy left the parlor in the last moments of Larken and Emmy's tirade. Chloe and Fetch stood in the shadows of the hallway wide-eyed. "You heard?" queried E., who noticed their obvious consternation.

"We heard clear in the kitchen, and even old, deaf Uncle Marcel heard," whispered Fetch.

Chloe was not at all pleased. "It took us a while to calm him down, but he's asleep in his rocker now."

"Doesn't this take you back to when they were kids? Larken and Emmy, I mean."

Ivy's recollection brought some relief to Chloe and Fetch, and the group nodded in mutual remembrance.

"Oh, yeah," piped Runner. After a moment he asked, "We're going to San Francisco?"

Aunt E. saw the incredulous faces of Chloe and Fetch. She put her arms around them and tried to soften the blow. "'Bout all we can do. Pack us up for the train tomorrow. Whatever we left in town, steal from here."

E. smiled reassuringly at Chloe and Fetch as the voices of Larken and Emmy rose once again to a fevered pitch. "Never you mind them; they'll wind down directly. Where are Finch, Billy, and Alice?"

Fetch answered, "They left over a while ago for town to do some shoppin'."

"Huh," mused E., "how odd."

Finch, Billy, and Alice returned to Fairlake Farm early that evening with two wagonloads of purchases. Alice crossed the front porch and entered the hall issuing orders. She called out to Chloe and Fetch to help Billy and Finch unload the wagons, adding as they scurried past her, "We need all the help we can muster."

Larken and Emmy still sat on the floor of the parlor strewing papers, with a newly refilled sherry decanter between them. Aunt E. reclined on the settee, and Runner and Ivy sat on the floor beside her. These two jumped to their feet as Alice stormed into the parlor. Alice seized the decanter from Larken's hand and thrust it into Runner's, ordering, "Take this and lock it up, and throw out these awful flowers. Ivy, go make pots of coffee and set out biscuits and ham. This will be a long, sleepless night. Larken, Emmy, this room's a mess. Clean it up and, E., help them, please. When this is in order, each of you go immediately to your respective bedroom and stay there until further notice."

As if in a trance, they all obeyed without questioning.

Alice's next orders were to Fetch and Chloe, who stood among the packages in the hallway. "Go to the attic, bring down the traveling cases, and deliver them to the front upstairs hall. When that is done, Fetch, get Runner and feed and water the horses."

Alice, Finch, and Billy systematically delivered the purchases to their assigned bedrooms, leaving four extra bundles in the hall tagged for Ivy and Runner.

Emmy sat on her bed fingering the many dresses. "I can't believe this."

E. stood inside the door. "She did the same for me."

Alice pushed past E. and entered Emmy's bedroom. "Each of you ladies has the same number of dresses, similar in style more or less: three are plain and one is frilly. Remember my shopping was hurried. These were the best offered and will just have to do. Of course, you have your fancy gowns, the ones you were wearing when you arrived. Now, go into the hall and select your traveling cases. Here are Ivy and Chloe to help you pack. Larken has Runner and Billy to see to him."

"Mama." Emmy embraced Alice. "Mama, you are wonderful for all you have done for us. I hope to be more like you someday."

Alice held Emmy close and whispered, "You will be in time, dearest Emmy, of this I am sure."

Emmy and Ivy packed quickly and silently, each respecting the other's private thoughts. Ivy broke the silence. "She, your mama, Miss Alice, bought me a pair of shoes to replace the ones I left in New Orleans."

The wagons were loaded and the horses hitched. All had been accomplished, as Alice had intended, by dawn of the new day. Everyone assembled at the front of the house. Uncle Marcel sat in his rocker. Ivy crouched beside her grandfather and wept. Chloe stood behind her daughter, with one hand placed protectively on old Marcel's shoulder and the other clutching a kerchief that wiped away her unbidden tears. Runner and Fetch sat on the steps, their heads bowed low. Runner had his arm around his daddy, and the two rocked back and forth in loving mourning. Larken and Billy sat together on the wagon seat, and Emmy and her parents stood close by with E.

Uncle Marcel rose to his feet and addressed the Lord above in a voice loud enough for all to hear. He spoke with the grace and assurance of the very old. After Marcel had thanked his Maker for all good things, he turned his attention to those near him.

"Children, every time we meet we say this might be it. When we lose sight of one or the other, we say this may be our last time. When you come home here, where are you coming? Nowhere permanent. Now, you know the truth. Where's our true home?" Marcel lifted his eyes, scanned the heavens, and raised outstretched arms. Just then the pink dawn broke over the timber trees in the eastern sky. "Now, when you go home there, you're really goin' some place, and there you don't have to say good-bye."

Fetch climbed up on the wagon seat next to Larken. Billy, now standing next to the wagon, reached up to squeeze his only son's hand for what he felt was the last time. Larken squeezed back and looked into his father's face, but neither had words to say.

Runner hoisted a dazed and slightly hysterical Emmy

into the wagon. Ivy and E. helped pull her up, and then Runner jumped on the back.

"Better hurry to meet that train, Daddy."

"Runner, I know these horses better than you!"

Finch reached up and shook Larken's hand. "Now when Bates shows up—yes, we know about Bates—we'll fend him off and hopefully be able to confuse him."

Larken gratefully nodded his head. "If anyone can muddle Bates, you can. But be careful; he's mean."

Alice had the last word. "Don't be hard in your heart with Garnet. If we'd let things go on, you'd have had no financial future."

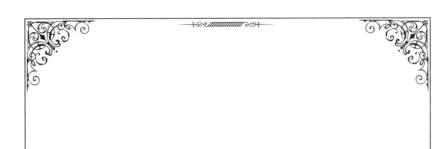

Chapter Six

Good heaven! What sorrows gloomed that parting day,
That called them from their native walks away;
When the poor exiles, every pleasure past,
Hung round the bowers, and fondly looked their last . . .

OLIVER GOLDSMITH

By 1867, with the advent of the railroad and the Western expansion, the small town of Independence, Missouri, had burst forth into burgeoning growth and incessant activity. It was from here that wagon trains left on the Oregon Trail, as hundreds of pioneers responded to the government's urging to settle and farm the newly acquired virgin lands.

Small merchants stockpiled fortunes simply by supplying the necessities for the westward-bound travelers and accommodating the wagon masters and cavalry on the layover between trips and sorties. Opportunists of every description met the train to hawk their wares. Boys, some barely old enough to carry small parcels, hounded the arriving passengers for pocket money as they loaded the wagons and carts bound for the many wagon train offices surrounding the depot.

Hotels, saloons, and stables sprang up overnight, as did smokehouses for drying beef. Mercantile stores competed in prices, and feed and seed stores advertised saplings for the planting of orchards.

The forges of the smithies never cooled down, and the noise of their hammers striking the anvils trilled all night long. The tethered beasts whinnied and neighed in objection to their confinement, nervously waiting to be freshly shod for their long journeys.

The wagon wheels and mule teams stirred the dust continuously, so that men covered their faces in kerchiefs like masks and frequented the saloons to slake their thirst and salve their dry throats.

Having braved the hard wooden benches, the cinders blowing through the windows, the acrid fumes, and the nauseating odor of the unwashed masses of passengers on the train, Emmy, E., and Ivy cleaved to each other for strength and support as they faced another grueling scene. Independence, Missouri, was a mass of dust, heat, and people. They were used to the bustling streets of Paris or London, but this was unadulterated chaos. This civilization was not at all civilized to their way of thinking. The three stood on the platform of the depot, staring in dismay at the confusion before them, covering their ears to drown out the racket and their faces to avoid the grime and the dust.

Larken and Runner unloaded the last of their baggage, and Larken impatiently fended off the hordes of youths who vied for his attention. He shouted at two of the least obnoxious boys who were already shoving a pushcart in his direction. "Is there a wagon train outfit around here?"

The larger boy hollered back as he loaded the cart with their luggage. "You rich?"

Larken grinned and shook his head. "No."

Watching the lad and his younger accomplice count their many bags, Larken was momentarily amused at their astute observation and impressed by their nerve. The boy eyed Larken in disbelief, shrugged his shoulders, and pointed to a small shed several yards behind the substantial building that housed the wagon train offices.

"Then yonder's the one for you."

Larken read the sign that squeaked on rusted hinges from the front-stoop railing. "Belmont's."

The smaller boy stared at Emmy in awe and, when she smiled, he ducked his head and blushed. "You shore is clean, ma'am."

Emmy took a small coin from her purse and pressed it into his grubby hand. He nodded his thanks and quickly took off with his friend, pushing the loaded cart to the shed, where they dumped the luggage in a heap. Then, laughing and counting their "take," the boys sprinted with the empty cart down the middle of the road, in and out between mules and wagons. Emmy good-naturedly shook her fist after them, and Larken, still grinning, entered the wagon train office.

Emmy sat on a bench outside the shed. The roof's eaves offered a bit of shade from the stifling heat of the sun overhead. She fanned for breath and wiped the smudges of dirt from her forehead. Her muslin traveling dress blended into the dirt and dust around her. *Mama chose this dress wisely, just as if she'd been here before.* A tear made a streak down her cheek. As miserable as she was, Emmy found herself dozing. She awakened with a start when Larken returned and, for a moment, she lost her bearings. He sat on the bench beside her and spread out the papers with the wagon train instructions.

"Where is everybody?"

"Store." She pointed down the road. "They wanted a chew."

Emmy leaned against Larken's shoulder and glanced over at the papers. "What's all this?"

"Rules and provisions for the trip. Says we leave tomorrow at daybreak."

"Stop it; I'm too tired to laugh at your pathetic jokes."

"Daybreak, no joke." Larken added, "Since we don't know the distance between Bates and us, the sooner we get out of here, the better. Actually, we're lucky we don't have to wait a few days."

Emmy nodded without a fuss as she scanned the wagon train instruction papers and noted, "Funny. There's not one word about servants or food or stock or laundry."

Larken patted her hand. "It's a given; they probably show up just in time to leave."

Runner, E., and Ivy approached the shed laden with packages.

"Hey!" Larken called out above the noise of a mule team passing between them. "I've only bought the two wagons!" And Larken said to himself, *Thank you, Billy, for slipping me the extra money.*

"Got some chew and rock candy." Runner handed Larken one of the sacks. "And here's a fine bottle of libation for our hotel room."

Ivy opened a parcel for Emmy to see. "We bought sunbonnets; the patterns aren't bad."

E. untied her package. "See, darlings, checkers and cribbage and new playing cards, like civilized people."

"Where are we going to stay tonight, and how are we going to get this stuff there?" Runner motioned toward the large pile of luggage.

"To answer your first question: on the west side of town in our wagons. We leave at sunup." Larken waved his hand at the dismayed faces of the three. "Don't for one minute forget Bates. We need distance, and leaving before the next train arrives here tomorrow, well, that's our safest move."

Around the corner of the depot, in a flurry of dust, ran the two boys, pushing their cart. Cheerfully they called out, "Halloo, time to move on, Mr. Blakemore."

"And there, Runner, is the answer to your second question."

The west side of town was even noisier and busier than the depot. However, a large hotel offered public bathhouses for both ladies and gents. Even though all the rooms at the hotel were occupied, the women took full advantage of the hotel's amenities. They rested on the hotel verandah and sipped cooled sassafras tea and dined on chicken stew and hard rolls.

After their rest time they felt refreshed enough to tackle organizing their newly acquired provisions in the wagons. Larken and Runner were embarrassed to admit that although they were both experienced in handling horses and wagons, the bridling and saddling and rigging for the carriages had always been done by the horse grooms in the barns. They tried to mimic, without much success, the other men working to get their wagons ready for the morning departure.

It had been a contentious day, so when Aunt E. brought out the sherry bottle with a few tin cups, Larken and Runner thought one drink would be just the thing they needed to keep them going. Emmy and Ivy, having repacked the cooking utensils, again, so they would not rattle in the wagon, both gladly accepted the sherry. After the fourth round of drinks, it was decided unanimously that the rest of the packing would be best left until morning.

E., Ivy, and Emmy stretched out in the wagon to sleep a few hours before dawn. Shortly thereafter Larken and Runner crawled into the back of the other wagon to nap a while.

It was only a miracle and the heat inside the wagon that caused Larken to awaken as early as he did. He sat up and punched Runner. In the darkness he heard the noises of activity and knew they had better get moving.

Larken's nervous voice awakened the women. "It's time to move!" He held up a strap and to Runner said, "Where's the other side of this thing?"

"The mule?" Runner's muffled voice called out from beneath the wagon.

"The leather thing." Larken sounded impatient and

irritated.

Emmy poked her head out of the wagon. "The sun's coming. Just start throwing things in. Ivy, you help Aunt E."

E. yawned and stretched her cramped legs. "What time is it?"

Ivy raised a flap and peered out toward the east. "It's gonna be light soon, doesn't matter what time it is."

Larken's tired voice rose above the shouts of the other men as the wagon train's departure drew near. He was totally agitated and exhausted. "Runner, is this thing tight enough?"

Runner checked the harness. "Tight enough for my money."

"What the hell does that mean?" Larken was immediately sorry for his sharp response to his old friend's attempt to ease the tension.

Runner put his arm around Larken and whispered kindly, "Means I don't know any more than you."

The fevered pitch of voices and the bustle of preparations were now replaced with a still hush of anticipation as the wagon train awaited the final command.

Larken stood with the others outside the wagons and issued his final orders. "Look, the sun's coming up. E., you ride with Runner and straighten that wagon as we go. Emmy, you and Ivy do the same in this one."

All was in place and ready. The mules snorted, and the horse pawed the dirt and shook its mane. The sun was bright and blinding, and the silence was pierced with a shrill "Hi-Ho" as Mr. Belmont, the wagon master, sounded the departure.

All moved, with one exception. Emmy and Ivy's wagon stood still. The mules walked away, completely unhitched.

An angry Belmont rode up on his horse and, with the help of the other men close by, got the mules back in place and hitched them properly to the wagon. A few remarks were made to Larken but, in general, the men stifled their amusement. Emmy could not contain her hysterical laughter. Larken roughly seized the reins from her and, shoving her aside, growled, "Shut up, damnit!"

Chapter Seven

The sun descending in the West,
The evening star does shine;
The birds are silent in their nest,
And I must seek for mine.

WILLIAM BLAKE

L eon McInally and his wife, May, found the five eccentric people in the train's last two wagons entertaining and in dire need of their help. After the first morning's fiasco, Larken had quietly offered Leon payment for his expertise and his assistance. Mr. McInally refused at first, but after a week on the trail and repeated threats from Belmont, he reconsidered and accepted Larken's offer. Leon was amazed at Larken and Runner's inability to savvy manual labor and their total ignorance of the basics necessary for survival. He remarked discreetly to May, "Even the black man's hands are soft." Leon taught Larken and Runner how to quickly harness and unharness the mules, keep the tack fit and in order, and start and douse a campfire. The wagon wheels needed constant tightening and the canvas flaps required mending and securing.

May shared trail recipes with Ivy and helped with the cooking. She learned checkers from Aunt E. Though May was younger than Emmy, she was wiser through hard experience. May wasn't pretty, but thin and pale; her mouth and temples were already creased with lines, her little bony hands rough and calloused. Emmy loved May's gentle ways, but was increasingly perplexed at her consistent patience with and respect for her husband, Leon.

At first Leon and May were alarmed by Emmy and Larken's bickering. But in time they learned not to take the Blakemore's outbursts too seriously. Eventually they became more amused than concerned with their banter. Each night the McInallys reviewed the day, whispering in the privacy of their wagon, gossiping and giggling over the barbs and retorts of the Blakemores.

Ivy's goodness gladdened May's soul, and the two reverent spirits became devoted friends. May confided in Ivy, revealing her plain and impoverished past. Ivy and E. delighted May with their descriptions of Paris, New York, and New Orleans. These places May would never see, and she begged them to repeat their stories over and over.

Over the days and weeks the friends became more familiar, and Emmy probed May's good heart for the secrets to her marriage. Leon was not handsome; he was not educated; he wasn't even clever. But May's devotion to him made Emmy envious and sad at her own plight.

One day in the late afternoon, the two women sat in the shade of the wagon. The train stopped early that day so the men could make some needed repairs. Emmy sighed as she watched May apply salve to her blistered hands.

"May, how did you two know of your love?" Emmy raised her eyes in apology. "Stop me and tell me to hush if I'm getting too personal."

May lowered her voice to a whisper. "We didn't. My brother and Leon's father betrothed us as children. We've just tried, that's all, and love and respect have grown."

Larken walked around the side of the wagon leading his horse. "There's a farm near here," he said, as he cinched the saddle's girth. "A chap named Collins lives there and raises vegetables; Leon and Runner and I are going over to buy some. Get a pot of water boiling for supper."

The women watched the men depart. Runner's long legs dangled as he rode behind Larken with his arms around Larken's waist. Leon rode beside them. At the top of the hill, Larken slowed the horse and scanned the horizon. Leon reined in his horse, looking in the same direction.

"Someone following you?" Leon asked.

"Yeah," replied Larken.

From that day on, Leon wanted to keep a cautious watch on Runner and Larken's flank.

"There's smoke over the trees." Runner pointed up in the sky. "I guess Farmer Collins is cooking." Rounding a bend on the worn path, the men spied a small cabin in a clearing.

"Looks like he just lit that fire," Leon observed. The men called out as they approached but received no reply. They dismounted, tied the horses, and, calling again, entered the cabin.

They found him in his garden. He hadn't been dead for long.

"Guess his heart just gave out," Runner whispered reverently.

They dug a grave and topped it with a crude cross. Runner prayed aloud over the mound of dirt, and the three men wiped their eyes unashamedly. The finality gave Larken an uneasy feeling that he didn't like. This solitary man in the open country: Larken did not quite understand why a man he did not know could bring him emotions such as this.

After putting out the fire, they locked Farmer Collins' cabin door and took along his old horse and hound with them. The men halted their horses at the edge of the lush garden. Runner spoke quietly under his breath. "Let's get what we come for so as not to shame the man by wasting his toil."

The three pulled up turnips, onions, radishes, and a sack full of sweet potatoes, tying the vegetables to their saddles. When they neared the edge of the clearing, they met a group of men from their train, bound to buy vegetables. Larken waved them to stop and told them what had happened.

"Help yourselves to the garden. It's free for the taking." As the men rode off, the hound broke loose and ran back toward the farm.

The three men returned to the wagon train in silence. The loneliness overwhelmed Larken with an unexplained grief. He thought, *I didn't know that man.* Rubbing the gold wedding band with his thumb, he tried to recall his Mother's face. "Runner, why did he choose to live alone?"

"Don't know. Some folks are scared of loving; hurts too much in the losing."

⊹⊙℃/////////⌁⊙⊹

The next morning the wagon train departed. The dust rose in puffs in a dry relentless wind, stinging their faces, and the sun baked and smothered their bodies. Emmy rode beside Larken in the wagon, puzzled by his moodiness. The evening before, when Runner and Leon told them about the vegetable farmer's death, Larken said nothing and withdrew after supper.

Runner pulled Emmy aside and said, "Let him be." Larken never joined them for drink and checkers, but sat outside for most of the night.

Emmy tried all morning to make Larken angry or to make him laugh. This day as they rode along he seemed indifferent.

Larken glanced over at Emmy, amused at the sight of her. Two kerchiefs covered her forehead and neck beneath her sunbonnet. Her face was grimy with dirt and her red curls poked out stringy and damp. A blob of thick milk curd was spread across her nose in a futile attempt to ward off freckles and sunburn.

Emmy squirmed in discomfort. "How far do you think we go in a day?"

"Two, maybe three thousand miles, maybe." Larken's ridiculous reply failed to shut Emmy up.

"We've been at this for three weeks. I'm hot. Aren't you hot?" Emmy thought, *Damn it, Larken, talk to me.*

"Yeah." Larken stared straight ahead.

"You are hot but you don't want to talk about it?" She nudged his side.

"Yeah." Larken stared ahead.

"Why not? I'm hot." Emmy pulled up her skirt and

wiggled out of her petticoat.

Larken glanced her way briefly. "It makes me hotter to talk about how hot it is."

Emmy covered her face with her petticoat. "This dust is stifling. How can you breathe?"

Larken jerked her petticoat from her and wiped his face with it. "I haven't drawn a breath since we left."

"But you don't want to talk about it. If we weren't always the last to be ready to go, we wouldn't always get stuck at the back in the dust. Where are we anyway?"

Eyeing Larken's clenched jaw, Emmy was secretly pleased with herself. *At least I'm making him angry.*

Larken thrust her petticoat back into her arms. "It's hot as hell, the air is full of dust, and I haven't the vaguest concept of where we are. Now, either shut up or throw yourself under the wagon wheels. Can you do one or the other, please?"

Emmy smiled to herself behind her petticoat. *Larken's anger beats that awful indifferent pouting any day. His anger I can handle.*

She reached up and turned his face toward her and, smiling sweetly, finished him off with, "Geez! I'm hot." Larken kissed her hard on the mouth.

Chapter Eight

Curse not the king; no not in thy thought; and curse not
the rich in thy bed chamber; for a bird of the air shall carry
the voice, and that which have wings shall tell the matter.

ECCLESIASTES 10:20

The United States Army felt it had largely abated the "Indian Problem." The government signed treaties with the Indians, and, though renegade factions popped up on occasion, the real threat to the Western settlements came from the outlaws. These men formed pockets of gangs, drawing their members from the deserters representing both sides of the recent Civil War. The army's best men had been called back from the Western outposts to participate in that war, leaving a vast area unprotected.

The outlaws were resourceful, and an amazing network of cooperation existed among them. The gang leaders were not always riffraff but, quite often, astute opportunists taking advantage of the vacuum of law, order, and authority.

They were a menace to the normal progress of civilization, and the U.S. government formed a relentless effort to ferret them out of their hiding places and hang them. The outlaws were now challenged to thwart the determination of the best officers of the United States Cavalry.

Bates entered the saloon at Mitchell Pass, also called Scott's Bluff. He ordered a whiskey and surveyed the crowded room. The whiskey was bad and he spat it out, ordering the bartender over his way to pour another and to "do better this time."

The bartender looked at Bates. "Yes, sir, I can oblige." His hand shook as he poured the whiskey. He had seen all sorts, but in this one he looked into the yellow eyes of a snake.

Bates gulped the liquor and seemed satisfied. "You seen a man called Blakemore?"

"Don't know the name."

"Dandy, an' always travels with two highfalutin' women an' two darkies."

"Oh, yeah. They come in here stockin' whiskey fer the trip."

"Trip west?" Bates questioned.

"Yeah. He a friend of yours?"

Bates grabbed the bartender's arm. "I do the askin'. Gimme that bottle."

Satisfied, Bates walked out of the saloon and into the street as a small group of cavalry rode up. Ducking his head, he hurried out of their way.

The captain called out to two boys rolling a hoop. "Hey there, boys."

"Yes, sir?"

"You seen or heard of Victor Brock or a man called Pinky?"

"Yes, sir. They was through here a while back an' braggin' 'bout how they done took a load of money, shot a man, an' got caught. Then some stupid jake leg let 'em get away."

"Is that right?"

"Who are you?"

"Captain Jake Leg."

The boy was scared he'd sassed an officer and ran off.

The captain, a man named Harris, spoke to his corporal. "Vic and Pinky are probably back in the Roost."

The corporal shook his head. "If we don't bust that Roost open, it'll be your butt, sir."

Captain Harris, unmoved and confident, replied to his corporal, "Keep tight in your own butt, Corporal. Camp the men just outside of town. We'll head for Fort Laramie in the morning."

Bates had taken it all in. He leaned against an unhitched

wagon out of the soldier's view but within earshot. He had come to enjoy stalking. Bates believed himself smart and clever. The more information he had, the better. Also, out here folks thinned out and paths crossed. Today's stranger might be tomorrow's enemy or important source of information. He had the goods on Blakemore: The man owed lots of money and Bates would get a cut when he brought him in. Bates hated this conflict of interests. He dreamed of killing Blakemore slowly and had several methods of torture in mind, yet delivering him alive would make Bates wealthy. He would get Blakemore one way or another. He was moving in closer every day. After he got him, then what? The stalking was delicious. He'd ride on the flank of the cavalry tomorrow, keeping sight of them to Fort Laramie. Tipping the bottle dry, Bates weaved his way into the saloon for a refill.

A few days later in Fort Laramie, Larken and Leon rolled a new wagon wheel from the back of the blacksmith's shed. As they rounded the corner, Larken pulled Leon back and they flattened themselves against the shed wall. Leon McInally instinctively and furtively sidled into the shadows and heeded Larken's motion for silence. Larken's attention was fixed on Captain Harris and his salute to his superior officer. Colonel Fenton descended the steps of the Fort's headquarters. Harris dismounted his horse, and the two officers shook hands and engaged in covert conversation.

Larken wiped the sweat from his forehead and broke the silence. "I'll swear and be damned."

"What?" Leon spoke in a whisper and placed a reassuring hand on Larken's shoulder.

"I knew them years ago at school. We had a pleasant enough acquaintance back then, but since my leaving there was not under the best or fairest of circumstances it might be more comfortable if I avoided them all together."

Larken's past dubious amusements had followed him all the way from his days at West Point. Six months before the gunfire at Fort Sumter he had been expelled after trifling with the Commandant's daughter, who took Larken more seriously than he had intended. When Larken told the Commandant of his childhood betrothal to his second cousin he was unceremoniously shown the gate. Just at the time when speculation of war between the states turned toward reality, Larken was sent packing from West Point.

Larken mused. *Also, this probably would not be the appropriate time to reacquaint myself with these good men, since, apparently, me and my companions are wanted.*

Taking care, Larken and Leon returned to the wagon train unobserved.

Larken's main nemesis, Bates, lost a day outside of Scott's Bluff when his horse went lame—unquestionably the gift of a benevolent Providence. Bates, consequently, had lost sight of the cavalry unit.

The wagon train camped outside the west gate of Fort Laramie for three days, making repairs and packing in fresh supplies. It was wise to cross the mountains in early summer before the snows came, and Belmont was rightly anxious to get started. He issued orders for an early morning departure and rode the line of wagons to check the readiness of his travelers. He soon spied Larken and Runner laboriously hoisting the wagon as Leon attempted to set the new wheel in place.

Belmont, irritated, grumbled under his breath. "Blakemore again!" Dismounting, he shouted, "What the hell, Mr. McInally? I expected better judgment from you." He approached Larken's wagon and continued his tirade. "This is damn fool's folly. It's almost dusk. You've had three days to see to this. Get it done."

On this evening before the next day's departure from Fort Laramie, Ivy settled May to stirring the stew and Aunt E.

to stoking the fire. While the two ladies performed the easy tasks and chatted incessantly, Ivy snared Emmy to help her bind and hoist the McInally's provisions into their wagon.

Ivy suspected May's condition; she knew the signs. Though she and Runner had no living children, she had carried, in the early days of their marriage, two babies to almost full term. Ivy therefore kept a discreet but careful watch over her friend, carrying the heavier loads and insisting on more frequent periods of rest.

A harmonica played a wistful tune amid the murmuring voices and occasional shouts that came from the many campfires. A horned owl screeched and the horses snorted and the cattle lowed.

Suddenly the sound of splintering wood, and the ensuing thud of a wagon falling, struck terror into the hearts of all within earshot. In moments, torches lit the blackened night, and men's voices arose, shrill and high-pitched, intermingled with the wails of the womenfolk.

Larken tried in vain to pull Leon's broken body from under the wagon wheel, but Leon's chest was crushed. It had happened so quickly. Larken could not put the pieces together of exactly how Leon had come to be under the enormous weight of wagon and wheel. Several men rushed in to help, but Leon was losing life fast. The wagon wheel was finally lifted and Leon's body pulled free. May was there, kneeling, caressing, pleading for her husband to stay with her.

Leon McInally died just before midnight. May sat with him dry-eyed as stone and crooned and whispered to her beloved. As Leon's spirit escaped, a cool refreshing breeze blew, and the gathered mourners marveled that a chorus of birds sang from the top perch of an old gnarled tree.

May stood and relinquished Leon's body to the care of others. She stoically reached out to Larken and, as she fainted, Larken caught her frail little form in his strong arms. He stared for a moment at the limp body of May in his arms. Runner stepped in to help Larken carry May to her wagon.

After they placed her gently on the blankets in the wagon, the women, including Emmy, E., and Ivy, cautiously took up their vigil. Larken walked back to their wagons without a word.

The camp was hushed in reverence. Even the animals' voices were stilled. Aunt E. and Ivy sat by May all through the night. The flickering glow of candlelight showed dimly through the canvas of the McInally wagon. Little ones nearby were lulled to sleep by Ivy's "Balm in Gilead." Women, and men too, wept as Ivy lifted her grieving voice in hope and wailed the refrain, "To heal the sin-sick soul."

Runner looked up as Emmy returned from one of the many trips she had made to the McInally wagon. She had gone back and forth this long night, never quite sure where she was needed most. Larken's ashen face frightened her, and she grieved almost more for Larken than for May.

"Ivy with her still?" Runner asked. Emmy nodded to Runner but kept her eyes fixed on Larken. Runner nodded back, "I'll go to bed. She'll be with her the night through, most likely."

Larken looked up and spoke to Emmy in a hoarse whisper. "Did Aunt E. go to bed?"

Runner added more wood to the fire and hesitated to hear Emmy's reply. "They're all three talking. Seems that May's going to have a baby." Now the tears began to pour from Emmy's eyes and she sobbed. "Aunt E. asked May if she told Leon about the baby before he died. You know what? She didn't. Do you know why? She didn't want him to worry about her. She promised him that she would be strong. She wanted him to die in peace. She said that if he was to know about the baby, God would be the one doing the telling."

Emmy knelt by Larken and laid her head on his knees. Runner moved silently away but paused in the shadow of the wagon to hear Emmy's next words, "Larken, I wish I could be the kind of wife May was."

Larken stroked her hair and replied, "Maybe you could be a better wife if you were married to a man like Leon. Go to bed, Emmy, for a while; there's little left of this night."

Runner had heard. His bowed head rose to see the

first hint of dawn in the eastern sky, and the dull ache in his heart lightened.

In the early hours of the morning, Larken sat staring into the campfire. Runner stood from time to time and added chips of wood to enliven the dying embers. The other men returned from Fort Laramie where they had taken Leon's body to be buried in the graveyard by the cavalrymen. The Colonel had arranged lodging for May. An eastbound wagon train would take her back to Missouri within the month.

Chapter Nine

> . . . my wicked Life and my solitary Life began
> both on a Day.
>
> DANIEL DEFOE

The wagon train departed Fort Laramie one day behind schedule. Less than a week later, violent thunderstorms and torrential rains wrought havoc on the train's progress, necessitating the constant repairing of wagon tarps and the oiling of stiffened saddle and bridle leather. The trail ruts were thickly mired. One wagon after another bogged down.

A proud and overly zealous Belmont shouldered his responsibilities, deeming any deviation from orders a personal affront. Delay could prove hazardous to the train if early snow fell in the looming mountains. Belmont's impatience erupted into miserable fury when a bolt of lightning struck a tree, killing his horse that was tied up there and destroying two of his supply wagons. He vented his frustration on Larken. The blame was not well founded, for Runner and Larken had managed to ready their outfit each morning against all odds. Many a bet had been placed to the contrary, Belmont being the chief loser.

Larken's mood since Leon McInally's death had been somber and unresponsive. He seemed oblivious to Belmont's abusive tirades. Runner, silent and protective, worked beside Larken during the day, and at night Runner would listen to Larken talk out his grief with a bottle of port between them.

Toward dusk on the eighth day of the drive from Fort Laramie, one last violent deluge came to a thundering halt, and clear, vibrant blue skies broke through the clouds to the west. The blinding sunset poured its soothing warmth over the plains, and the weather-weary travelers emerged from their shelters to build campfires and cook and replenish their dwindling provisions.

On this first fair evening, E. and Ivy delighted in the preparation of supper and chatted incessantly. A playful breeze fluttered their skirts and lifted their spirits. Larken strolled past them without a word and, bottle in hand, made his way toward the shadows of the makeshift horse corral. Emmy's worried gaze followed Larken out of sight. Runner noticed, reading her expression. He squatted beside her and patted her hand. He pointed his finger at her tin of untouched food and gently persuaded, "You eat, Darlin'."

"I'm too upset to eat. Where is he, Runner? There's no fussin' and no fun." Emmy bit her lip but a sob escaped her.

Runner encircled her in one strong arm and whispered, "Right now he's sortin' things out. He'll be his ol' rascal self soon enough."

Emmy held back her tears and mustered a faint smile. She reached for her supper and took a bite, welcoming the kindly nod of approval from Runner.

"This is good, Aunt E. Thank you, Ivy. Take some food to Larken, Runner, and coax him to eat. There's a lot for him to sort out."

Larken did eat the supper Runner brought him. Through the evening hours Emmy could hear the murmur of their conversation and an occasional chuckle. She sat through the night huddled on the wagon seat, wrapped in the cherished nap quilt Alice had made her when she was a baby. It was one of the few keepsakes she had brought with her from her mother's house. In the privacy of darkness, her tears flowed freely and somewhat relieved her homesick heart. Emmy did not necessarily miss her home at Fairlake Farm, but she did miss the gaiety of the life they left behind. She was aware of Runner and Larken's quiet, sober return to the camp about midnight.

Emmy crawled back inside the wagon and, with a hope-ful sigh, lay down next to her soundly sleeping Aunt E. She touched her aunt's quiet form gently and whispered to herself. *She's always just let me be.* Emmy, now calm, slept.

Larken had seen Emmy huddled on the wagon seat and watched her retreat inside as he and Runner parted for the night. He adjusted his saddle for a pillow and wrapped a horse blanket over his shoulders against the night chill. He tucked his boots inside the bedroll to avoid varmint invasion. Stretching his long legs, Larken flexed his toes almost in a fit of mirth. It was good to lie here with a clear head, to rest on this starry night. *I do vex you sorely, don't I, Emmy.* And Larken slept, reproved in a peaceful reverie. This blessed night, he felt free of the sick, fitful uneasi-ness brought on by the menace of Bates.

Larken awakened slowly to the rooster's crow and the ensuing chatter of birds. The cool breeze of early morning refreshed his sweating forehead. He lay still, eyes closed, and reveled in the glad sensations of his interrupted dream. In the dream he was a small boy and Emmy was a baby. Larken smiled as he recalled the memory. Emmy had taken her first baby steps in total confidence toward his outstretched arms, preferring and trusting him over the doting and coaxing of anyone else. A sharp and unaccustomed pang of conscience over this new responsibility of being a husband unsettled him. He had always felt deeply for Emmy, but this new relationship of marriage was awesome and overwhelming. He was afraid he could not live up to being the kind of husband he felt Emmy deserved.

Without warning, Larken was socked in the jaw and a rough hand grabbed him by the throat. Belmont's grunting voice was hoarse and exasperated. "This is the last morning we'll wait on you, Mr. Blakemore. You and your family been holding us up every morning. No more!"

Larken was dragged from his bedroll gagging and retching. Belmont, shouting obscenities, rolled him over in the dirt face down and, in repeated yanks, hauled him by his hair to the icy water of the horse trough. With little strength left, Larken struggled and gasped for air as Belmont repeatedly doused his head in the putrid water. Adding final insult to the previous injury, Belmont hauled Larken upright and, wheeling him about, flung him downhill into the animal-dung pit.

With the advantage over a startled, stunned, almost drowned Larken, Belmont advanced toward him with fists clenched, ready for a fight. A crowd had gathered quickly, with shouts and groans of excitement and disbelief. They fell silent as Emmy pushed through them to Runner, who now stood defiantly between Belmont and Larken. Emmy's wail pierced the deadly hush. "Runner, Oh God, Runner, help him!"

Larken began to laugh hysterically. He squatted in the muddy filth and made no bodily move but to sputter water and muck from his mouth. Belmont lowered his fists and barked out. "We leave now." He looked around at the crowd and continued, "Everyone be ready." He stomped off. The crowd muttered its disapproval of the wagon master's excessive action, but quickly dispersed.

With matted hair and crusted body, Larken, with Runner's help, hitched the mules while the ladies hastily prepared to depart.

They had not been on the trail five minutes before Emmy smiled sweetly at Larken and said, "Lord, you stink. And I'm hungry."

Larked laughed at her. "I do stink."

There was no need to salt the wounds of the wagon master's chagrin. Belmont's anger lingered in his stare over the next two weeks, which he vehemently fixed on them as he would ride the lines of the wagon train back and forth daily. E. pointed out, and rightly so, that Belmont's pride would be assuaged at cost to them.

Though Larken did not want to admit it, Belmont's outrage had spurred him to work harder and faster upon rising in the mornings. He and Runner talked to other men in the wagon train about the fastest ways to hitch the mules, break camp, and keep their wagons prepared. They encouraged E. and Ivy to watch closely and learn from the women the best habits for tidying up the campsite and wagon before retiring for bed. Emmy even learned some new campfire recipes that did not require as many pots and pans to be cleaned and stowed. They had become so efficient that there were actually a few mornings when they were not the last wagons to pull out and get in the line.

Belmont still spoke gruffly to Larken, if at all. Larken did not feel as though they had redeemed themselves completely, but he was proud of his little group. He knew it was Belmont's responsibility to keep the whole wagon train on schedule in order to make the mountain passes before snowfall, so they would have to keep up their good work.

One evening, though, Larken decided it was time for a little fun.

"We have all pulled together these last few weeks, and I think we've mastered this trail living. We have worked hard, so tonight let's get everything ready early and open a bottle for just a few drinks and . . ." He winked at Ivy, "a little Chinese checkers."

By the time of the full-moon's rising they were ready for the morning's departure. They opened a bottle of port to toast their combined efforts and pulled out the Chinese checkers board and began playing. Having decided to keep watch over each other, just in case they got too carried away, they crowded into one wagon, with one or two awake while the others slept. Emmy complained, "How come I have to stay up first?"

Runner needled her with a tweak to her chin and playfully retorted. "Because not one of us can wake you before you're ready."

Ivy moved her marble to set herself up for the win and mused. "We're taking turns so we won't be late and get left behind."

Instead of sipping, Emmy gulped her cup of port. It tasted so good after so much work. She pushed her legs hard against Larken's ribs, stretched, and yawned. She slurred her reply. "Ivy, you're only acting that way 'cause you're ahead in checknese chiners."

Larken rubbed his side and moved Emmy's feet, taking the cup from her. As she tried to snatch it back he laughingly held it out of reach, teasing her. "Don't take this as criticism, but you're a little drunk and a little bitchy."

Emmy replied with a grin, cheered by the return to their usual sarcastic banter. "It was my upbringing." She reached inside her little bag, removed her nightdress, and pulled it over her day clothes, tugging down and smoothing it to her satisfaction.

Larken watched her, bemused at her childish routine of things even in these odd circumstances. Emmy's little fist was closed throughout this maneuver, still holding tightly to her set of marbles. Ivy and E. were falling asleep, and Emmy searched under them to retrieve the large marble sack; she counted the marbles, and plopped them back in one by one. Seeing that Larken watched her without disdain, Emmy put her head against his shoulder and sighed. "I'm just gonna take a tiny little catnap."

Larken let her stay but, slapping her lightly on the cheek, filled her cup with a sip of port, and offered her a bit more. "No, no you aren't. We'll talk."

He sat her up. Seeing Runner grinning at them but nodding fast toward sleep, Larken tried hard to think of something to say, something to discuss. "Why were you called Runner?"

But Runner was barely able to respond. "I was known . . . for my . . . speed." And Runner passed out.

Emmy handed her cup to Larken, which he filled, as well as one more for himself: anything to keep them up and talking. Emmy took a genteel sip and, smiling, noted, "Look, it's just us. You and me. We don't give in to drink."

Larken, agreeing with her, pulled her head back against his shoulder. "I'm at my best when I'm vulgarly drunk.

Shall I make sublime and enduring love to my chaste cousin-wife? It would keep us awake and occupied."

Emmy did not stir. She realized, even if she was a bit inebriated, that her reply was of importance in the scheme of things. "Stop drooling and button your trousers, Larken. I'd sooner welcome a good vomit after a hard night drinking than to stir a sheet with you."

Larken laughed and, while he held her close, they stayed quiet and fell asleep.

Aunt E., as usual the earliest to awaken, attempted to extricate her stiffened legs, which were pinned down and cramped beneath Ivy's heavily sleeping body. E. felt an urgent need to visit the wooded thicket adjacent to the camp.

Most mornings it was dark inside the wagon, but not so this day. An ominous orange glow filtered through the canvas cover. E. scrambled over the others and breathlessly poked her head outside to verify what her fast-beating heart already knew. Daybreak had come some time ago. She jumped from the entrance to the ground and, spinning around in every direction, broke the deadly silence, shrieking, "We've been abandoned!"

A large black buzzard answered her shriek with a

piercing caw, frightening her. Swooping and flapping its wings, it landed in a tree nearby. E. fell to the ground and covered her head.

Runner, Ivy, and Larken scrambled down from the wagon in fitful consternation and confusion, rudely aroused by the simultaneous shrill bugle of bird and aunt. Emmy awakened slowly to the commotion that invaded her sweet reverie of home and her soft down bed, of her mother's tapping foot, and her clock's ticking. A fly buzzed her nose and mouth, and she brushed it away from the drool of her lips. Emmy's head ached and her eyes stung from sweat trickling down her forehead. Her hair was damp and sticky, and, when she tried to sit up, she found it was painfully stuck to the melted tar of the wagon tarp. Outside, the others heard Emmy's moans of agony and disgust as she tore her red curls loose. They turned in unison to receive her hysterical tirade. Standing in the wagon's entrance, mute, with her hands outstretched toward the merciless sun, Emmy circled her arms, motioning in horror at the empty expanse. There was no one there but them, no other wagons, no other people.

❦

Emmy sat on a stool on the shaded side of one of the

two wagons. As E. and Ivy snipped matted curls with scissors and combed tar from strands near her scalp, Emmy grimaced in pain and shrieked an occasional "ouch." With most of the painful procedure done, Emmy lowered her voice, whispering for the hearing solely of her aunt and Ivy. "Now I guess we have Larken to lead us through this God forsaken wilderness!"

But Larken listened from the sunny side of the wagon out of view of the women. He and Runner had tended the mules and returned unnoticed. Larken rounded the corner and startled Emmy. He faced her in eager anticipation of a spat.

Because of the dreadful circumstances, there was need for clear thinking. Larken had no clue and no direction, and a good set-to with Emmy was in tall order; it would borrow time. He replied with conviction. "I can hold my own!"

Emmy lowered her head into a bucket of rainwater and glared at Larken upside down. "I doubt that!" She continued gasping for breath and growling, "We might still be with the wagon train if you'd . . ."

Larken jerked the lye soap from Ivy's hands and, pushing her aside, began to scrub Emmy's hair, holding her struggling body firmly with his other strong arm. "If I'd what?" He scrubbed harder. "If I'd never gone to sleep? Well, I did go to sleep, and they left us; so we're here now, and fighting won't get us anywhere."

Larken released his hold and Emmy, freeing herself, upset the bucket of water and stood screaming at Larken. Her beautiful hair was bobbed short in odd places: uneven, standing stiff and straight out from her face. Her nightgown was streaked with black tar and dirty water stain, and its silk ribbons were wet and shriveled. She sobbed. "We aren't anywhere. Where would you have us go?"

Larken observed his precious mess of a wife, so childlike, so pathetic. He knew he must stay in control for her sake, and for them all. He pointed his finger at her and scolded. "One more word and I'll tell you exactly where you can go."

After a sparse supper the five desolate travelers spent the night in fitful sleep, in lonesome, dark isolation. At dawn they began preparations to go. But where and in which direction? Fort Laramie was nearly two weeks behind them, and Larken was not sure they could keep to the trail the whole way back. Larken had decided the obvious, that is, to head west, with the sun to their backs. He had no idea where this would take them, but northwest would be the wagon train's destination and, therein, the mountains and Bates. Bates by now had probably found out they were traveling with Belmont's group. There was no way Larken and Runner could tackle either of these alone with three defenseless women.

The women cooked a filling breakfast: oatmeal, dried beef, and cornbread. Ivy sat in the wagon this early morning, gazing out at the cloudless sky and already sweltering horizon. She stared mournfully at the sickening vultures, which kept circling, waiting. Larken and Emmy resumed their bickering at daybreak, and their continued fussing was wearing on her nerves. Though Ivy usually found herself amused with them, right now they were not funny.

She closed her eyes and rocked herself, folding her hands in prayer. She quietly wailed her sacred song, stabbing at the heart of the awful silence of this uninhabited wilderness: "There is a balm in Gilead," she sobbed with the passion of her Island forebears, "to heal the sin-sick soul."

Runner dropped the iron skillet he was stowing in their supply wagon and ran to Ivy; pulling her down into his arms, he gently hushed her.

Aunt E., who was accustomed to Ivy's soulful singing, did not realize the depth of her emotional outburst. She reacted to Runner and Ivy flippantly. "Your 'balm' sounds to me more like dry bones in this barren land. Where in the hell is Gilead anyway?"

Emmy called out from the back of the wagon. "Doesn't matter, you can bet Larken can't find it."

Larken, adjusting the harness on the mules, yelled

back at Emmy, "Just shut up, will you?"

E. muttered to herself now with renewed concern. It's going to be hard to make a party out of this mess.

Emmy crawled out of the wagon and made a swipe at Larken with her hand-mirror. She had been looking at her reflection: red splotches, freckles, ruined hair. She was livid. "I wasn't talking to you, Larken."

Larken grabbed Emmy's wrist and the mirror fell into the dirt; Larken's heel shattered the glass. "I heard ya."

He walked away from them some distance and, throwing his head toward heaven, howled with maniacal laughter and lifted his arms, both to rebuke and implore. One large black buzzard left the treetop. In one encircling swoop, it splattered bird droppings on Larken's shoulder and down his back. Larken chased after the bird, flapping his arms like wings, shouting and laughing. "What the hell difference does it make why or how we're here? We are here and we'd better do something. No! Wait! Let's just live out here for the rest of our lives, in the dust, with the damned birds and the thistles and the Indians and the port and the squirrels and the nuts."

With some relief Emmy, Runner, Ivy, and E. joined Larken in his hysterical laughter. When the revelry slowed and a semblance of calm quieted them, Ivy with a serenely radiant smile said, "Oh, Larken, honey, Gilead is here."

She pressed her hands to her bosom. "Gilead is here in my heart and He's in your heart too."

Runner smiled. "Larken, better listen to her; she knows things."

Larken hugged Ivy and said, "You've told me that a hundred times, but sometimes I just need reminding."

Larken nodded and continued. "There're some trees out there; let's go find some water."

On the far side of a rocky hill, within shouting distance of the wagons, two Indians crouched. From their vantage point they had watched all that had taken place since early morning. They were silent, for their sign language allowed them noiseless conversation. However, on occasion they had to muffle their laughter. The Indians could not comprehend what circumstances would bring two sensible men out alone with their women. They decided the men must be loco and that the Great Spirit had favored them with an easy take of horses and provisions. Larken's sudden outburst and flapping arms confirmed all they were thinking. When Runner and Larken started out for water, leaving the women unattended, the Indians were assured of their good fortune and made their move toward the camp.

Ivy and E. washed Larken's shirt and Emmy's clothes and secured them to the back of the wagon to dry. Emmy changed into her light, calico traveling dress to be ready to leave when Larken and Runner returned with fresh water. When the wagon was all packed, the women rested in the shade of the wagon, fanning away flies and mosquitoes and discussing Bates. Larken and Runner discussed Bates only out of earshot of the ladies, but the three women were well aware of the danger of Bates. Now that the wagon train had deserted them they would be an easy ambush. Before he left, Larken had handed E., the best shot of the three, his revolver; she laid it on the wagon seat.

Aunt E. was the first to see the two Indians standing beside the back wagon. She froze with fear and began to babble, her eyes fixed and staring beyond Ivy and Emmy. With forced composure E. spoke in a high and weakened voice, waving her hands nervously in the direction of the Indians. "Company! How perfectly marvelous! Darlings, aren't you tickled blushing to see company?"

Ivy and Emmy turned around with curiosity as the grinning Indians advanced toward the three now horror-stricken women.

Ivy muttered, "Blushing?"

Emmy trembled but returned a smile and cocked her head flirtatiously. "Why, I could just d-i-die for some company." She prayed for courage and continued. "We've all forgotten our manners. I am Mrs. Larken Blakemore; this is my aunt, Miss E. Ferrell, and our dear friend, Ivy. All formerly of Louisiana."

E. edged toward the revolver while continuing Emmy's line of conversation. "She says 'formerly' because we are moving out West. Well, this is west, but I mean farther out. Much farther!"

The Indians ignored E. and Emmy; both looked at Ivy, who stood still and quiet, staring and unblinking. Out of the corner of her eye, Emmy saw E., almost within reach of the revolver. But suddenly one of the Indians stealthily reached for E. Emmy tried valiantly to divert their attention.

"San Francisco. Have either of you been there?" Emmy was sickened, for she could smell their dung-smeared bodies as she approached them.

The Indian held Aunt E.'s arm gently but with authority and backed her away from the wagon, and they moved beside Emmy. She defiantly faced him, and E. spoke up. "I like men who aren't given to brash verbosity, don't you, Emmy?"

"It's the first thing I notice about a man. And would you look at that beautiful feather and how it sets off his eyes, Aunt E., Ivy?" Emmy gasped as the other Indian swiftly grabbed her and covered her mouth with his hand to shut her up.

E. swung loose from the other Indian's grasp momentarily and replied to Emmy as if both were gossiping at a garden party. "I don't dare blink for fear of missing one single glance." The Indian grabbed her arm again, this time with more force. In terror, E. looked up into his face, her knees buckled, and she fainted into the arms of the Indian.

Meanwhile, Larken and Runner had discovered an abundant supply of water from an underground spring and had filled four bags full and two buckets to the brim. Thus their return was slow and cautious, as they did not want to spill one precious drop. Larken and Runner heard the incessant chatter of the women, but, not hearing male voices, they approached the camp unalarmed.

The Indians were foraging for food and whatever else they could carry when Runner and Larken saw them. They dropped their buckets and bags of water and ran shouting after the Indians. The two Indians took off for the hill toward their horses. Then Runner and Larken saw, to their horror, the three women lying on the ground, staked by their skirts and gagged.

Larken ran for his rifle and fired as the Indians came riding past the camp, whooping and hollering. The trailing Indian fell from his horse.

Larken stood stunned, watching as the surviving Indian rode away. Runner bent down and untied the women. Larken turned and squatted over the body, blood pooling on the dirt and the rock. Larken's shot had only stunned him, but when the Indian fell from his horse, his head landed on a large smooth rock protruding from the grassy ground. The violence disgusted Larken.

"Why did you shoot him?" Emmy sobbed, as she knelt by the lifeless body.

Larken jerked her to her feet. He was enraged. "Would you rather I thank him for what they did to you all?"

Runner sat with his arms encircling both E. and Ivy, calming their hysteria.

Emmy continued to cry. "Oh Larken, all they did was take some food."

Larken pulled her shaking little body to him. "Food? That's it?"

Aunt E., with compassion, reached for Larken's hand. "You couldn't have known, Larken."

Larken stood up and groaned from the depth of his sorrowful agony. "Shouldn't we bury him?"

Runner shook his head. "The other'll come back for his own, and who knows how many he'll bring with him. We better get out of here now. Get up!"

The ladies jumped into the back of the wagons. Larken

leapt onto the wagon seat, turned quickly to see that Emmy was safely in the back, and whipped the mules into action. Emmy, curled up, pulled blankets over her head as if she could hide and make it all go away. Runner followed in the other wagon with E. and Ivy. It was all Runner could do to hold the reins, since he was trembling from head to toe. E. and Ivy, terrified, were crouched low, peering out the back to see if they were being followed. They held on tight as the wagon lurched and jumped over the ground.

***

Bates rode at a good clip. His experience as a tracker told him he was not far behind his prey. Out of the corner of his eye a glimmer of light caught his attention. Thinking it could be a trace, he veered his horse toward it.

Just then the Indian was cautiously walking his horse back. Only having his knife and tomahawk for weapons, he wanted to be sure that the White Men and their guns were out of sight. Suddenly he heard hoof beats and instantly shied his horse back to be still. He flattened his body to the ground where he could see the campsite and his brother lying dead on the ground. Bates approached on his horse, and seeing the remnants of the Blakemore camp, he smelled blood. The wagon tracks were fresh.

There were broken mirror shards on the ground. *That's what caught his eye.* He saw the bloody Indian and thinking he was dead, smiled. *It's not every day you come upon a dead Indian for the taking. That scalp would look good on my belt.*

The Indian on the hill watched as Bates savagely grabbed his brother by the hair and reached for his knife. Suddenly, the fallen Indian came to and reached for his tormentor. The Indian on the hill cried out as Bates scalped his brother, his brother who had not been dead until now. After removing the scalp and tying it to his belt, Bates raised his knife again, this time thrusting it through the scalped Indian's forehead. The Indian up on the hill ripped the tomahawk from his girdle, but then realized he was too far from the man. Having witnessed this desecration, he recorded in his mind every dismal feature of Bates' countenance. He would not kill him now, but would stalk him and hunt him like some mad animal. He would track them both, the one who had wounded the body and the one who had molested and killed the spirit. He had indeed come back for his own.

Chapter Ten

Lord, be my help, for I am in great distress.

DANIEL DEFOE

R unner and Larken agreed on traveling toward the southwest, wherever that might take them. They still trailed their two horses, loosely tied to the last wagon, and they were saddled and bridled and ready. Larken and Emmy rode together on the wagon seat, and she was quiet and subdued after the morning's exhausting encounter with the Indians. Larken did not feel safe to make camp, and he searched the horizon for somewhere to give them cover.

Runner had changed seats with E. and Ivy. Now he sat at the rear of the last wagon, rifle loaded, ever watchful and alert for the danger they knew lurked behind them. Every now and then he would crawl toward the front seat to reassure E. and Ivy and to encourage his trudging pair of mules.

The day became overcast; no rain relieved the dust and no sun guided them. Emmy stood up in the wagon to look back. She said to Larken, "I wonder if Bates has given up on us."

Larken pulled on Emmy's skirt. "Sit down or you'll fall. Besides, there's no sense in being an easier target. The answer to your question is I don't know."

Emmy pulled her skirt away. "I was just waving at Aunt E. and Ivy. You almost made me fall, grabbing like that. I know you don't know, but what do you think?"

Taking Emmy's chin firmly in his rough hand, Larken turned her head to meet his stern, serious eyes. "We're wanted in every state in the Union to the tune of roughly seventeen thousand dollars. I've got a mad Indian who wants my ass as well as my scalp, and I have no idea where Bates is. You'll have to forgive me if I'm a bit preoccupied."

Emmy held Larken's stare. Her blue gingham sunbonnet, bought new in Independence but now faded and grimy, fell away from her head, revealing her shameful hair. Tears mingled with dirt streaked down her cheeks. She could taste the salt of her tears and her nose ran, but she was so frightened she no longer cared. "Geez! You're grumpy," she wailed.

Larken put his arm around her and held her close to his side. Emmy wiped her nose on his sleeve.

There was a copse of trees, Larken noticed, that would offer a degree of cover. He headed for the large shade trees, thinking he could leave the others there and ride ahead to scout out their next move. Larken stopped the wagon and jumped to the ground. Nervously he looked around. *Was it safe enough?*

In wild frustration he yelled, "Where is the sun? Which way is west? Thousands of people have left their homes and families to come out here; where the hell is everybody? This place is like a giant tomb." Breathing heavily but calming down, he asked Runner to water the animals and, needlessly, reminded him to be alert.

Days of too much worry and looking over their shoulders made them both somewhat edgy. Runner got down from his rear sentinel perch in the wagon, his rifle ready. *Did he see an Indian behind that tree? Did he see Bates behind that rock, the one over there?* Runner shook his head to clear his thoughts and, keeping his eyes fixed on the horizon, whispered to Larken. "We got to keep moving; no tellin' where Bates or that Indian is."

Emmy looked at the view around the trees. "Are we lost?"

Larken patted Emmy's tousled head. Her red curls

were starting to grow back, haloed and childlike. He sighed as he held one lovely strand in his hand and spoke softly. "Lost? If we were only lost, we'd be in good shape. Then at least we'd have some place to try to find. The way it is now, I don't even know if we're lost."

Larken turned aside to speak to Runner. "Before we go any farther I need to see what's up ahead. Untie my horse, Runner; I'm going to ride up ahead. Stay here and keep an eye out for that Indian. You and I both know he's out there. His vengeance is just, so I'd rather be done in by the Indian than that low-down Bates."

"You want me to go?"

"No, old friend."

Larken's horse was ready for a run. After a short while he reined in his horse. Larken stopped in both amazement and confusion. He was in the midst of very high hills, each overlapping another, with grass here and there in tufts. The wagons would not be able to climb the hills, but a man on horseback could easily ascend them. Larken made his way around one and then another, baffled because he seemed to be going in circles. He retraced his route and tried again. He repeated the maneuver several times, but he could not find a route suitable for the wagon.

And then he heard voices and laughter.

Larken turned his head slowly, scanning the hill above.

Two men stood leaning against a smooth out-crop of granite toward the summit. They were smoking cigars. Their laughter was infectious and Larken, overcome with both shock and exultation, dismounted his horse and led him up the hill, roaring all the distance with the laughter of a mad man. He reached the strangers, out of breath and weak in the knees. "Thank God. Can't say how grateful I am to see you. I am in need of directions."

"You jist been 'bout ever direction there is, mister," one man said with a sardonic smirk.

Larken extended his hand to one and then the other of the two men, and the men cautiously shook hands. "My name is Larken Blakemore. I'm afraid I haven't a card; forgive me."

One of the men elbowed his companion. "Dang, Bobby, I think I gave my last card to that nice man at the Grand National Bank in Denver." The two men chuckled over their private joke, excluding Larken but at the same time scrutinizing him.

Larken saw that their hands never left the gun holsters at their sides. He noted that the tall, skinny guy was left-handed. "My family and I are looking for San Francisco. Is it anywhere near here?"

The shorter of the two men answered. "Not even close. I'm Bobby Gary. This is my associate, Slick Lindon."

"How do you do." Larken nodded politely. "I'm not even close?"

The men were well-outfitted: expensive boots, beaver hats. How curious, thought Larken.

"Why San Francisco?" asked Slick, offering Larken a cigar.

Larken accepted the offering with a slight bow, bit off the end and spit it to the ground. Slick handed him his lit cigar, and Larken used it to light his own. He inhaled the first puff with savor and recalled the satisfaction of easier days, when cigars were just one of the luxuries he took for granted. "It's a ridiculous predicament really. I can't stay in Louisiana; can't go north or south, so my only real option is west."

"What are you wanted for?" Slick eyed Larken closely, thinking to himself, *Is this man a fool or is he damned clever?*

Bobby snorted. "Only thing he could be wanted for is smelling to high heaven."

"I apologize for that, but we haven't come across an inn or a bathing house in our travels."

Slick and Bobby rocked with laughter and Bobby wheezed. "I mean you smell awful pretty."

Larken saw each man relax his gun hold. They even seemed to be enjoying him, so he continued: "You're too kind. We do have toilet water, of course, but that can hardly compare with a proper bath." Just to be sassy, Larken blew a couple of smoke rings with sheer delight.

"Hardly," Slick answered, and grabbed a smoke ring in his fist. "You gigging us, Blakemore? Not that I ain't interested in talkin' personal hygiene, but are you wanted or not?"

"What would make you think that?" Larken tapped down his glee, assuming a sober reserve. "Why all the questions?"

"You can't go nowhere but out here, an' you don't seem the sort fer here. You got, I see, assorted studs in the buttonholes of that fancy blouse. Your trousers are citified, and you got Slick droolin' over that gold watch and chain. Fellas in Leadville was sportin' them when we was last there. You're a good-lookin' cuss, Mr. Blakemore, but a trifle fancy. Jist sounds like you're needin' a place to hide. And," Bobby continued, "we're in a position to do the askin' 'cause there're four of us: me, Slick, and these here guns."

The long-absent sun burst forth its blinding rays, and dancing spots blurred Larken's vision. Bobby waved his weapon, indicating his desire for further conversation. Larken's eyes adjusted, and, seeing his most obvious predicament, he complied. "It's not anything so dramatic. I just left a few debts back East and at home, and I haven't the money to repay them as yet."

"You mean banks?" Slick wasn't sure he was following Larken's highfalutin talk, but it was worth a try to figure it out.

"Yes, and gambling houses, hotels, some individuals. We intend to stay out here only as long as it takes to pay it all off." Larken felt himself showing off, saying too much to these total strangers.

Bobby nodded with mutual understanding. "To wait out the law."

"The law? No, these are debts. I didn't steal the money. I thought I'd be able to pay it all back. I couldn't, so my credit is somewhat . . . blemished." Larken didn't think he was getting his point across. It was as if both Bobby and Slick had jumped to some wild conclusion and were holding onto it for dear life.

Slick, catching on, was highly pleased with himself. It was somewhat like conversing with his and Bobby's boss, Big Vic. Took effort for sure, but the reward was educating. "Now that's a interest'n way to say it. I know how that is and it ain't a easy feelin'."

Bobby and Slick relaxed, smiling at Larken, almost friendly, but still behind their guns. Bobby continued, "We work fer a man who was blemished to the grand total of fifteen thousand dollars. It was a record where we come from. How blemished are you?"

Larken blushed. "Only slightly more."

Bobby and Slick now stood on level ground facing Larken with rapt attention. "How much more?" Bobby whispered as if the three were sharing a secret.

"What does it matter as long as I don't owe you?"

Slick put his gun to Larken's head. "Don't matter a damn."

"Seventeen thousand, more or less," Larken whispered back, swallowing hard.

Bobby screeched and Larken jumped. "You took off with seventeen thousand dollars and started shufflin' out here to some place you don't even know about? You're a cool thief, Mr. Blakemore."

"I am not a thief." Larken was now more indignant than afraid.

Bobby ignored Larken's denial. "You spent money you didn't have, knowin' you didn't have it, and you took the goods jist the same. What's that called where you come from?"

Larken refused to succumb to their insinuations and replied with dignity. "Having a line of credit."

Bobby and Slick talked together, ignoring Larken in their conversation. "He sure do make thievin' sound fancy, don't he?" Slick glanced sideways at Larken with a slight smirk of admiration.

"Sure would be a feather in our caps was we to bring in a man who stole the most," Bobby noted.

"It would fer a fact. We got this nice valley no badge ever seen. I'd like to eavesdrop on him and Big Vic matchin' sums and one-uppance. Bobby, have you ever heard the like of Blakemore's gift of gab?"

Larken spoke to himself out loud. "But I understand in California . . ."

Bobby interrupted. "There's law in California now, Mr. Blakemore. I don't want to upset you but I gotta tell you that you are a thief. This place we got is safe fer people like you an' me, what's got little prices on 'em."

"Men who steal and murder?" Larken was defiant.

"Men with lines of credit an' short tempers. That puts it in your way of talkin', if you please, but it don't change the matter." Bobby fanned the air with his hat. "Cool down, mister. What's more, don't be scared of men who done murder. Nobody likes to kill."

"What about Pinky?" Bobby interjected. "Slick, that one enjoys killin'."

Slick nodded. "Well, most don't like it."

Larken looked hard at them. "Have you murdered anyone?"

"Only while protecting recently acquired capital, but,

I got to tell you, I can't eat meat for a week after." Bobby grimaced.

Larken weighed one way out of this mess with another and came to no reasonable conclusion. He needed to get back to the wagons soon, with or without the outlaws. Bobby's last remark convinced him that more trouble likely lay ahead of them than behind; in truth, it was a toss-up. He'd try to take his leave now. "Gentlemen, you're kind to offer your valley, but I just don't think we'd fit in."

Both men closed in on him and Slick took the reins of his horse from his hand. "You been ridin' round the entrance fer the past hour 'fore we met," Bobby remarked with menace. "And we can't hardly let you ride off after comin' so close, can we?"

Larken bargained. "I'm a man of my word. I vow not to tell."

"That's a good trait in a man, ain't it, Bobby?"

"Yeah, but all I know is you're a thief, and thieves can't be trusted, I'm sorry to say. We'll go back and get your family and go into Robber's Roost together."

The decision was made for Larken. With no recourse, he amiably inquired, "Will my family be safe there?"

Bobby and Slick assured him that all would be well. Bobby answered Larken with one hand on his shoulder and the other holding the gun on him. "Oh yeah. There's a armed guard at every entrance. Kind of gives you a secure feelin' knowin' nobody kin get in or out without bein' seen, don't it?"

"Frightfully." Larken was oddly relieved. Here was an armed escort into a valley where Bates and the Indian couldn't find them, at least not for a while.

Bobby patted Larken on the back. "For stealin' the most, you'll have a important status with the boys. Hell, fer seventeen grand, it won't matter that you never killed no one. You didn't, did you?"

Larken immediately thought of the Indian but didn't think it wise to own up to that unfortunate killing, in case it might bring more trouble. He quickly replied, "No, of course not!"

"You'll be right popular all right, but you best be watchful of that uppity attitude you got 'bout killin'." Slick advised.

Larken held his tongue, keeping his thoughts to himself. *First Bates, then Belmont, then the Indian, and now I have these two charming new associates to introduce to my family. I'm under some sort of curse.*

Slick disappeared behind the boulder and returned, leading his and Bobby's horses while motioning for Larken to mount.

Just then a gunshot rang out, echoing through the

trees and carrying its report high into the hills. Larken's horse shied sideways, dragging him in mid mount. Slick dismounted and gave Larken a boost into the saddle. Both men could see that Larken was badly shaken. They knew a secret path into the hills above the trees that was totally hidden from view from the valley below.

They rode silently and, in half the time it had taken Larken when he rode out, they returned to a point just above the two wagons. Larken stared down, shocked and half-crazed at what he saw. Bates held Emmy tightly. Runner, E., and Ivy were tied up at gunpoint and one of Runner's mules lay dead.

Bobby clamped a gloved hand over Larken's mouth before he could yell out and whispered, "Who's that man?"

"He says I took his money." Larken's voice quivered.

"Did you?" Slick asked evenly.

Larken was now grateful for these two outlaws. Their very profession might offer him some hope in this dreadful plight, so he replied truthfully. "Doesn't matter. It was a fair game."

Slick leaned in on Larken's other side, across his saddle horn, and in a low voice insured his confidence. "He know you haven't got the money?"

"Yeah, I think," Larken replied, weak with worry.

Slick continued. "Then he's wantin' to collect a reward

on you."

Bobby and Slick agreed on a plan in seconds, and Bobby ordered Larken, "Ride on down and get him up here some way. We'll take care of him."

Larken felt the wonderful resurgence of power, the confidence of holding a winning hand. He rode down into full view of Bates. He dismounted and spoke to Bates, all the while looking only at him. Emmy's horrified expression gave Larken only a moment's pause. "Bates, I'm flattered that you always seem to want to be wherever I am."

"You're comin' back with me, Blakemore." Bates' face reddened with anger at Larken's habitual arrogance. Bates thought, *Cocky bastard, and he's not even armed!*

Larken was proud of his little group. They uttered not a peep so he might hold Bates' attention. The outlaws seemed to intuitively trust that Larken had a plan and that the plan was now in progress. Larken knew that Runner lay there, silently grieving over the unnecessary, sadistic slaughter of his poor, innocent mule.

Larken answered Bates, shaking his head. "To the contrary, that won't do you any good."

Bates cackled. "The reward will do me a lot of good."

Larken knew Bates was greedy, so he played his high card. "There's more here than any reward would pay."

Bates showed his hand all right. Using Emmy as a

shield, his beady eyes brightened and he drooled spit down Emmy's cheek. "You're a sly one, Blakemore. You had the money all the time?"

Emmy squirmed to free a hand and wipe the slime away, and Bates squeezed her roughly and spat more insult on her hair. Larken looked away in disgust. *Hold on, Emmy, this weasel will pay for that in just a little while.* Larken spoke this vow inaudibly.

"Now Bates," Larken continued, "I'm not fool enough to pay for things when all those gullible people trusted my good name and my fabricated credit."

Bates looked up the hill from which Larken had just ridden and smiled. "You come up with me."

Larken hesitated. "Let her go first."

Bates put the gun to Emmy's neck and snarled, "Not 'til I see that money."

Dear God in heaven, this is working. Hold on, Emmy my girl. Larken held this hope in his thoughts and with feigned resignation he replied hoarsely, "Okay."

"Larken!" In disbelief Emmy called to him for help.

Larken turned to go and, looking at her over his shoulder, he winked. "Don't worry, dear. I'm sure Bates is a man of his word."

Bates coaxed them along, his gun now crammed in Emmy's side, and answered them both with anticipation as he wheezed at the climb. "If there's enough money up this hill, you won't see my face again."

Emmy was confused at Larken's lighthearted wink. *Can't he see that I am terrified? There is no money. Why is he leading Bates on in this hoax? Bates will kill us for lying.* "But, Larken," she sobbed, "there's not..."

"There's not anything we can do. Bates has us, Emmy, so shut up!"

The butt of Bobby's gun came down with accurate force on Bates' skull as Slick tore Emmy out of his clutch. She screamed and Larken cheered, as Bates dropped to the ground. *Wow, what a pair this Bobby and Slick are: not seen or heard, then whack!* he thought with great respect. Larken shook their hands repeatedly. He turned to Emmy and held out his arms. "You okay?"

Emmy responded with tears of relief and joy and clung to Larken. After a few minutes, when she had calmed down, Emmy looked at Bobby and Slick. They were eyeing her with obvious admiration, and they immediately removed their hats. Emmy blushed and smiled as her heroes openly gawked at her beauty. "Yes, I'm okay. Invigorated. If only there was music, then I could dance. Larken, who are your little friends?"

An impish grin spread across Larken's face as he introduced Bobby Gary and Slick Lindon to his wife. "And," he added, "they're thieves."

Emmy's eyes bugged out and her hand flew to her mouth to suppress her shock. Bobby and Slick smiled proudly. Bobby, who was truly affected by her appreciation, addressed Emmy with all the gentility he could muster. "Welcome to Robber's Roost, ma'am."

Chapter Eleven

I give you plain warning 'fair sirs', that you
Had better consult how to bear yourselves
Under these circumstances than give way
To such misplaced merriment.

SIR WALTER SCOTT

olonel Fenton sat at his desk in the headquarters of the United States Cavalry at Fort Laramie. It was a stifling day in the middle of August 1867. A gust of hot air from the one open window blew his papers to the floor, scattering them about. He cursed in his attempt to gather them back in order. The papers were gritty with dirt, and his throat was parched and dry. The colonel swallowed the last of his whiskey and, hiding the emptied glass under his desk, stood up in response to a knock on his office door. A "what now" thought crossed his mind as he granted entrance and returned the customary salute to the officer who entered. "Colonel Fenton?" Captain Harris grinned.

Colonel Fenton's face relaxed into a broad smile, and

he hurriedly offered Harris a chair. "Sit, Tom, it's been a while."

"Almost two months and a promotion for you, sir."

"Yeah." Colonel Fenton looked around his shabby office. "They gave me a raise, made me a colonel, and then stuck me here."

Harris nodded in agreement regarding the meager accommodations, notably unsuitable for a colonel. "To bring law and order to the lawless West."

"Indeed," replied Fenton. "Nobody comes to this hell hole for fun. You wired you needed my help?"

Harris frowned in earnest. "You know of the gang run by Victor Brock?"

Colonel Fenton tipped his chair back against the window ledge and lifted his long, booted legs to rest atop the pile of stacked papers on his desk. He was at ease with Tom Harris. "Big Vic? Know of him? Why?"

Harris felt free to stand and pace back and forth in front of the colonel's desk. He had a sorry confession to make, but no better hands to lay it in than the colonel's. "He, Brock, and his partner pulled a train job. We were tipped off and got there just after the partner shot a U.S. Mint guard." Harris hesitated, obviously embarrassed. "They got away as we were taking them to face charges."

Colonel Fenton didn't seem surprised and nodded.

"That happens."

Though relieved, Harris was agitated. He leaned forward and pounded the colonel's desk with his fists. "What are my chances of getting to them out there?"

Colonel Fenton swung his legs to the floor and stood to look out the open window, away from Harris, with his arms clasped behind his back. "None," he replied. Several minutes passed in silence between the two officers. A trapped wasp buzzed its way to freedom through the open window and Colonel Fenton took a swat at it as it passed. Turning back to Harris, he continued. "Brock and his boys stay in a place called Robber's Roost, southeast Utah Territory, a sort of "King's X" for outlaws."

Harris nodded. "I've heard of it. I was sent to flush the place out."

Colonel Fenton knew that Harris was an eager, ambitious, young captain. He also knew that he, Fenton, was tired of this place and the endless, fruitless pursuit of the "phantom" gangs. He would not discourage Harris but he would offer a stern warning. "Same here. Before you knew you'd found the place, you'd be dead. I've lost some good men at the Roost."

Harris hoped his question would not overstep the friendship and relaxed atmosphere with his superior, but his zeal spurred him to say, "So, what're you doing about it?"

Fenton was not offended and decided to play honest and straight with the young man. "Drinking a lot of whiskey. Waiting. Word is the gangs are getting smaller. There are fewer of them, but they still have the advantage."

"How long have you been waiting?"

"Two and a half years."

Harris whistled. "That's a lot of whiskey. You mind if I go down alone and take a whiff?"

Colonel Fenton considered the young officer too promising to waste, but he was resigned and concluded their visit with advice. "Closest town is Moab. There's a bartender there, name's Jobe. He knows all and says nothing. Start with him but be careful. You do too good a job and you might end up a colonel in a joint like this."

Fenton removed his glass from under the desk. He opened a side drawer, took out a bottle and another glass, and poured them both a drink.

<hr />

Slick stood straddled over Bates' sprawled body. "Want me to finish him off, Mr. Blakemore? Since you're above killin', I'll do it for you; but you got to give the word, as he's your concern."

"No, don't kill him. You say where you're taking us no

one can get in or out without warning? Bring him along with us down into the canyon. We'll tie him up and leave him down there alongside Runner's dead mule. When he finally comes to, the stench and the buzzards will make him wish you'd shot him."

Slick hoisted Bates over his shoulder with a grunt and followed Bobby, Larken, and Emmy back into the canyon. They immediately freed Runner, E., and Ivy amid detailed explanations and introductions, and then securely bound Bates with his own ropes.

"This is jus' me," Slick snorted, "but I got no good feelin' about this man Bates. He's cussed to kill a innocent critter fer nothin', and he's the first white man I ever saw sportin' a Indian's scalp on his belt." Slick added one more nonfatal pop on Bates' skull for good measure.

"Now that the niceties are over, I request, Mr. Blakemore, Mr. Runner, and you ladies, that you lay down here at my feet any and all firearms or weapons in your possession. That includes knives, or even a hat pin." Bobby smiled but issued the orders with his gun trained on Larken. When this was accomplished, Bobby continued. "Mr. Runner, you help Slick tie them two horses what knows each other—yours and Mr. Blakemore's—to the back of this first wagon. Then hitch that live mule to a single harness and drag his dead partner over here next to Bates, as Mr. Blakemore has requested. Trail this man's horse at the back of the second wagon." Bobby kicked Bates with his boot.

"It's gettin' up late in the day. So far, so good. I don't want any talkin', ladies, just movin'. Climb up into that back wagon and go all the way inside, and then drop them flaps. We're gonna secure you in so you can't see out. No argument, no complainin', just get along. You'll be a'right. Mr. Slick'll drive your lone mule. Mr. Blakemore, you and Mr. Runner do the same in this first wagon. Go on inside and don't consider a peek. I'll be out here settin' sideways on the wagon seat, drivin' these two mules. Our horses'll trail 'cause they know we're headed home. Be smart, Mr. Blakemore; any trouble and Slick takes off with your women. If we get on, we'll be in the Roost 'fore sundown. Once inside, we'll let you look out and see your new home. How's that?"

Bobby Gary couldn't recall a better day. He was bringin' in the prize. He just wished Big Vic had been here to see his organizational aptitudes. Of course, if Big Vic had been here, he'd have done all the ordering. He was like that.

Imprisoned in the semi-darkness of the wagon, the three women sat huddled together and hushed. They strained to hear Bobby's further orders to Larken and Runner. Ivy rubbed salve on their wrists, raw from Bate's merciless binding, and softly crooned her prayers for deliverance. She was calm and grateful to have escaped Bates, so she quietly offered up her requests for their continued protection.

With the movement of the wagon their unknown journey began, and each one looked at the others with an identical, quizzical expression of helplessness. "Who are they and where are they taking us?" Aunt E. broke the silence, whispering to Emmy.

Emmy smiled faintly, recalling her skillful rescue from Bates. "They're not all bad, really—kindly thieves. They are taking us to their hideout, a place called Robber's Roost. We'll be detained but, I guess, safe. It's certainly not San Francisco."

"You know, Larken," Runner began as their wagon lurched forward, "I've been saved killin' a man. I was thinking of lots of mean ways to avenge that poor mule. I'd sure hate to be in Bates' boots when he wakes up by that carcass."

"Wouldn't you hate to be the mule if he came back to life lying there next to that stinking Bates!" Larken laughing turned toward Runner.

Runner, with his tear-streaked face, started laughing too. "At least that mule's been used for something more than pulling a load; he's serving justice now."

Bobby, gruff, but smiling at hearing their laughter, said, "You two hush up in there."

Larken, still grinning, whispered, "There's no one I'd rather be in this mess with, headed for the Lord knows where, than you, Runner. Memorize the motion, Runner, and how long it takes when we go down and when we climb."

At intervals along the way, sentinels called out passwords and Bobby obliged with the prearranged response.

"What's going on?" Larken shouted.

"Calm down, Mr. Blakemore, and never you mind; those are the voices of your fortification. Relax and rest assured."

"Yeah, relax. Well, why not? Might as well. You know, Runner, I've always talked my way out before, kept in control. I got no smart answers to this one."

Runner and Larken rode on in silent concentration, nodding at each other as the wagon altered its direction. After some time, about an hour of mental notation, Runner protested. "What good is this doing?"

"Don't know, but it's passed the time for sure."

After a twenty-minute descent, the wagon leveled off. Slick and Bobby slowed the mules to a final stop and threw back the flaps. "Come on out now and see, while there's light left." Bobby called to Larken and Runner as he raced back to the women and offered his hand to Emmy with the poise of a cavalier.

They stood facing a large frame house. The canyon walls were so tall and steep around the house that twilight had set in the valley, even though the sun was still high in the western sky.

"This place here's as good as any. There's a clearin' behind the house be good fer plantin' if you want. Got the biggest tree in the Roost out back." Bobby knew this was the only available place and he thought, *It might just be suitable for these highfalutin' folks.* He was mighty pleased with his arrangements.

The house, not being easily defended from attack, had stood empty for some time. The other gangs in the Roost usually chose to live in the many caves in the cliff walls that lined the canyon known as Robber's Roost.

Emmy was shocked, for, though the house was plenty big, it was badly in need of repair. Even in the shadows of early evening, the dirt piled on the dilapidated steps and porch was apparent. The entrance was vacant and dark; its door lay in the yard. No telling what one would find nesting inside.

Larken looked around. Plenty of grounds surrounded the house and the small sturdy barn; in Larken's mind it was well-situated on high land, with a rocky creek running behind it at the base of a bluff that led up to a steep cliff. "With work, this place could be fixed. Is there any place around where we can buy supplies?"

Slick pointed down the trail that continued past the house. "Weems' place is up the Roost ten minutes. Post Office Tree's jist outside the other entrance. That's the tree with a box nailed to it. The guard'll take your letters and put 'em in; jist be careful what you say."

"Why, does he read the letters?" Aunt E. was settling in. Her optimistic foresight saw the possibilities of a reasonably comfortable home. She was exhausted with travel, and even outlaws were better than no society at all.

Slick had taken a liking to E., who he considered less nervous than the younger one and able to take care of herself. "Those letters got to be read, ma'am. A man with a grudge an' a pencil's as quick to kill as a man with a gun. Can't have that."

"Lord, no, Mr. Lindon. Then we'd lose that secure feeling you were telling us about." E. was pleased with herself for remembering Slick's surname. Mr. Slick Lindon was thoroughly charmed.

Larken had a more practical question. "I'm assuming, Bobby, that you have the authority to offer us this house. Are you sure the previous owners of this land and house won't want to reclaim them?"

"Not likely. They're all dead, Mr. Blakemore."

Runner, returning from the barn to tend the animals, entered in on the tail end of Bobby and Larken's conversation. As he handed Bobby the reins to Bates' horse, he warily asked, "How'd they die?"

"Natural causes." Slick chuckled as he and Bobby shared yet another one of their private jokes. "They stole from Big Vic and Pinky, so, *naturally*, they shot 'em. Well, folks—Mr. Blakemore, Mr. Runner, and ladies—Slick and I better git along and report in with Big Vic and Pinky. With their tempers we sure don't want'em wondering where we are. We'll take along Bates' horse as payment fer our trouble and services rendered on your behalf. Good night all and, as Parson would say, God bless."

The realization began to dawn on Emmy that this burned out shack was going to be her new home and, in her mind, she might never leave. The emotional impact of all the recent events came rushing in on her, and she began to ramble with detached horror. "A year ago this week, I was written up in the newspaper for a party I gave. They said I was like the sun coming over the horizon of the social world for the very first time."

Larken, knowing Emmy's hysterical reverie would have to play itself out, took her gently by the shoulders and placed her out of the way. "Aunt E., you and Ivy start getting the stuff out of the wagons. Choose whatever we might use tonight. We've got a little whiskey; bring it out."

Emmy did not stay where Larken put her but wandered among them, in and out, murmuring. "I wore emerald green and had an emerald comb in my hair, and I didn't sit out one dance."

Runner walked by Emmy with a lantern from the wagon. "Emmy, I remember that dress and you made a right pretty picture dancing that night." He continued on by her to hand Larken some bedding and then up to the front of the house.

Larken said, "I think Emmy's adjusting well."

Runner hollered back in a few minutes. "We best set up camp outside, until we see if we'll be safe inside. Floor looks rotted, but I won't be able to see good until daylight. We got a good water well next to the back porch that I found when I watered the horses. Also, I dug up some turnips and a couple of taters for a soup."

Runner handed Ivy the turnips. Ivy responded, "I'll start a fire for the water." Emmy continued, "We danced all night and ate caviar at three." The rest went about their duties, and they made no reproofs of Emmy.

"That caviar was some of the best we ever had." Ivy smiled an indulgent smile toward Emmy as she danced about in some wildflowers.

Larken licked his lips at the memory. "I wish we had some of that caviar right now."

Runner added in with a laugh, "And champagne. Remember that champagne, cold and bubbly."

"Just whisky for us tonight, old friend." Larken patted Runner on the back.

<hr />

Larken then looked to Ivy, "Is there anything we should do for Emmy?"

"Bless her soul, what with the heat and no decent food and not enough water, not to mention Indians and that Bates breathin' down her neck, and now this Roost place, I think Emmy deserves to go a little off balance. Maybe she jus' glad to be alive. Let her chatter a while," Ivy said as the fire caught.

E. spoke from inside the wagon. "Caviar? Um, that reminds me. We could use some dried bacon and flour from Weems' place in the morning."

Ivy clapped her hands. "I hope he's got some rock candy. Get me some for sure."

Ivy sat Emmy down on a crate and patted her hand. "Honey, what special treat might you want brought from the store?"

Emmy stared into the dark, and her voice was still on the edge of forlorn. "I bet there's not even a cotillion here. Where will we dance and have parties and gossip?"

Larken squatted down beside Emmy, offering her a small glass of whiskey. In a moment she took a sip and enjoyed the burn. Then she gulped the rest of the glass and looked at Larken and smiled gratefully. For the first time she looked Larken in the eye and asked, "Are we going to be all right?"

Larken caressed her hand and consoled her. "I think so."

<hr/>

The last embers of their supper campfire glowed blue, rekindled by a gentle breeze. A full moon cast eerie reflections of light on their future home. Emmy, after eating a bit, was refreshed and quieted. She looked around and took it all in. She held Larken's hand. Unspoken thoughts passed between them.

<hr/>

Runner and Larken set out early the next morning. They passed numerous shacks dotting the slope of fertile land, and most seemed uninhabited. Gray smoke wisped forth from some of the chimneys with an inviting aroma. Across a creek running to the left of the road, one more shack was situated down in a valley, on the banks of the small river. A young girl stood near the door beating a rug; she waved at them with her broom. They returned her cordial greeting, both feeling quite neighborly.

"Man, am I hungry. Let's get us some breakfast fixin's and head home in a hurry. It's been a month since we ate right." Runner rubbed his stomach and switched the mule to a faster pace.

Larken grinned in agreement. "I'm with you ol' friend, but we've got to load up a lot more provisions on this trip than just our breakfast."

Rounding a sharp bend in the road, Runner avoided a collision with three fast-trotting horsemen, stopping abruptly. Relieved but angry, they turned in their wagon seat, swearing and shaking their fists. The three horsemen had stopped down the road; turning in their saddles and staring, they waved and rode on with boisterous shouts and laughter.

Runner climbed down from the wagon to reassure and praise his mule. He noticed a placard on the fence running next to the road. Runner motioned to Larken to read the faded, splintery sign. "Haggar Cattle Company—Trespass and Get Shot." Runner and Larken got back on the road in a hurry to avoid any more unpleasant confrontations. They rode on in silence, bemused and sharing the same thoughts.

The morning was quiet once more, save for the mule's clip-clop and the birds' daybreak chattering. Down the road ahead where the creek narrowed, Larken and Runner saw a man and a dog approaching from the other side. Smooth stepping stones, about eight of them, had been placed for crossing the swiftly running water. The black dog yapped and splashed and swam. The man was clad in a long black robe, a clergyman. He lifted his cassock above his boots as he hopped from one stone to the next, a curious sight to see. As they passed, the man waved and the dog barked a welcome. Larken and Runner returned the greeting as the poor man's right foot slipped from the last stone and went out from under him into the water. He immediately recovered his balance but had to keep shaking the water out of his boot with every step. It was a funny sight, but they stifled their laughter to avoid the embarrassment of one who might turn out to be a friend or an enemy.

The Weems' store was just a larger shack than the ones they'd passed. The proprietor sat perched on the porch railing. As they drew to a halt, he set aside a piece of wood and his whittling knife and stepped toward them with his hand extended. "So you're Mr. Blakemore and Mr. Runner. I been waitin' for you all mornin'."

"All morning? Why, it's just twenty minutes past dawn. How did you know who we . . ." Larken was interrupted and hardly got in another word with Weems, on that day or on any other occasion.

"Don't stand there on formality. Seventeen thousand! It's believed to be a record. Come on in."

The store was crammed full from the floor to the ceiling. Flour sacks rested on lard tins, and tools were stuck at different angles in the piles, with handles sticking out every which way. It was a mass of unorganized mess, as was Weems himself. He appeared to be about seventy years old, mostly bald, with a fringe of dirty gray sideburns. His shirt was buttonless, revealing a white hairy chest, and his trousers were tied with a rope below his flabby, sunburned belly. Weems' reddish face was fleshy, and his tiny blue eyes twinkled with excitement.

Larken cordially shook hands with Weems. "How do you know so much?" Weems shrugged off the question. "So, you plannin' to fix up the house before you plant?"

Larken replied in good humor. "Thought we might."

There was a slight commotion behind the counter as three hound dogs rose up simultaneously and yawned. Runner and Larken returned the contagious yawns. The room was almost stifled with camphor, but Weems did not show any signs of drowsiness in the pungent air. The hounds gawked sleepily and went back down from view behind the counter.

Weems handed Runner a roll of string and a knife and, grunting instructions, pointed at a pile of goods. "Winter comes earlier here than down where you come from. Better plant first. Got all you need packed up already."

Larken was somewhat taken aback at Weems' information and ingenuity and spoke with due respect. "Then what do I owe you?"

Runner had cut several pieces of string. Weems reached for a couple and began to tie up a bundle; he motioned and mumbled for Runner to do the same. In his own time, Weems replied to Larken. "Credit's good here, Mr. Blakemore. You need anything I ain't got, I make a run down to LaSal Mercantile at Moab once a month."

Now, ignoring Larken, Weems addressed Runner. "Put plenty of chew in a extra bag for you an' the aunt, and here's rock candy for your missus."

Runner, now won over, ventured a presumptuous request. "You put in any whiskey?"

Weems carefully handed Runner a couple of parcels. "First thing I packed. Two bottles of my best."

The black dog they had seen at the creek bounded

into the store, knocking Runner off his haunches; shaking water from its soggy fur all over him, it licked his face. Then leaping over the counter, the dog roused the sleeping hounds. There were a couple of dog groans and growls, and the black intruder leapt back over the counter as its master entered the store. Runner and Larken grinned at the sound of the man's step-squash step-squash as he walked toward them.

The clergyman gave a firm command to his errant dog. "Sit, Praiseworthy."

Praiseworthy, whose unbelievably long legs had vaulted her over the counter, now folded them under her body and crept with obedient penitence toward her owner. The tall, regal dog was a lovely creature, black as night, with a white fluff on her chest and four white-tipped paws. Her eyes glistened with intelligent wonder and suggested wolf in her pedigree. Larken and Runner looked the pair over in amazed admiration.

The clergyman was about fifty, slender, and slightly gray. His face was both hard and kind. He wore the white collar and long black cassock of a priest and carried a dilapidated Bible with a tattered hole clear through the middle of it. The man sighed as he handed the Bible to the store owner. "Weems, you got another Bible?"

Weems held the Book up to the light and put his eye to

the hole. He reached behind the counter and handed the man a replacement. "Take care of this one. I only got one left back there. These'll have to last you till I go to town."

Gesturing toward Larken and Runner, Weems introduced them. "Parson, this is Mr. Blakemore an' Mr. Runner. Seventeen thousand."

Parson gave Larken and Runner a hearty handshake and, with deference, addressed them. "I heard. Welcome to the Roost, boys."

Seeing Runner and Larken's fixed stare on the ruined Bible that Weems continued to examine, Parson gave answer to their questioning. "Boys around here take that 'eye fer a eye' stuff literal."

His jovial expression faded, and a hardness came like a cloud to cover his lighthearted countenance as he spoke to Weems. "You seen the paper out on me?" Weems nodded his affirmation and added, "Your bounty runs out the end of this year."

Runner exclaimed in amazement. "You're a preacher and you're wanted?"

Parson waved the question away as if it were irrelevant and returned his hands into a pious pose. "Misunderstandin'. The payroll men misunderstood that I was takin' the money for their own good. Money is the root of all evil, Mr. Runner."

With that matter sufficiently settled according to Parson's way of explaining pertinent issues, he turned to Weems and asked, "Big Vic and Pinky back from their last job?"

Weems shook his head and replied. "No, but I hear they did all right. Cavalry was all over 'em, but they got away."

Parson sighed with obvious relief and for a moment bowed his head as if in prayer. "Good, good. You seen Lela?" he asked Weems, a tender smile appearing on his face.

Weems answered with distinct kindness. "She was in yesterday." He smiled in much the same way as Parson had. Both men paused in their conversation as mutual gladness shone on their hardened faces at the mention of the name "Lela." Parson sweetly added, "Never kin find her when the weather's pretty."

Larken cleared his throat and, not wanting to break the effect of this oddly sacred conversation, asked in a hushed voice. "Is Lela your daughter?"

Parson smiled and placed a gentle hand on Larken's shoulder and answered. "She thinks she's everybody's daughter."

Parson turned toward the door of the store with the obedient Praiseworthy at his heel. His stride still sounded the step-squash.

Larken and Runner openly grinned, reminded of their

first sight that morning of this most unusual man and dog. Parson returned their smiles knowingly and without embarrassment.

He waved a good-bye to them. "Well, got to go bless the Haggar brothers. They are goin' fer a load of cattle in the mornin'." Parson stopped and came back in as if there were something he had forgotten to say or do.

Weems crossed to the far corner of the store and, opening the lid of an old pipe stove, reverently placed the now useless Bible on the coals and set it afire. Runner and Larken watched the ritual and, though neither of them uttered a word, their thoughts were identical: *This society has created its own set of rules based upon propriety and a code of ethics that most outsiders would not expect.*

As the Bible burned, Parson nodded his approval to Weems. With his scrutinizing eyes fixed on Larken and Runner, he hesitated. "Say, I heard somebody shot a Indian about fifteen miles out of the north entrance to the Roost." The hardness in Parson's face had returned.

With nauseating uneasiness, Larken felt that Parson's statement was mostly addressed to him. Covering up, Larken avoided the penetrating hold of the clergyman's perception and, looking up toward the rafters of the store for divine help and sweating profusely, mumbled. "Did they?"

Parson grabbed Larken's clammy hand and shook it.

Wiping the moisture he had received from the handshake on his cassock, he and his dog made their departure. On leaving, Parson got in his final remark. "Jist somethin' I heard. Well, nice to meet you. Thanks, Weems."

Larken and Runner were both stunned and concerned over the encounter with Parson; he seemed a man of most odd and contrary wisdom and affection. They discussed him all the way home that morning. The two agreed that they liked him and that in some way he was interested in their welfare and on their side.

As the two approached the clearing and spied their new home on the hill, Runner shivered as he spoke. "Yes, I like Parson all right but he scares me." Runner paused. "But then, that is true of all we've met so far in this place. Larken, did you see all the stones piled at the side of Weems' store? Tombstones, restin' and waitin'."

"This place is of a different sort than any I've ever known." Larken agreed. "Runner, let's keep this morning's encounter and conversation to ourselves, away from the women. If we are perplexed, there is no way we could explain it all without alarming them. As for Parson, he is like a Merlin, a wizard. He sees the good and the bad from a different point of view than the rest of us."

Runner nodded. "I think he was warning us. He's going to search us out and get to the core of things, the truth.

It's almost as if he is testing our worth for some reason. We are not his friends yet, but he hopes for us to be."

"Yeah, but for sure we can take nothing for granted in this place. Runner, we are prisoners here, held in a jail with folks who follow their own set of rules. One misstep in our ignorance and we're goners without really knowing why."

Chapter Twelve

May we presume to say, that at thy birth,
New joy was sprung in heaven as well as here on earth.

JOHN DRYDEN

For the next few days, the five new "inmates" of the Roost worked feverishly with excitement and without incident. They cleaned and repaired from dawn until dark, with much joking and laughter. They felt amazingly free of all worry, aided by the shouts of encouragement from the various groups of horsemen who periodically halted at the bottom of the hill and stood curiously watching from the road. Not one ever offered to help them. Emmy, with a pout, questioned Larken about the Roost's inhabitants' lack of hospitality. He assured her that this was right, somehow, judging by the way things were done in this place.

"They are checking us out, testing our mettle," Larken explained. "Don't you feel the need to succeed? I do."

One evening, just at dusk, they received their first visitor.

He stood on the repaired porch admiring the smoothness of the planed and restored planks, perfectly fitted without gaps; he knocked on the open front door and tested its swing from the newly installed hinges. The visitor was pleased. An attractive Negro woman to whom he bowed low and removed his hat greeted him first.

"Good evening, ma'am; you are Mrs. Runner, I presume."

"Yes, sir, I am called Ivy," she replied.

Parson smiled and said, "So nice to meet you, Ivy. May I ask, what is your Christian name?"

Blushing, Ivy returned Parson's smile. "Oh, yes, sir, my Christian name is Zita Yvette; I was named for my grandmother and my great-grandmother."

"What a beautiful name, but I do prefer Ivy," he replied as he took her hand. "God sees into your heart, and He is glad."

Ivy hesitated as Emmy stepped in front of her.

"And you are Mrs. Larken Blakemore." The gentleman said this with such gallantry that Emmy's heart skipped a beat, honored to be called by that name for the first time.

Their unexpected guest looked past Emmy and acknowledged E. "And you are the beautiful aunt."

E.'s blush was full-blown as he extended his hand to her. "And you must be Parson." She felt as giddy as a schoolgirl, and she asked him to come in.

"I have come to bless this home, and before I enter I will pray to God from this very threshold."

Larken and Runner, having heard the newly familiar voice, entered from the kitchen and stood behind their womenfolk. Larken nodded, "Good day to you, Parson."

Following his lead, they all bowed their heads. "Oh God, be with these good folk as they try to make this hell of a hovel into a decent home, a home of peace and refuse." (Parson meant to say "refuge," but there was something accurate in both words under the circumstances.)

Emmy held out her hand to Parson and graciously led him inside her new home. "You must be Parson. Larken told me about you. I don't as yet know whether to thank you or cuss you for the blessing."

Emmy felt a surge of security in the strength of Parson's rough hand, for he held hers tightly. His head cocked to one side, he replied out of the corner of his mouth. "That's all right. Around here my blessing is a gamble."

Emmy giggled as she pulled her hand away and reached for the one chair in the so-called parlor. Larken held the back of the chair firmly in his two hands. "Sit down, Parson, but don't lean back or it will give way. It's a bit down on our list for fixing."

"Don't want to keep you from your work." Parson spoke

to them all as he accepted a glass of sherry from Aunt E.

Everyone hovered around their first guest as he bent one way and then the other to look past them and take in the miraculous, quick restoration of the truly grand old house. He was amazed. True, there was no furniture, but that would be remedied shortly, when Weems returned from Moab with the ordered purchases for the house. Parson had never seen Weems as jovial as he now was at buying these folk their furnishings, even on credit. Such an important position as being privy to the newest gossip about the Blakemores had placed the proverbial feather in Weems' cap and filled his store all day with the boys of the Roost eager to hear.

Parson had watched this house go up when it was first built and knew the floor plan. Too, he had visited here on several occasions before the former owner had gotten cocky and taken too many liberties according to the rules of the gangs of the Roost. The original building of the house had set Weems up in business, for a lot of money had been spent on it.

As Larken refilled Parson's glass with their prized sherry, he asked, "Did you ever find your little girl?"

Parson swallowed his second sherry in one gulp and smacked his lips with approval. He handed Larken the glass and waved it away cordially. "That's more than enough hospitality, Mr. Blakemore. Caught up with Lela jist this mornin'. She'll likely be by here. She don't see womenfolk much 'cept fer Ma Haggar, and Lela thinks she's really a man." Parson placed his fingertips together, pursed his lips, and nodded his head in thoughtful agreement. "Can't blame her. Ma don't work at feminine much."

Runner stood patiently to the side of the gathering, mustering up courage to ask the parson a question. He weighed the possibility of rejection, still feeling some reluctance to be too personal with this man. When there was a natural pause in the conversation, Runner ventured forth. "Those men, Big Vic and Pinky, did you ever find them?"

Without hesitation, Parson took Runner into his confidence. "Heard they done fine on a train job back East. Missouri, I think. That was their boys, Slick and Bobby, what brought you in. Keep expectin' to hear that one shot the other."

"Slick and Bobby?" Larken interrupted.

"Naw, Vic an' Pinky."

Parson was irritated at Larken's mistaken conclusion. His face hardened and then relaxed. *It was a good thing, his dropping by, for these Blakemores sure needed his direction and his savvy.*

Larken said, "I thought they were partners."

Parson stood to leave and ended the discussion with

what he intended to be the final remark. "Last I heard. Well, I got to go. Got a early funeral tomorrow."

With all the talk about robbing and killing, Emmy gasped at the thought of a funeral and offered her condolences. "I'm sorry."

Off-handedly, Parson replied as he took his leave. "Don't be; he asked fer it."

The Blakemores stood at the door and watched Parson walk his long legged gait down the path and into the dark. They were completely bewildered. Aunt E. spoke for them all. "That man is a preacher?"

Lowering his voice slightly, Larken replied. "With a foot in heaven and a foot in hell."

Closing the front door, they were startled by a shrill whistle, followed by an interval of silence broken by the distant barking of a dog and a shout that pierced the still, dark night. "Heel, Praiseworthy."

For three days a gentle rain fell intermittently and softened the hardened earth. The large garden plot had lain fallow for several seasons now, and the Haggar brothers' stray cattle had wandered in, providing in their droppings nourishment to the impoverished soil. The Haggars occupied the most land in the Roost, and their farthest pasture to the south bordered Larken's newly acquired acreage.

Larken and Runner repaired the neglected, broken-down fence to keep out the trespassing animals, and established the line of ownership to what was proudly called by all of the Roost, "The Blakemore Spread." Packets of seeds, brought from Weems' store, were waiting on the back porch entrance to the kitchen with hoe, spade, string, and all other necessary implements for the tilling and the sowing.

On the fourth day, the rain ceased and the sheltered birds greeted the warm sunshine and fresh coolness of the morning with warbling song. Amid much chirping and chattering, they foraged for food and bathed in puddles. Larken and Runner scattered them to flight, bounding down the back steps early in glad anticipation of starting the long-awaited planting project. They had studied the manual and were ready.

Toward midmorning, after several hours of spading, they unwound the ball of string, stretching and binding it with pegs at different intervals to designate the rows. Runner began to hoe at the farthest end from the house as Larken squatted in the dirt to check the lines.

The first he saw of Lela was her shadow, which fell over him as she knelt beside him and spoke. "You got a bad eye fer straight, mister."

Larken, keeping his attention on the string, replied defensively. "I meant to do it that way."

Lela leaned across Larken's knee and, making her own judgment, sat back on her haunches and shrugged. "Then you done good."

Larken stood up, pulling her up beside him. Lela was about ten years old and engagingly pretty. This was the girl who had waved at them with her broom the first day they had ridden into Weems' store.

She wore a brown gingham dress and expensive, black-patent boots. Her light brown hair was sun-streaked with gold and held neatly back from her face with a new pink ribbon. A locket on a black silk rope fell nearly to her waist. Above tanned cheeks, her blue eyes fixed inquisitively on Larken. She screwed up her lightly freckled nose and bit her lower lip thoughtfully, starring at him. Larken was enchanted.

To avoid the girl's piercing blue eyes, he looked out toward Runner and waved. Larken thought, *I feel as if she's looking clear inside me.* And to break the spell she cast over him, he asked, "Where'd you come from?"

"Fort Worth." Lela answered quickly and with a smile. She seemed pleased. And indeed she was very pleased with the progress of their acquaintance, just as she had planned.

Larken shook his head in order to correct her line of thinking. "I mean just now."

She pointed toward the large oak tree. "I been watchin' you from over there." She persisted in her examination: "Was you ever in Fort Worth?"

Larken replied, "Yeah," nonchalantly turning his face away.

He was amused but did not want to offend her in the least, should she think he was laughing at her. This child was no fool. She was highly intelligent, earnest, and blatantly honest, and he already valued her friendship. Bending over and loosening the first peg, Larken handed it to the girl, motioning for her to straighten the line. She adjusted it a bit to the right and pounded it back into the dirt with her fist. She stood for a moment eyeing the row.

Satisfied, the girl scampered and squatted from one peg to another until she reached Runner, who had been leaning on his hoe and watching all the while. Larken saw them exchange a word or two and shake hands.

When she returned, the girl resumed her inquiry. "Was you there New Year's Eve, 1856?"

"Where?"

"Fort Worth."

"No," Larken replied as he walked the second row, now easily setting the pegs.

She stayed with him, nodding her approval at his work. "You sure?"

Larken hesitated before beginning the third row. The cool, early morning breeze became sultry hot as the sun rose over the sharp hills in the East. Taking his kerchief from his back pocket and wiping his forehead, he answered her emphatically. "I'm sure."

She stared at him in disappointed disbelief. Larken was sorry that he had upset her and, lowering his voice, he gently asked, "Why? Were you there?"

Lela removed a delicately embroidered handkerchief from her sleeve and, dabbing perspiration from her upper lip and temples, she whispered to him in the sweetest confidence. "My mama was. I's born the next October."

Larken could not help but think of Emmy at the same age. He had always taken Emmy's girlish concerns seriously. The intimacy of true friendship had been theirs from the beginning. He sighed as he whispered back. "Where's your mama now?"

The girl clapped her hands and raised her arms skyward in affirmation. "In heaven with God."

Larken responded reverently. "I am sorry."

She looked at Larken with concern, pursed her lips, and frowned. A cloud of anguish fell over her entire countenance momentarily. When she recovered, the girl spoke like a sage giving counsel. "There's worser places to end up. Parson said."

Larken was relieved at the return to a conversation that he could handle. He couldn't fathom why a conventional "I'm sorry" had thrown the child into consternation. He ventured, "I met Parson at Weems' store. Is he a good man?"

She nodded with delight and her little chest heaved with pride as she answered his question. "Used to have a whole church to tend to down in Prescott."

Runner had gained on them with his hoeing. He kept his distance so as not to interfere in what seemed to him to be a private talk, but he did strain his ears to eavesdrop all he could without interrupting. Now and then Emmy or Ivy or Aunt E. appeared on the back steps, and Runner motioned to them to stay put.

Larken had now pegged and lined six rows of the ten he had mapped out for the garden; the girl worked beside him as they visited.

He asked, "Where is Prescott?"

"Arizona Territory. You don't know much, do you?" Her remark was not rude but gentled with the soft voice of concern. *This man sure needs me aside him*, she thought for a moment, smiling to herself.

"Parson was leadin' a Easter service down there when another preacher got mean drinkin' an' shot Parson bad, so Parson shot him back an' he died, an' so Parson come up here. Besides preachin' an' prayin', he does cavalry hold-ups, 'cause those men is doin' good an' they shouldn't ought to ask fer pay fer doin' what's right." She swallowed hard, out of breath but satisfied.

Larken followed her account, nodding along in agreement, with some sympathy for Parson's plight, until it took its odd turn of justification for robbery. He was appalled but checked his reaction with a noncommittal question. "Is that right?"

"Sure. Parson said." She replied with affirmation.

Larken posed the obvious. "And Parson's always right?"

"He's the servant of the Lord an' the mouth of God hisself." She pronounced this proclamation with her firm little legs set apart and her hands on her hips.

Larken knew better than to argue. The child's immovable loyalty was commendable, if misplaced.

"So, you live with your daddy?" he asked her, having drawn this conclusion.

She shook her head. "Not exactly with him. I know he's here somewhere."

They had finished the rows. The girl followed Larken to the back porch to get the packets of seeds. Ivy had put out a pitcher of water and some cups. Lela could see the women through the kitchen window; she waved at them.

Larken handed her a cup as he drank his water thirstily. The child took the cup carefully in both hands and crossed the newly tilled garden, gingerly stepping over the stretched string. Without spilling a drop, she offered her cup to Runner. Larken saw Runner bow with appreciation as he accepted her gift.

The child did not return to the porch but instead headed for the oak tree. A muslin bonnet had been left there, and now she sat cross-legged on the grass and removed the pink ribbon from her hair. She then started to braid her hair. Runner and the three women in the kitchen beheld the lovely young girl and were smitten.

Larken poured two cups of water and went over to sit beside her.

Deftly she tied the two braids in place across the top of her head with her pink ribbon, tucking the braids into her bonnet and leaving its sashes loose. She thanked Larken as she took the cup from him, exclaiming, "This sun's fierce!"

The two sat in silence for some time, listening to the sounds of midmorning: the droning of bees, the whir of gnats, which they both brushed away, the far-off bellowing of the Haggar brothers' cattle, the far-off bay of Weems' hounds, the bark of Praiseworthy in reply, the murmur of women's voices from the house. They sat there together, a man and a child, and shared their contentment.

Larken spoke. "Have you ever seen him, your Pa?"

"Lots of times. I jist don't know fer sure which one he is, even if I'm lookin' right at him. When my mama was dyin', she told me, she said, 'Lela, your pa is good at his work an' he's a pretty man'." She looked at Larken's handsome face longingly. "You sure you wasn't in Fort Wo...?"

Larken interrupted her. "Positive. What else did your mama say?"

Lela moved to rest her body against the tree and, stretching her legs out in front of her, leaned her head back. Her eyelids were heavy and she spoke in a drowsy monotone. "Said when she was gone to git up to the Roost an' find him."

Larken saw that she was tired, so he ventured to ask only one more question. "Didn't she tell you his name?"

The child closed her eyes and, for a moment, recalled the vision of her mother. She held the locket tightly in her fist. A little sadly, she replied to Larken's question, "My mama was fevery and couldn't . . . or didn't, know his name."

Larken felt it best to leave her to nap a bit if she would. He quietly eased away toward the back porch to gather the rest of the packets of seeds. Runner was there, as were the three women, and he silenced their inquisitive urges with a firm "Later."

Runner and Larken planted half of the rows by noon and decided to take a break for lunch. They were standing by the well washing off the dirt when they saw Lela dart for the garden. She lifted up each sack and examined the label, then dug up some of the newly planted seed.

Larken exclaimed under his breath. "What the hell?"

He sauntered over to her and resumed their morning conversation as unperturbedly as he could. "Who takes care of you? Where do you live?"

She was frowning and seemed displeased with his planting, but turned her head his way and grinned. Her reply was impertinent, impish, and long-winded, as if she had something more important to discuss but would humor him with an answer.

"With Parson mostly. But the women, when they is any, like to make on over me; an' the men, they bring me clothes an' things I need, like this ribbon. Haggar Brothers brung it from Kansas City jist fer me. Parson tells me good from bad, an' he says he don't care who I come from 'cause God sent me same as anybody."

Larken felt launched, as he often did with Emmy, into an argument that he never intended. His reply was typical and disagreeable.

"And you spend your days asking men if they were in

Fort Worth on New Year's Eve, 1856. Did it ever occur to you that there were a lot of men in Fort Worth on that night who didn't know your mother? A lot of men can't remember where they were on any New Year's Eve. I saw you, didn't I, on that first morning we rode to Weems' store? You were beating a rug outside Parson's cabin, the one across the river."

"Maybe." Her blue eyes flashed at him. "You're pretty sure talkin' fer a man jist planted zinnias an' named the row squash."

"What are you talking about? The package says squash." Thoroughly irritated, Larken raged.

Lela held out her palm. "Look at the seed. Can't help what the package calls 'em. Zinny seeds grow zinnias." She was sorry he was so upset. She wanted to help him, so she softly encouraged. "Nothing wrong with zinnias."

Larken lowered his voice, now speaking to her kindly but with dismay. "Nothing, except you can't eat them." He saw Runner duck around the corner of the house, most probably to stifle his laughter.

"Maybe not," she continued, making a sweep with her arms in gesture toward the other rows. "But you'll have a whole lotta beans, squash, and onions."

Larken bellowed good-naturedly. "Is that what's in the rows labeled peas, corn, and beets?"

The girl giggled at their return to pleasantries. "Yeah, but you planted 'em right so they oughta come up good."

Larken tugged the pink ribbon in her hair and winked. They giggled together.

"Why do they put the seed in the wrong packages?" He knew full well what her answer would be.

"So they kin sell 'em to people like you what don't know the difference, I guess." Lela smiled for a moment and then frowned in serious thought as she abruptly changed the subject. "Hear you stoled money you meant to pay back. Where you gonna git that kind o' money?"

Larken took his time answering her. He sensed she already had a plan to offer him, schemed in her uncanny little head as she spoke. He rolled up each of his sleeves precisely to the elbow. She watched him admiringly and waited for his reply.

"Thought I'd worry about that after we got settled." He glanced at her to see if she was satisfied.

The child shook a scolding finger at him. "If you worry, you can't pray. An' if you pray, you don't have to worry. If I had that big house an' those women to see to it, I think I might rent out rooms to some of the boys 'round here what come in with thick pockets."

Her idea was brilliant, and really their only solution, Larken thought. *Let those who go out and rob return and willingly pay off his debts!* Trying to hide his enthusiasm, he cautiously replied. "You think those men would pay?"

"Fer a good meal, a hot bath, an' a clean room, you bet. But that's jist what I was thinkin' I might do if I was you." Lela started walking away, smiling slightly to herself. She had finished with this day's visit, its purpose accomplished.

Larken called after her. "I'd thought about doing just that."

She knew better and let him know it with a shrug of her shoulders and an indifferent, "Uh huh."

He was not ready for her to go, so he caught up with her and took her hand, grateful for knowing her. He shook her little hand and introduced himself. "I am Larken. Larken Blakemore. Will you come back to see me?"

Lela laughed out loud. "Got any more to plant?"

Larken laughed with her. "Yeah, and I'd like to know what I'm planting."

She nodded. "I'll be back when the furniture comes. That your woman over there?" She pointed to Emmy, who was heading toward the clothesline with a basket of laundry. "She's pretty but she's as stupid as you. She your wife?"

"Yes, she's my wife and she's worse, if you can believe it." Larken wondered if Emmy heard them and if she could be as amused at these remarks as he was.

"Judgin's the Lord's work. Keep it up an' you'll burn in hell. Parson said. I seen her doin' the washin' in the spring water; puts orange in your clothes. You drink from the spring an' you wash from the river."

Lela waved at Runner in the garden and at the women she knew were watching her toward the back of the house. Emmy had heard, for she set her basket on the ground and began to examine the washing.

"I'll tell her," Larken called out after Lela, as she disappeared around the corner of the house.

Larken looked down at his orange-stained shirt and laughed. He pulled it off over his head and wiped his face and tousled his sweaty hair with it. Emmy stood a few feet away with a bucket of cool well water and a cloth, admiring Larken's physique. His gambling-salon pallor was now tanned and ruddy and his shoulders muscled and handsome.

Larken felt Emmy's presence and turned toward her as she spoke. "I thought you might like to cool off; your neck is burning."

Emmy dipped the cloth in the cool water and gently laid it on Larken's neck and back. "I can feel it!" He winced. "Your hands are rough."

Emmy slapped his sunburn and fumed defensively. "I can't help it!" She poured the remaining well water down his back and soaked his trousers.

Larken shivered with delight at the refreshing douse and, softening his voice to a whisper, replied with intimacy. "No, I know you can't help it."

He then looked up and shaded his eyes to see if he could still see Lela. Larken asked Emmy, "Did you see that little girl? She's a sassy know-it-all."

"She's cute. You spent the whole morning with her and, from my observation, enjoyed her company." Emmy obviously approved, and Larken nodded his head slowly in thoughtful agreement.

Larken brought Emmy close to his side and stood with her, surveying their garden. "Yeah," he remarked with satisfaction. "By the way, I've decided to plant beans, potatoes, and onions."

Emmy chuckled and threw a wry smile at Larken. "And zinnias?"

He tweaked her nose. "So you heard?"

"Your voice carries. And what's more, what'd she say about renting rooms in the house and your women doing the work?" Emmy looked at her calloused hands and scowled. "Would you even consider inviting those cut-throats in?"

"Seems like a good idea." Larken took her hands in his and faced her squarely. "Emmy, I don't like this place any more than you do. But the only way to get out is to pay back those debts."

Emmy knew that Larken was probably right, but she was still apprehensive. "I know," she sighed with resignation. "But we'd be living with murderers and thieves."

Larken agreed. "But don't you see that we'd be robbing them of their booty?"

Emmy pulled away from Larken. "I think we should talk it over with the rest of the family. Give me your shirt; I'm going to the river for wash water."

"What? Not the spring?" Larken teased. Emmy made a comic face and they laughed at each other.

Weems had still not arrived with their new furniture from Moab so they improvised a dining room table with sawhorses and planks laid across, and most of the group sat upon barrels and crates; Aunt E., presiding in their one chair, towered above them.

They were gathered together as a family to discuss the precarious future. Larken was the first to address the situation. "We just create snobbery; snobbery pays. That's what Aunt E. did when she sold the house in New Orleans to be used as a hotel and casino."

E. spoke from her lofty place of honor. "From the carriage trade to the outlaw trade."

Emmy agreed. "Yeah, catering to cutthroats."

Larken stood and began to pace back and forth, forming in his mind the final appeal to this democratic assembly. Everyone sat quietly and awaited his oration.

Larken now stood by Aunt E., tall next to her. Clearing his throat, he began. "We'd only take the cutthroats who steal enough to afford Blakemore House. Look, I can't . . . We've got to make some money. This is the only way I can think of."

They looked at each other and nodded in agreement.

Emmy spoke the final verdict for them all. "Then there's no point in a vote."

Aunt E. banged her tin cup on the table like a judge's gavel. "Blakemore House it is."

Runner filled their cups for a nightcap and a toast. They were glad to be together, and they laughed as they tidied up the meager fare and began to make ready for bed. They were surely all for one and one for all.

Larken took Emmy's hand as he walked toward the back porch door. "There's a breeze out. I'm going for a walk. You want to come?"

"I guess," she said and held on to his hand.

Larken could feel in her small wrist the pulse of her pounding heart. The many stars brightened the dark night; the delicious odor of the garden's earth filled their nostrils as a gentle breeze brought its fragrance for their delight. From the ground a small, white object fluttered to their feet. Larken picked it up knowingly and pressed it into Emmy's hand. It was Lela's delicately embroidered handkerchief.

Emmy and Larken walked around the corner of the house, loath to retire on this refreshingly cool and tranquil evening. The others had gone to the wagons, for they would continue to sleep there until Weems returned from Moab with beds and bedding. The myriad of stars lighted the path and the surrounding land down to the road that led to Weems' place; their twinkling was mirrored on the nearby creek like sparks of fire. Larken and Emmy stood still and listened to the water's flowing and the distant lowing of cattle. The house was now settled in darkness, so they were startled when Lela jumped down from the top porch steps and faced them with the warmest of greetings and a knowing smile of approval.

"I'll put out the word that we're open for business." And then she was gone.

Larken scratched his head. "Do you think, Emmy, that she's been out here all evening?"

"Seems so."

Emmy sat on the middle step examining her rough, sore

hands. Her eyes welled with tears and she began to sob. "I've got calluses on my hands and feet, my hair feels like straw, and my face looks like leather. I've lost so much weight that my bosoms have withered; I couldn't come up with a half-inch of cleavage if I shoved them up over the back of my head!" She shook her hair loose and untied the ribbon.

Larken sat beside her, took the ribbon, and tied her hair back, smoothing it around her face. He wiped Emmy's tears and her nose with his fingers and tweaked her nose. Forcing a weak smile, Emmy touched his shoulder. She looked at him for a moment, then stood up and entered the empty house. Larken looked after her fondly and thought it best to let her go.

The moon had risen and now outshone with brilliance the light of the stars. Larken walked toward the wagons engrossed in thought. Runner had left an oil lamp burning and Larken lit a cigar by its flame, sitting on the ground by the lamp to keep vigil until Emmy returned. He did not see the lone Indian standing on the cliff above him, silently watching.

Chapter Thirteen

The House should become the church of childhood,
the table and hearth a holy rite.

REVEREND HORACE BUSHNELL

eems received the news of the proposed Blakemore House taking in lodgers while he was still in Moab. Knowing the layout of the house, he made additional purchases to accommodate paying clientele. Once again, the house would provide his good fortune. He was willing to extend Blakemore's credit but now he had a shoo-in, for he would be the sole provider of all the supplies needed to run a small hotel. Weems went so far as to consider refurbishing the old broken-down privy and bought extra lumber to erect a private facility for the ladies of the House. At Larken's request, Weems made the inquiries necessary to purchase a surprised luxury for the ladies. He could now promise delivery of the said item before Christmas.

Wagon after wagon, seven in all, rolled up in front of Blakemore House in orderly fashion, accompanied by hordes of men who systematically unloaded the furnishings under Weems' direction. There were arguments and an occasional gunshot, which Weems squelched with authority.

It was a fair day with the recent cool weather holding. The excitement grew to a fevered pitch as Parson blessed each item. E., Emmy, and Ivy instructed the men.

In the parlor, an armchair covered in crimson velvet was placed on either side of the fireplace, with a matching settee facing them. Behind the settee were four straight chairs around a card table, and a large cabinet with drawers and shelves was set against the front parlor wall. The opposite wall was left vacant at Larken's request. Lela skipped in and out, followed by Praiseworthy, and begged to be allowed to wind the mahogany mantle clock.

Two small side tables held a couple of garish, atrocious oil lamps in blue, red, bottle green, and yellow glass; these were Weems' delight and a gift, as he put it, "for a house warmin'."

A mirrored hat stand stood against the wall in the front hall entrance. Weems designated the long, narrow room to the left of the stairway as the office. It took six men to lug the roll-top desk into the house; only by dismantling the desk into its parts were the men able to maneuver the turn through the skinny door into the office. Progress in moving was delayed when each man fought to take a turn spinning and rearing back in the desk's companion swivel chair.

Weems outfitted the common eating room with a large dining table and matching sideboard, with four chairs on one side of the table and two at each end. A long bench was placed at the far side of the table.

There were howls and whistles and unsavory remarks when the four double beds were hoisted up the narrow stairway to the four rooms above; the shouts reached a raucous pitch when the chamber pots and spittoons were unloaded. A mirrored washstand dressing table was placed in each of these rooms. Bunk beds occupied the sun porch that ran along upstairs above the office. A fine single bed and dresser were set in the small private room at the back of the sun porch; these items were coveted with apparent jealousy among the men.

The ladies received bundles of cloth, new sewing baskets, and crates of dishes. The movers rolled barrels of liquor up the front steps on planks, amid boisterous shouts of approval. At Weems' suggestion, Larken uncorked a couple of bottles and passed them around among the men.

Slick followed Aunt E. all over the house, bowing and

praising with all the courtly manner he could muster. He stayed at her elbow to lift and to reach, to tote and to squat. Weems presented Aunt E. with her very own, specially ordered, dressmaker's dummy. Slick, out of deference to Aunt E.'s feminine sensibilities, modestly wrapped it in a blanket and escorted the form to the second floor. Aunt E. handled Slick with her charm, but ducked away on several occasions when his ardor became unmanageable.

Late that afternoon the exhausted ladies sat in the three rocking chairs, which were the last of the furniture unloaded that day. The chairs were a kind and thoughtful gesture, an added nicety, and they had more than expressed their gratitude to a blushing and thoroughly satisfied Mr. Weems. The ladies approved most of his choices. As they picked through their new sewing baskets and measured bits of fabric, they laughed quietly over Weems' gift of the multicolored oil lamps.

Emmy leaned over her sewing, frowning. "This fabric keeps bunching up. What am I doing wrong?"

Aunt E. held up her cloth piece to examine it. "I don't know; mine's doing the same thing."

Ivy, apparently having the same problem, ripped her threads out in disgust and stood up, arching and rubbing her sore back. Spying Lela coming up the road, Ivy smiled to herself and thought, *Darlin' little thing*. Her backache eased immediately as she announced to the others: "Look there, it's Lela."

Lela came along, waving her greeting to the welcoming women. She was carrying a doll in her arms and a scrap of cloth. She pecked each one of them lightly with a kiss on the cheek. "I come to sew with you. Is it okay?"

They all nodded their pleasure at her presence. Emmy included her in their work by asking Lela's advice. "Maybe you can tell us what we're doing wrong."

Lela looked at each individual piece of sewing. She handed Emmy her doll as she took Emmy's cloth and examined it closely. "You're pullin' them gathers too tight. Makes it bunch up and it wastes cloth."

Watching over their shoulders, Lela commented her approval as each pulled the threads out and started over. Satisfied, she perched on the porch railing with her back against the post. She drew her legs up, stuffing her petticoat and pink-and-green calico skirt between them, and, cradling her doll in the folds, laid her piece of cloth across her bare knees. Smoothing the cloth with the palms of her hands, Lela concentrated with a slight frown and pursed lips.

Aunt E. sighed with delight at the sight of the precious child. "Who's your friend there?"

Lela sat the doll in her lap to face Aunt E. and proceeded with a proper formal introduction. "Her name's

Martha. Named her after the lady what waited on Jesus in the Book. Parson give her to me."

Ivy was gratified but looked away. By now she knew that one accepted Lela's bursts of faith without inquiry. One just took them in and let them abide.

"You put the word out we were taking boarders?" Ivy asked after a long pause.

Lela measured the cloth this way and that across the doll. It was a lovely piece of purple taffeta, and quite pretty in contrast to the doll's painted china face.

In time, she answered Ivy. "Yes, an' I prayed, too."

Emmy looked at her chapped hands and broken nails and replied sarcastically. "Well, we're ready for them."

Lela reacted to Emmy's complaints as if they were tedious for her to bear. She replied on the defensive and a bit out of sorts. "Maybe God ain't ready. Can't tell God when. Parson said He don't like that."

Emmy's face flushed red and Lela was sorry. Looking at Emmy with apology, she changed the subject.

"I'm gonna make Martha a dress for church. Parson says there's churches where women dress proper an' I got to finish her fancy dress 'fore one's built here."

Aunt E. looked at the girl with disbelief. "Do you think someone will build a church here?"

Lela swung her legs down from the railing and, tucking Martha under her arm, she pulled up her hose and smoothed them, one leg and then the other. She weighed her answer to Aunt E. carefully. Lela wished to be firm but not as preachy as she was with Emmy.

She replied with a smile at E. "Sure," Lela said sweetly. "I been prayin' fer one. With God, askin' is gittin'." Then she asked E. gently. "Don't you know 'bout prayin'?"

Lela eased herself down from the railing and walked behind them, admiring their sewing.

E. sputtered her reply. "Yes, but . . ."

Lela paused at E.'s rocker. "There's no buts with God. Parson said." Lela patted E.'s handiwork and hugged her. "See," she pointed out, "see how the gathers does smoother when they ain't so tight?"

Emmy felt affection for the girl, but she remained somewhat on the defensive, since Lela had the upper hand. Lela had a way of winning arguments to her own satisfaction.

Emmy quizzed her. "You've made curtains before?"

Lela answered with an assured "yes." Then she added, laughing, "Made Parson's twice; first ones was burnt up."

Ivy stood up abruptly and turned her back on them to hide her amusement. She entered the house, calling back over her shoulder. "I'm going in to start supper." E. followed immediately behind Ivy for much the same reason.

They embraced in the entrance hall, stifling their giggles.

Lela heard them and saw that Emmy had too. She sat in the vacated rocker beside Emmy and spoke softly for just the two of them to hear. "I like bein' here with you." She paused for a moment and then continued. "I never seen a whole family together before. You're blessed, Miss Emmy."

Emmy reached for Lela's hand and squeezed it. She knew that Lela was right. She would admit it, and she would be at peace with this unusual child.

"I guess we are. Would you like to stay and have supper with us?"

Lela's eyes widened as she gushed forth her pleasure at the invitation she had longed for. Clapping her palms together and leaning intimately close to Emmy, she breathlessly inquired. "Would I have a place at the table?"

"Of course." Emmy responded without hesitation, thinking to herself, *What a simple offer I have made and what a joyful acceptance I have received.*

Lela jumped up and skipped toward the door. Emmy joined her, imitating her skip, and they entered the house arm in arm. Lela held them back for a moment and whispered. "Where would my place be?"

"I think," said Emmy, "Larken would want you right by him. He likes pretty girls."

Lela smiled. "I know. I seen him lookin' at you. Kin I go in an' help like family?"

Emmy answered with approval. "I think they'd like that." Lela had already entered the kitchen, and Emmy heard Ivy and E.'s enthusiastic greetings.

Their guest did indeed help with supper, then sat proudly between Larken and Runner, intermittently popping up to wait on them all when needed. As they filled their plates from the fine china serving bowls, Lela requested that "grace" be said. She gave a nod to Ivy, as always giving credit to Parson for instigating such matters. Ivy's return of thanks was more formal than Lela was accustomed to, but Lela was satisfied.

When dinner was finished, Lela was the first up to clear the dishes from the table. On one of several trips to and from the table, Lela paused momentarily behind Larken and laid one of her braids to the back of his head, comparing the color of his hair to hers. Larken did not notice but Emmy and E. did, and later in privacy the two spoke together of Lela's odd gesture.

They visited around the dining table, with Larken and Runner smoking cigars and E. and Ivy enjoying an after-supper chew. Lela and Emmy sucked on peppermints. They discussed the details of their new venture into inn-keeping. "What'll they pay; what can we get away with?"

Larken asked, blowing smoke rings to catch up with Runner's and entertain the ladies. Ivy opened two windows in the kitchen at the back of the house, and E. opened one of the broad parlor windows in the front, both laughing good-naturedly while fanning the room with their aprons.

Lela followed Larken's line of thinking. "With a bath, a clean bed, an' good food like this, I 'spect you could ask maybe up to three a night."

"You think?" Larken spoke to Lela with deference, valuing her advice in the family discussion.

"Yeah, 'course. Parson, he paid nearly four at a place over in Denver, but they had rugs nailed down an' a tub in every room an' bedposts with gold painted on 'em." Lela smiled to herself, pleased with the picture she had drawn for them.

Runner and Larken looked away from her with raised eyebrows, and the ladies fidgeted, wiping off crumbs and refolding previously folded napkins; they all avoided Lela's dancing blue eyes, innocent and delighted with her colorful description.

Startled by a loud bang at the front door, Lela rose in a flash, and Larken moved fast to catch her by the sleeve and hold her back.

"Lela! You women take her upstairs," he ordered.

Lela resisted Larken's hold. "It might be somebody I

know."

Ivy and E. swiftly encircled her and, with Emmy pushing from behind, they ushered Lela through the hall and up the stairs.

A loud, gruff voice demanded through the partially open door. "Open up."

Runner quickly handed Larken his gun. Neither was surprised to find it unloaded. Larken shrugged and, whispering loudly so as to be heard above the continued impatient pounding, exclaimed to Runner. "They won't know it's not loaded."

Lela called out from the top of the stairs. "Peek out and see if he's ugly."

Larken peered out the crack in the door and hollered back to Lela. "Huge. I'm not a good judge of men's looks, but I'd say, without feeling terribly guilty, that he is one of your uglier men."

The pounding and demanding shouts from outside continued. Lela knew who it was, and was amazed at the forbearance of the usually impatient man who now awaited entrance.

"Is the door locked?" She hollered out to Larken, assuming it must be so.

Larken shouted back. "No."

The door swung wide open, banging against the wall;

in single file, seven men entered. The lead man amiably shook hands with Larken and introduced himself as Victor Brock. At close range, the tall burly man, though not ugly, was certainly strong-featured, craggy, and weather-worn. The hand that shook Larken's was formidable, and Larken checked to see if his five fingers were intact.

The second man, who wanted to force an introduction, nudged Big Vic. He was rightly named Pinky. Pink he was, from the top of his head of thinning, wispy, strawberry strands and sunburned scalp. He was covered in tanned rosy freckles, which multiplied in abundance over his face, ears, and neck.

Slick and Bobby bowed pleasantly, renewing their acquaintance with Larken and Runner. The last three to enter were not introduced and stood in the shadows of the hall, inseparable. One was a young Indian with no expression at all; another was an older man, tall, skinny, and mean looking; the third was a pretty, cocky kid who acted a little silly as he stood in the corner of the hallway.

Big Vic startled them all with his resounding shout. "Lela."

He turned to the grinning boy and ordered him forth. "Choirboy, get that package."

Larken took note that this so-called Choirboy obeyed Big Vic only after receiving a nod from the man called

Pinky. A kind of tense pecking order existed in the gang that Larken gathered were to be his first hotel guests.

As Choirboy retreated outside, Big Vic, in his booming voice, admonished Larken. "Mr. Blakemore, you should keep your gun loaded and your door locked."

Lela, who jumped from the stairs into the open arms of Big Vic, interrupted Larken's attempt at an indignant retort.

"What'd you bring me?" Lela cajoled wistfully.

Pinky's lower lip pouted. "Ain't you glad to see me?"

"Sure I am," Lela replied sweetly and reached for Pinky's calloused hand.

Choirboy returned with the package and handed it to Big Vic, who squatted down to Lela's height. Emmy and E. moved closer to see. They were a bit less nervous than when the men first barged in, but were mutually horrified at the thought of these men as guests and at their familiarity with Lela.

Runner never took his eyes off the two gents in the shadows. He noted that the tall older man fidgeted and scowled and that the Indian's face remained vacant. He shuddered at the thought of them sleeping under his roof, this night or any other. Slick and Bobby no longer worried him, and the big man seemed intelligent. The pink man was an overgrown brat. And the pretty boy: *Well*, Runner thought, *I'd like to wipe that insipid grin off his girlish face.*

Larken's attention remained on Big Vic. *He's the one who has the tighter grip on Lela,* he thought.

Lela squealed with pleasure as she lifted a pair of shoes and a doll's dress from the box. "It's a dress fer Martha! An' some shoes fer me!"

She rubbed the soft leather with her fingers and placed her hands inside each one, lifting them up to inhale the delicious odor of fine tanned leather. Delicately placing the shoes aside, she smoothed the doll's lavender lace dress approvingly.

She looked up at Big Vic. "Did you find me them beads?"

Vic measured the new shoes to Lela's patent boots. His voice was less booming as he mused to himself and to her. "The shoes are too big," he sighed, "but you'll be needing them soon." He pulled out of his blouse and over his head some glass beads. "Lavender, like you asked for." The big man handed her the beads abruptly and, clearing his throat, stood up and moved away from Lela.

Pinky moved in and took Big Vic's place beside Lela. He, too, knelt down to her level as he whined, "I was gonna wear 'em back here fer you; he did instead."

Lela patted Pinky's cheek and he blushed crimson. "I know you would've. Thank you both."

Having spoken to the two and hopefully shown them equal appreciation, Lela turned to Larken and waved her little arms to include Runner and the ladies.

"An' thank you fer the place at your table. I got to git over to Parson's. He's learning me a attitude a night. We're up to the peacemakers whom the Lord called blessed."

Emmy had moved closer to Lela; giving her a hug, she placed the shoes and dress in the box and E. handed her the lid.

Ivy walked Lela toward the door as Big Vic's voice boomed her departure. "Then you run along. Give him my best."

Pinky called after her into the dark night. "Give him my best, too."

Aunt E. put her hand to her throat; she was touched as the sweet little voice trailed back to them from the road. "I will."

A mid-October storm was approaching, with winds picking up and howling through the Roost. Gusts of wind brought a few leaves through the front door, and they briefly danced around the guests' feet in the hallway.

Larken returned to business. He once again extended his hand to the big man. "Is there something we can do for you, Mr. Brock?"

"I'm called Big Vic." Amid the distant rumble of thunder,

Big Vic's voice rose louder, like that of a deaf man trying to hear and be heard. "This is Pinky. You've already met Bobby and Slick." He pointed to the vacant-eyed Indian. "This is Mute"; and to the tall older man, "This is Jim"; and to the kid, "This is Choirboy. We have come for lodging."

Larken withdrew his crushed fingers for the second time that evening and laid them in his left palm to recover. He counseled to himself. *Avoid shaking hands with Big Vic or, for that matter, any of these ruffians.* Considering his reply to the big man's request, he further counseled himself. *Stay in control.*

With complete business aplomb, Larken proceeded. "We can accommodate you, if you don't mind doubling up."

Big Vic nodded in agreement. "Not at all. Boys, bring in our things. Pinky, see to it."

Pinky's face reddened once more in embarrassment, as he grudgingly followed Vic's orders.

Big Vic addressed Larken with a wry smirk of friendliness, as though conferring with an equal. "I understand you've bested my record at seventeen thousand."

Not wanting to make this formidable, craggy, mountain of a man angry, Larken hesitated, weighing his reply carefully. "I had help, and it was done over a long period of time. I was never really . . ."

Big Vic interrupted. "I'm not threatened by your great

success, Mr. Blakemore."

Larken stuttered, on the defensive. "But I didn't actually rob people."

Big Vic laughed, slapping Larken on the back. "You have an extended line of credit—an amusing way to put it. Call it what you like, the result is the same."

Larken was irritated and moved away from the big man, thinking, *Not necessarily.*

"I assume you will want to be paid daily?"

Though Larken had come out on the short end of the previous confrontation with Big Vic, he now felt the important matter of bargaining was to his advantage. Fully recovered, he responded quickly.

"That's right; three dollars a man per day."

"A nose-bleeding sum." Vic's retort was, however, accompanied by a nod of acceptance of terms.

Larken held the reins once again and took advantage. "With good reason. I'm sure you're used to the best. By charging that much, we weed out undesirables, making our preferred guests more comfortable."

Swallowing the bait of Larken's snobbish approach, Big Vic extended his hand to Larken to shake the final approval. Larken winced, but proffered his fingers for what he hoped would be the last crunch from the big man's hand.

Larken's clever mind served him well again. He had always preferred the challenge of the wits over the battle of the fists. He smiled to himself. *This works on men but rarely on Emmy.*

He concluded the arrangements: "Breakfast will be at seven. Just to keep it from slipping your mind . . ." Larken held out his hand for payment.

Big Vic counted out some money and gave it to Larken. He chuckled. "It would have troubled me had I forgotten." He surveyed the layout of the house. "This will be fine." Vic was pleased not only with the accommodations but also with the man, Blakemore.

During the negotiations, Pinky and the other men unloaded their belongings into the front hall. The storm had broken into a steady downpour, so the men hurried and dumped and scattered their gear in all directions. Runner assisted them, and the women stood in the dining room entrance, staring in dismay at the confusion.

They voiced their concern to each other. Emmy was vexed with the set time of breakfast at seven. She glared at Larken every time he looked her way, but he ignored her.

Larken, totally in charge, continued. "There are two rooms: one very large and another small, private one."

Big Vic took Larken's cue and responded. "I will manage in the small room and the rest of you will put in together."

Pinky was furious. Bobby and Slick carried their belongings along with Big Vic's, who followed them up the stairs.

Shaking with rage, Pinky shouted above the thunder and rain, "I'm not bunkin' with the help."

Big Vic turned on the stair and, with the violence of the storm expressed across his grim face, shouted back with deliberate sarcasm. "As you wish; it's a clear night."

Emmy sat cross-legged on her new bed, staring at her blistered hands and broken nails. Blakemore House was finally quiet on its first night of occupancy. She patted the soft mattress, which was a gloriously welcome relief after the last months of hard, cramped accommodations. She slipped shyly into her nightgown, giggling at the snoring men and yet apprehensive at their proximity to her room. There was no lock on her door and the walls were thin. *With so little privacy here*, Emmy thought, *there is probably no future for our marriage.* She was shocked at her desire and deliberately put the ridiculous thoughts from her mind.

Emmy's bedroom door creaked slightly and opened slowly as Larken slipped in. Her heart skipped a beat with fright and, though she was relieved, she frowned with disapproval.

Larken grinned and set a sack on her bed. "Look inside. We've just earned money for the first time in our lives, Cousin." He took a bottle from under his arm and a glass from each pocket and set them on the dresser.

Emmy glanced into the sack, picked it up, and shook it, unimpressed. She sighed with disgust. "I don't like earning money."

Larken kept his back to her and gripped the dresser's edge. He was both angry and hurt, and he responded through clenched teeth, steadying his voice. "You are im-damn-possible to please!"

Emmy ignored both his remark and its tone and continued her own line of thinking. "I was just sitting here wondering if, on the night I made my debut, my parents thought they were introducing me to society so I could end up being a maid to cutthroats and thieves."

Larken poured their drinks, sloshing them over with his still-shaking hands. He wiped the spill with the sleeve of his blouse. Taking his time in replying, he turned slowly to offer her a glass. Emmy reached for it and smiled, nodding gratefully. Larken saw the red, rough fingers that clasped the stem and softened. He said with a sarcastic grin, "I know they did. I remember drinking to it." He raised his glass in a salute to her before he took a sip.

Emmy took a gulp and hiccupped at the strength of the

drink. She glanced sideways at Larken and frowned.

Moving the only chair in the room to sit beside her bed, Larken propped his boots, ankles crossed, on the footboard. He looked at her, waiting for whatever was next on her list of grievances, balancing his glass on his chest.

Emmy proceeded. "And what was that? Seven o'clock breakfast? What were you thinking?"

Larken thought his answer was both obvious and reasonable, so he answered her calmly. "These people get up so early, I thought seven might be considered lunch."

But Emmy was not in a reasonable mood. She spoke in whispers, irritated at their lack of true privacy. She paused to listen. As the snores of the men continued, so did she. "Eating at seven in the morning has to be bad for you. And that means we have to be up by five to get it fixed and served. Our first night and I hate it already."

"I think you'd better get used to it," Larken replied, firmly resolved.

Emmy knelt at the foot of the bed and pounded Larken's boots with her fists. Her auburn hair fell disheveled over his feet. She cried like a child throwing a tantrum. "I will not! Go in there and tell them we will serve at a decent ten o'clock."

Larken lifted his legs, throwing her small body back on the bed. He stood up, dropped his glass to the floor, and grabbed her by both elbows, lifting her to her feet and bringing her close.

His breath consumed her as he warned in a low hiss. "Ten? You go wake the devil and his demons out of a dead sleep and tell them yourself."

Emmy stared Larken down. Her face blotched with red spots and her heart beat fiercely. "You're a coward. You've always been a coward." She lowered her eyes away from his.

Releasing her, Larken picked up his overturned glass and refilled it. "You bet I am. That's why I'm still alive." He spoke to her quietly and she heard.

Larken stood by Emmy's bed. Neither of them spoke for several minutes.

Emmy broke the silence. Taking several deep breaths and staring at nothing, she reminisced. "Remember that country home outside London? We got up early there to hunt, but that was for fun."

Larken nodded, remembering the carefree days spent in Europe sitting out the American Civil War. Since the family's hope of a commissioned post for Larken via West Point had died when he was abruptly expelled, Garnet and Alice had felt the only other alternative to keep their sole male heir safe had been to pack him up with a good deal of the family's money and send him across the Atlantic

Ocean. Shortly before the firing on Fort Sumter, Aunt E., Emmy, Larken, Ivy, and Runner sailed for Europe, where they regaled in luxurious splendor until long after Lee surrendered at Appomattox. "That was a grand time. The little bald earl running after you with his tongue hanging out."

Emmy handed Larken her glass for a refill. She giggled and blushed. "He was adorable. If I'd married him, I could sleep late tomorrow."

Larken smiled at her and teased. "Yes, but you'd have to sleep with him tonight."

Emmy twittered with delight at the bawdy turn of their argument. "That's nasty."

"Um. Well, Darling, Ivy and Runner are taking turns staying up so they can wake the rest of us. Larken spoke as he took the empty glass from her and placed it beside his on the dresser. He lowered the wick of the oil lamp and, deftly removing his boots, slid into bed next to her. Emmy forcefully shoved him onto the floor with her feet.

Laughing hard and low, Larken gathered his boots and crawled toward the door. On all fours, he whispered. "Good night, Cousin."

"Larken?" Emmy sat up alarmed. Larken peered up over the end of her bed. "What?"

"You don't think any of those vile snakes would try to come and overtake me, do you?" Emmy put her hand over her mouth, her eyes wide with apprehension.

Larken consoled her. "If one did, he'd never live to tell about it."

Very pleased, Emmy responded. "You'd protect me?"

Rubbing his back where he hit the floor, he grinned at her. "I wouldn't have to."

Larken rose up over the end of the bed and kissed the sole of her foot. She wiped the kiss away with the other foot. He gave her one long, last smile and crawled quietly out the door, shutting it securely. Emmy reached for the kissed foot and held it in her hand until she slept.

Chapter Fourteen

Come, o thou traveler unknown,
whom still I hold but cannot see.
My company before is gone,
and I am left alone with Thee.

CHARLES WESLEY

The previous night's storm subsided into a clear but chilly sun-drenched day.

As the warm fall days turned colder at night, the delightful fresh air blew in a north wind, with scattered snow flurries melting in mid-flight.

Runner built fires not only in the kitchen cookstove but also in the parlor fireplace, the latter an unnecessary but hospitable gesture to the first Blakemore House guests. Runner's move proved effective, for it was late into the morning before the ladies had finally prepared breakfast.

The men returned from the stable after seeing to their horses and gear; they glanced, impatiently questioning, toward the dining room. Larken and Runner, nervous over the delay, played host. They gathered the men before the parlor fire, engaging them in inane attempts at conversation.

The hungry guests ate the long-awaited meal ravenously. It was plentiful and delicious: oatmeal, flapjacks and syrup, grits, diced browned potatoes, back-strap bacon, and eggs cooked with fresh garden tomatoes and onions. The diners grunted and smiled their approval.

As Emmy, Aunt E., and Ivy cleared the table, Big Vic lit a cigar, reared back his chair, and spoke to them good-naturedly.

"That was a delicious meal, ladies, although it is ten o'clock. I thought you said breakfast was at seven, Mr. Blakemore."

Emmy, with a wry look at Larken, replied, "Mr. Blakemore often says seven when he really means ten."

Pinky, pounding the table with self-assumed authority, growled, "In the Roost, seven means seven."

Aunt E., pouring Pinky another cup of coffee, spoke intimately to him, smiling. "A delightful custom, Mr. Pinky."

Choirboy grinned through the whole exchange with his wide-eyed stare fixed on E. She felt uncomfortable and compelled to address him personally.

Aunt E. spoke gently with a motherly tone. "You're awful young to be away from home."

Choirboy was obviously pleased with her attention.

Smiling angelically, he continued, encouraging their conversation. "I'm almost nineteen. My maw says I got a baby face."

E. still stood by Pinky. She could feel the tension rising in him to pick a fight. She felt that her preferred presence by his side might balance that chip about to be knocked off his shoulder. Aunt E. set the coffeepot in front of him for his own personal disposal. She removed the china pot of zinnias from the center of the table just as a precaution.

"I'm sure your maw is proud of you," she observed to Choirboy.

Speaking from behind his perpetual grin, Choirboy stretched his neck in importance. "Hell, yes, she's proud. Done my first bank job when I was thirteen!"

"Don't be a braggart, boy." Big Vic verbally shook the wind out of Choirboy's sails. For a fleeting moment, they all saw the boy's ever-present smile turn into a grizzly grimace.

Slick felt that sometimes his boss ventured too far and ruffled the feathers of his subordinates unnecessarily, so he dared to intervene, "Not everyone has had the same opportunities you've had." With that show of support, Choirboy's clenched teeth eased back to his carefree smile.

Ignoring them all, Big Vic stood up as he spoke to Larken. "These are fine accommodations. First night of real rest I've enjoyed in a long stretch."

Pinky excused himself to E. and, nudging her aside,

stood to face both Larken and Big Vic in rebuttal. "I was up the whole damned night."

Bobby challenged Pinky. "I had a good sleep."

Pinky shouted back at him. "Your snorin' kept me up."

In an attempt to return to civility, Big Vic laughingly explained to his hosts. "We all snore, I'm afraid. When we bunk in the caves, we sound like bears."

Pinky was sorely agitated and continued to shout. "When we bunk in the caves, we all sleep in one room. An' I'm not sleepin' like the hire-ons again. This is as much my gang as yours, Vic."

"Actually, it isn't. I've tried to let you think so." Big Vic's expression was one of severe earnestness and his voice held a tone of pity.

In the deadly silence that followed, Jim and Mute rose from the table in unison, attached like Siamese twins, with their hands to their holsters.

Praiseworthy bounded into the house, closely followed by Parson and Lela. The big dog headed straight for Runner, whining gleefully and shaking moisture from her coat. Runner embraced this welcome show of friendship, hoping it would ease the tension. He hugged Praiseworthy's woolly neck, inhaling her doggy, earthy smell, and fondled the silky ears with affection.

Pinky paid their arrival no heed, shouting above the

commotion. "My father . . ."

Big Vic interrupted with rage. "Your father was my dearest friend. He and I started this gang when you were a pup. When he died, I took over. Keeping you on was only a favor to your old man, you bastard."

Pinky lunged at his throat and Vic, with his massive size alone, overpowered the smaller man, locking his arms behind his back with a firm hold.

Now having Pinky's immovable attention, Vic continued. "I know whereof I speak. Your mother serviced our old gang with great delight and appalling frequency. You were nearly grown before we could be sure who you took after. You were your father's greatest disappointment. Parson can bear me out."

Parson lowered his eyes, speaking almost inaudibly. "Vic, I . . ."

Vic demanded, "Tell him, Parson."

Parson spoke to Pinky reluctantly. "Yer ma, I heard tell, she was good at what she done and in the end was sorry, God rest her soul. An' yer pa, he tried hard not to hold your bein' what you was against you."

Pinky, having wrested his body free of Vic's hold on him, shook with rage and humiliation. He cried, violently gasping for breath.

"He tried hard? He made me what I am. If you hate me,

what do you call the girl? She's always lookin' fer someone to call her pa. At least I knew my pa's name."

Big Vic grabbed Pinky's finger, which was pointed at Lela, and bent it back until it cracked. Pinky howled in pain as Vic smashed his fist into Pinky's jaw and sent him sprawling across the dining room table, shattering china in all directions. Pinky rolled off the end of the table, grabbed a chair, and swung it wildly through the air at Big Vic, stunning him momentarily.

Emmy screamed as the falling chair knocked her to the floor. Larken and Runner helped her away from the melee and to the stairs, ushering Ivy and E. up with her.

Recovered, Vic flung into Pinky, smashing one blow after another, and Larken and Runner raced in to intercede. Lela stopped them. Pinky continued to punch at Vic's stomach and kicked him a mean blow to the groin, but the action threw Pinky off balance, and Big Vic knocked him to the floor.

Parson sat crouched in the corner, hanging on for dear life to his growling, barking dog.

Vic pulled a beaten, smarting Pinky up off the floor. Pinky reeled around like a drunken man for a moment, then snarled as he pointed at Mute, Jim, and Choirboy.

"We're gittin' outta here."

The three men pushed roughly past the cowering women on the stairs to gather their belongings and returned, shoving them aside and madly throwing one satchel after another into the front hall.

Pinky, still enraged, almost wrenched the front door off its hinges. He glowered at Parson, as Praiseworthy growled and snapped at him.

Pinky hissed a warning toward Parson. "You sided with him one too many times."

Parson stood with Big Vic on the porch, watching as Pinky and his men headed around the corner of the house toward the barn.

Runner peered past Vic and Parson as he joined them. "You reckon they'll leave our horses alone?"

"Yeah," replied Vic. "But when they ride off, go check just the same."

Parson was visibly shaking as he spoke. "Vic, I, the girl . . ."

Big Vic reentered the house and took Larken aside. "Larken, Bobby and Slick will clean up this mess. Could you see to taking Lela for awhile?"

Larken nodded his agreement. "We'd be glad to have her."

Big Vic's worried expression relaxed with gratitude and he continued. "We'll be leaving tomorrow. No need in bringing retribution on you, your family, and Lela."

After Pinky and his men rode away, shouting and shooting in the air, Big Vic, Bobby, and Slick headed for the barn behind Runner to check things out. Soon after, they too galloped away on some undisclosed mission, leaving Runner to walk back to the porch.

Parson stood on the porch with his arm around a shivering young girl, warming Lela from the chilly north wind and consoling her. Larken and Emmy, just inside the house, heard their interchange and both were saddened at the twisted knowledge of the child.

Lela kissed Parson's hand and he patted her gently. Lifting and holding her face, he advised her, as usual. "You'll be safer here than with me. I'm gonna try not to, but I might end up in the middle between Vic an' Pinky."

Tears streamed down Lela's cheeks, but she kept her eyes fixed on Parson's as she asked the question tearing at her heart. "There's gonna be a killin', ain't there?"

"I expect." As always, Parson answered Lela in the truth as he saw it.

The cool weather changed in a few days into a warm and balmy Indian summer. The garden flourished with vegetables, with pumpkins and strawberries, and with late-blooming flowers—zinnias of red and purple, and golden fall asters.

One group of men after another checked into the Blakemore House. There were new faces, comprising other gangs of the Roost. Throughout the remaining days of October, Big Vic, Pinky, and their cohorts were not seen in the vicinity of Blakemore House, not even on the frequent trips to Weems' store.

Larken and Runner graciously welcomed the various groups of bandits. As tough as these guests were, they paid promptly, obviously appreciating the luxury of clean beds and good food.

Larken wrote to his father: "The sky is bluer, the sun hotter, the rain harder, and always more needed. We are well. Ivy says the Lord is restoring our souls and I believe her. We never made it to San Francisco, due in part to my lack of persistence and in part to my lack of a sense of direction. I send you my love. Give my best to Aunt Alice and Uncle Finch. Tell them their Emmy is doing them proud. Your son, Larken. Post Office Tree, Utah Territory, October 1867."

Lela joined in with the women at their chores and, with the energy of her youth and industrious nature, cheerfully encouraged domestic perfection. She was forever at Emmy's side, asking questions about family in Louisiana and the world beyond. As she gathered information about

Emmy and Larken's odd relationship, she did not hesitate to encourage romance between the two of them. Lela relished the company of the women and delighted them with her affection. From the beginning Runner was her confidant, as he had been all summer when they planted the first seeds of the garden. Parson came daily to oversee the progress of his friends, keep a close eye on their safety, and instruct Lela in her catechism.

Mid-morning on a perfect autumn day, Ivy and Emmy scrubbed the last load of washing, while E. tidied the house after breakfast. Larken worked in the office at his ledger. The present residents of Blakemore House sat on the back-porch steps or stood out in the yard smoking.

It was a Sunday and most of them, recalling their childhood instruction, desisted from their line of work on the Sabbath. Parson found scriptural allowance for washing and accounting on this day, something along the lines of a loose quotation: the workman's worthiness of his hire, reaping and sowing, and cleanliness and Godliness.

Lela sat on the swing they had hung from a low limb of the oak tree. Parson leaned against the old gnarled tree lost in his preaching and teaching from the Bible. Lela and his assembled congregation, the outlaws, were spellbound, paying rapt attention as Parson's voice prophetically thundered forth. Lela fussed with her doll, interrupting at intervals to quietly ask Parson a question. He would have gladly continued until the noon hour but it was now hot and, their cigars smoked, the men began to drift into the house. Lela, knowing this to be their departure and pay-day, excused herself, patted Parson's hand and promised to return to him, then skipped after the guests.

Since the door to Larken's office was closed, Lela waited on the front porch of the house while the men passed back and forth, carrying their gear to the yard. Runner came around the corner of the house with a few of the men who were leading their saddled horses.

When the head outlaw, the last to emerge, brushed past her, Lela extended her hand, smiling sweetly. He reached into his pants pocket and handed her a sack. She swiftly counted the money and held out her hand to him once again, still smiling and squinting her eyes at him. The man laughed and handed her more. Satisfied, she thanked him and bid them all good day as they mounted and rode off.

Lela knocked on the office door, slowly turning the knob and identifying herself. She entered at Larken's insistence; he was bent over his ledger. She laid the sack of money on the desk in front of him and poured out its contents. Larken smiled at her while he counted, to the penny, the exact amount owed them.

"You're crafty for a ten-year-old." He faced her with a wide grin.

"Eleven," she replied, correcting him. "You know that first night I come for supper and sat by you, and got those beads and shoes, and a dress fer Martha from Big Vic?"

"But you didn't say a word," Larken replied, well recalling the event.

"Didn't need to; prayed to the Lord and got fer the askin' my best birthday ever." Lela spoke softly to Larken with simple, sweet sincerity.

Larken pushed back his chair and stood. He and Lela walked arm in arm into the front hall. They stood still at the dining room door, watching Emmy replace fresh flowers in the bowl on the table and stuff the wilted ones into her apron pocket. The late morning sun shone through the room's only window, highlighting her hair. "She's beautiful, Larken." Lela whispered and squeezed his hand.

"Yes, Lela, she is." Larken smiled down at the little girl.

※

They were without guests for a few days and caught up on the many chores that had been set aside. The tight schedule of feeding men and cleaning up after them had taken every waking hour.

It was late in the afternoon. Larken, Emmy, and E. had gone over to Weems' store and were expected back at any moment. Runner and Lela sat in the large wooden swing on the back porch, gently swaying, enjoying the breeze. It had rained earlier and was quite cool. There was a hint of approaching cold weather, and Runner wore his buckskin jacket and Lela her shawl. Ivy huddled next to Runner on the other side, napping against his shoulder. He was showing Lela how to reweave a hole in his straw hat.

They were thus occupied when a loud commotion and gunshots issued from the front of the house. Runner bolted forward around the house; Ivy and Lela entered through the back porch door. Larken was in the hall headed toward the front porch, where Emmy was greeting the new lodgers.

Runner stopped dead still when he saw Pinky, Mute, Jim, and Choirboy approaching the house. Pinky bypassed Emmy with an abrupt "howdy," and slapped a big wad of cash into Larken's left palm, pumping his arm in an exaggerated handshake.

Though the women hurriedly threw together a meal, the men ate heartily and seemed satisfied. Pinky did all the talking during supper, mostly to himself, laughing boisterously at his own jokes. Choirboy grinned with his mouth full and the others responded with an occasional grunt of assent. The meal seemed to gratify their huge appetites, Ivy and E. noticed with satisfaction and a great deal of relief. They were all a bit afraid of what Pinky would do if he was not agreeable, and they did not want to find out.

After two weeks of hosting Pinky and his gang, Larken's concerns about his lodgers grew. Late at night he heard muffled noises in the house, the front door opening and closing and then horses pounding out into the darkness. At dinner time each night, Pinky became more animated and rowdy with his men. They would openly joke about the stupidity of Big Vic as well as other gangs in the Roost. When Larken asked Pinky for the rent, he would produce large wads of cash from his pockets or even once from a muslin sack. The gang demanded privacy during dinner after the meal was served. And if Larken came upon them unexpectedly they would all hush their talking and look at him guiltily.

⊹⊙∙℮ //////////// ℈∙⊙⊹

Fortunately, the only meal Pinky's gang seemed to want was dinner, and they would wolf down large helpings of whatever was served. Emmy, E., and Ivy were exhausted with the planning and preparation for such large dinners every night, but at least it was only one meal a day.

Finished with dinner one night, Pinky's men followed him into the parlor. From the kitchen, Larken, Runner, and the women strained to hear what was being said in the main room. Lela watched Larken closely.

Larken whispered. "They leave at night and come back counting their money a few hours later. I got a few hints of this from Weems today. They've got to be pulling jobs inside the Roost. If that's what they're doing, I for sure don't like having them here, among other reasons."

Aunt E. was frightened, and she tugged at Larken's sleeve as she spoke in a low tone. "They pay well, even in advance, but it's not worth it, Larken."

"Lela, do you know what's going on?" Larken asked.

She looked as if she suspected something, but she shook her head "no."

"Wait here. I'm going to ask Pinky straight out." Larken left the kitchen before the others could object.

The gang sat around the card table counting money and laughing. As he entered the parlor, Larken noticed the first gesture from Mute he had yet seen. The Indian rubbed his hands greedily as he gawked at the money on the table. When Pinky saw Larken, he raised his hand to silence the men.

Larken spoke directly. "Pinky, I need to talk to you."

Jim sulked, mean-faced and grim. "He wants his pay."

Larken replied with a shrug. "I got my pay. That's not it."

Choirboy sauntered insipidly toward Larken, with his

hands outstretched, and whined like a kid playing hooky. "You're undid, Mr. Blakemore. We done something wrong?"

Larken faced them defiantly. "I think you are stealing from other gangs inside the Roost and, if you are, you're putting Lela and my family in danger. I want you to go."

Emmy slipped into the hall to open the front door and air out the heavy cigar smoke. In the shadows of the hat rack, she was unseen.

Pinky weighed Larken's ultimatum for a moment before he answered. He pouted childishly. "Vic's boys is as full of trouble an' you didn't throw them out."

Larken could hardly believe the immaturity of this grown man and wondered that he had a following of any kind. He was pathetically jealous.

It occurred to Larken to treat Pinky like a child in his reply. "Vic left before I had to ask him."

Pinky continued his whining. "I bet you the whole day's take we ain't near the problems Vic an' Bobby an' Slick was." He turned from mulish to mean with savage threats and boasts.

"It's them we been robbin', an' even if they figure it was us, they ain't coming near this place to git us. So, you see, Mr. Blakemore, we're all nice an' safe. Long as we pay fer our keep, we stay."

Pinky gathered up the rest of the money, and he and

his men headed up the stairs.

Larken stared after them, dumbfounded. He had underestimated Pinky. His was shrewd thinking, a smart move. He could bet that Pinky was settling down in Big Vic's previous private quarters behind the bunkroom. Larken swore under his breath. "Damnit."

The women had heard. Emmy came out of the shadows, and they all stood in the front hall dismayed. Runner remained just inside the kitchen door, working his left arm and holding his heart.

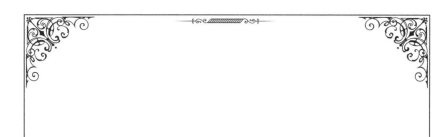

Chapter Fifteen

If ye be willing and obedient
Ye shall eat the good of the land.

Book of Isaiah 1:19

Pinky and his men stayed on well into November. They handled themselves tolerably, with no incidents to speak of. However, they were unpleasant, sullen guests and, as E. expressed it, "Creepy and obnoxious." She sighed with a faint smile, "I even long for the sight of Slick."

It snowed for several days in a row the week before Thanksgiving. Larken came down early one morning to build the fires before breakfast. Runner was ahead of him, as usual, standing in the entrance to the parlor. He had a quizzical but relieved grin on his face. "They're gone."

As he handed Larken the money the visitors had left, he continued, "I checked the barn. They cleared out."

"No message?" Larken asked as he counted the

money.

"Just this," Runner held up a smudged sheet of paper. It was scrawled all over in big print. It read simply, "We'll be back. Hold our place."

Cheerfully, they all enjoyed the reprieve and tidied things and aired out the house.

On a beautiful sunny morning, Saturday before the Thanksgiving holiday, Larken prepared to take the wagon to Weems' store. He was excited and told the family to keep watch on the road for his return. When Parson arrived the two men rode off together in high spirits, promising to be back before midday.

Sure enough, about eleven o'clock Parson and Larken rounded the turn, followed by Weems in his wagon. Runner and the women stood on the front porch, watching in astonishment. They all cried in unison, "A piano!"

The instrument was placed with care on the vacant north parlor wall. The circular top of its companion stool was covered in red velvet and swiveled up and down. The women polished the lustrous mahogany cabinet reverently and wiped each ivory key, sounding chords and taking turns playing remembered renditions. Weems ate with them and stayed all afternoon joining in their merriment.

Toward dusk of this most eventful day for them all, Runner rekindled and stoked the fire in the parlor at Parson's request. Weems was taking his leave when Parson detained him and ushered him in with the rest gathered around the piano. He ceremoniously seated Aunt E. on the stool and, taking his Bible, read and blessed and gave thanks. Parson gave a nod to E. who played the last few bars of the evening hymn for an introduction. Those knowing the words sang out, following Ivy's rich contralto lead, and Weems joined in with his humming monotone. "Softly now the light of day fades upon my sight away, free from care, from labor free, Lord, I would commune with thee . . ." Lela stood beside Parson holding Martha. She had dressed her doll in the lavender church dress.

Weems left the Roost the following day for Moab on his last sojourn for supplies until after Christmas. His empty wagon raced along at a fast clip. He was satisfied with life in general and whistled last evening's song.

Because his mind was preoccupied with plans for expanding the store, Weems was caught off-guard when the man stepped out of the brush at the side of the road. Being both friendly and nosy by nature, Weems slowed his mules. When he saw the face of the man, he regretted his lack of precaution. It was too late; he dared not reach for his shotgun.

The man grabbed hold of the bridle of one of Weems' mules, ordering him to stop. "You know a man, Blakemore?"

Less curious now and guarded, Weems asked, "If I don't know yer face, would I know yer name?"

The man inched toward Weems, slapping the rump of the mule. Those yellow eyes remained fixed on Weems all the while, making him sick to the pit of his stomach. For the life of him he could not look away, and those menacing eyes held his.

Impatiently the man growled a reply to Weems' question. "Not likely." He hissed, slobbering spit like venom at the corners of his mouth. "Blakemore."

Weems managed to look away as if pondering the name Blakemore. He shrugged his shoulders and replied evasively. "Heard the name somewhere."

A quick move and Weems instinctively looked back abruptly. The butt of a gun smashed the bridge of his nose. Blood gushed forth. Weems was too stunned to wipe it.

"Blakemore," the man persisted.

With blood coursing down his shirt and jacket and soaking his dungarees, Weems replied respectfully. "I seen him."

The man seemed to completely ignore Weems' condition and spoke to him in familiar confidence. "He ever come outta the Roost?"

Weems answered as if nothing was in the least bit amiss. "Never. An' the guard, he won't let nobody he don't know in."

Though the man kept his gun pointed at Weems' heart, he grinned flirtatiously at him. "You vouch me in."

Weems had never before seen such ugly, yellow, rotten, snaggled teeth. They were the same color as the man's eyes. He answered carefully. "The guard don't trust me; I ain't wanted. You a bounty hunter?"

Hoisting himself onto the wagon step, the man grasped Weems' jacket collar and jerked his head forward, impervious to the blood splattering down his sleeve. He held Weems by the throat, threatening. "I'm Blakemore's conscience. See this scalp? Yours'll hang with it if you tell you seen me."

Weems stared at the scalp, an Indian's, and shuddered. He gasped a whining reply. "Onliest reason I'm still breathin' is 'cause I don't tell nothin'."

The man let go of him and walked away into the brush. Weems sat still for a few moments and rubbed his scalp, and then he clucked at his mules and headed on his way to Moab.

On the crag of a butte high above the road, an Indian

squatted, watching both men from his vantage point. He kept his eyes on the man in the brush.

Later Weems entered the small but busy town of Moab, driving his rig past the saloon that was usually his first stop. But this day he made his way to the LaSal Mercantile to buy clothes to replace his bloody ones. The customers stared but no questions were asked, even though he was well known and on the friendliest of terms with the proprietor. After signing his ticket of credit and tucking his new purchases under each arm, Weems wandered over to the public bathhouse.

The change in his routine caused Weems to miss out on the drama that was unfolding at the saloon.

Captain Harris entered the saloon and walked up to the bar. He was without uniform, dressed roughly and as unkempt as most of the men; as he would have it, Harris was unnoticed by the locals.

The bartender, a barrel-chested, middle-aged man with carrot-red curly hair, was busy serving drinks at the poker table. Captain Harris bided his time and patiently scrutinized the crowd. The bartender returned to take Harris' order but the yokel slouched over the bar next to the captain butted in. "Jobe, gimme a cigar."

Jobe, grinning good-naturedly, reached into a tall humidor and pulled out the longest stogie Harris had ever seen. "You fathered a baby?" The man heehawed.

"I'm fixin' to." He stumbled and weaved out of the saloon.

Captain Harris spoke up, "Whiskey." Jobe placed a glass in front of him and, as he poured the drink, Harris inquired in a low voice. "Any chance of getting in on that game?"

Jobe replied in like manner, low and confidential. "Risky playin' cards with tempers you don't know. But it's an open table."

Harris took his drink and casually strolled over to the card table. He recalled Colonel Fenton's evaluation of the bartender, Jobe. "He knows all and says nothing."

The man shuffling the cards glanced up at Harris. "You wantin' in?"

Harris, still standing, replied. "You mind?"

The man shuffled twice more, taking his time. "You got money?"

"Some." Harris dropped more than "some" on the table as he spoke.

The dealer reached his long leg to the table next to them and, with the toe of his boot, dragged over a chair, questioning as Harris sat down. "Where you come from?"

Harris offered the information without hesitation as he stuck out his cupped hands and slid his money in front of him. "Fort Laramie."

As the dealer slapped the cards down for Harris to cut, he looked him in the eye for the first time, and held. "Army?"

Captain Harris was a pro. He held the man's gaze and stared him down, replying nonchalantly. "Stockade."

One of the other two men at the table entered the conversation and asked suspiciously. "How long you up there?"

Harris replied quickly. "Six months."

The man persisted. "I spent time up there an' I never seen you."

Harris was tensing up. It was too warm in the saloon. The morning had been plenty cold, but the midday sun had warmed things up, yet Jobe kept rekindling the stove. Harris stood up and removed his coat before he replied. He stalled for a plausible story. Harris thought of his colonel and the colonel's warnings about the place and the neurotically inquisitive men. And then he had it, as if offered to him on a silver platter by the colonel himself.

Easing back into his chair, Harris sorted his poker hand before replying. "Spent most of my time in the box."

His inquirer looked interested. "What were you in for?"

Here Harris played his trump card. "Desertion." He had their undivided attention. "Left my unit to bed Colonel Fenton's woman."

Disbelief was followed by howling laughter. The men laid down their cards and slapped their thighs with boisterous hooplas.

When the game resumed, the third player at the table asked his first question, the one Harris was waiting for, his lead-in for gathering information. It was an obvious, simple inquiry. "What're you doin' down here?"

Harris waved his arm to Jobe, indicating the next round of drinks was on him. He smiled to himself wickedly, knowing that all of his hospitality was paid for by the United States Cavalry.

Harris addressed his poker-playing pals. "Come to find a gang I heard about. Big Vic and Pinky's."

"You won't find 'em together. They split," confided one of Harris' new buddies.

Harris sat back to play cards and drink. Having heard his first bit of information, he was sure he would gather more.

<hr>

Lela scurried up the path to Parson's shack with her arms full. It was late in the afternoon of a cold, blustery December day, and she ducked her head down inside the hood of her green-plaid woolen wrapper to protect her face from the icy sleet that had fallen intermittently the last few hours. When she reached the door of the shack, she kicked it open without knocking and bounded in, dropping her bundles on the floor. Her arms now free, she pushed with all her might to shut and latch the door against the winter storm.

Parson had been lying on his cot against the wall trying to stay warm. He sat up as Lela, all smiles, entered. She retrieved her bundles and laid them at his feet before removing her mittens and cloak; then she sat down beside him on the cot. He took her little hands one at a time and warmed them between his large, rough old palms.

The room, though sparse in furniture, was cozy and cheerful. Muslin curtains hung at the two windows, and a blue calico tablecloth covered a table, with pewter plates set before four cane chairs. An ample fire blazed in the rock fireplace. A handsome maple rocker cushioned in calico sat in front of the fire; beside the rocker, a flat-top trunk served as a side table that held a finely etched glass oil lamp and several books. There were no pictures on the wall, but a very old and faded Navajo rug hung over the mantle of the fireplace. In the far corner stood a cupboard filled with knickknacks and assorted dishes. Pots and skillets hung on hooks on the wall on both sides of the cupboard. The one other table in the room was beside Parson's cot. It held the second of the pair of glass oil lamps, Parson's glasses, and his Bible. A curtained entrance led to a small back room where Lela kept her belongings and slept when she stayed with Parson.

Lela motioned for Parson to open one of the packages. He knew before he saw the contents that it was his favorite jacket, which she had taken away to be mended. He held it up while both of them admired the fine patching.

"Miss Ivy, she sewed it up fer you even better'n I could. It'll keep the wind out better now." Lela spoke gently, for she loved caring for Parson.

Parson was pleased that the Blakemores had become family to Lela and now included him too. "You tell her thank you fer me."

"Tell her yourself. You'll see her at Christmas supper," Lela reminded him, playfully scolding.

Parson implored the Lord with raised arms. "I'll tell her, I say unto you. Inasmuch as ye have did it unto one of my brethren, you might jist as well have did it unto me."

Lela sighed with delight. "You say it so pretty, Parson. I miss bein' with you."

They hugged each other and then sat quietly side by side for quite a while. Parson broke the silence. "Lela, your mama, she wanted the best fer you, an' right now that's stayin' on with Larken."

Lela twisted the tasseled belt of her navy flannel dress, intertwining it in her fingers and thoughtfully weighing her reply to Parson. She loved her new home and each one there, but her life and her heart were with Parson.

"They're real good to me. Feel like they're my family. I just worry 'bout you some, is all."

Parson sat there a moment or two, nodding his head with understanding. "An' I can't say it ain't lonesome with you gone. But I got two things fillin' my heart: you bein' safe an' my ghost."

Lela fought back tears of joyful gratitude. "Ain't God right fine to put that Holy Ghost in us?" She looked up at Parson as she spoke.

He saw the moisture glistening in her eyes, wide with wonder.

"Right fine." He patted her hand. "You're a good girl, Lela. Your mama, she'd be mighty proud." Parson stood up and stretched. Wandering to the window, he looked out. "The sleet stopped," he commented. "I'll fix us some coffee."

Lela unwrapped the remaining package and folded the new washing and drying cloths neatly in a stack. She handed Parson two new quilted hot pads as he reached for the kettle of boiling water. They sat beside each other once again on Parson's cot, sipping the steaming brew and inhaling its delicious aroma, just glad to be there together.

Lela quietly spoke her mind. "Mr. Pinky and Mr. Vic's gonna kill one another."

"I expect," Parson replied.

"I thought they was good men." Lela's voice was full of concern and she stared up at Parson, awaiting an explanation.

Parson shook his head in disgust. "Pinky, he'd kill to prove his worth. Vic, he'd do it to pay Pinky back. 'A eye fer a eye'."

Lela began to cry, pitifully and quietly. "Don't say it to me, say it to them. They might one of 'em be my daddy." Lela sobbed. "Stop 'em, Parson."

Parson took her cup and his and set them on the table by his cot. He lifted her chin and held her worried little face in his hands, praying for her understanding. "I can't do it, Lela."

Lela pleaded with him. "But why not? Blessed be them peacemakers, fer they gonna . . ."

Parson looked away from her. His expression was sad but his answer was firm. "It ain't my fight. An' I'm scared. Men git scared. These other men, they come an' go. But me, I made a solemn vow to see to you."

Parson stood up, pulling Lela to her feet and hugging

her close to him. With her face pressed against his chest she could feel the thump of his dear old heart.

She murmured, "Who'd you vow to?"

Parson looked over Lela's head through the window and out into the gray day. His thoughts traveled far away as he answered her. "God an' your mama an' . . ." He stopped.

Lela shook his arm, begging him to go on. "An' who? My daddy? You know who he is, Parson? Are you . . ."

Parson interrupted. "An' myself, that's who I vowed to. You belong with the Blakemores."

He reached for Lela's wrap and put it over her shoulders. He handed her mittens to her. She took the mittens from Parson and began to put them on, but Lela sat down once again on Parson's cot. When she patted the place beside her, Parson acquiesced.

Lela spoke to him in hopeful disbelief. "Why? Is Larken my daddy?"

Parson evaded her pathetic question. He wished for nothing in the world to ever trouble her and he was sorry about his stern face. But she had to understand. When he spoke, his voice was hard. "You might not be safe here."

Lela gently glanced sideways at Parson. "Was you there with my mama?" Parson hung his head in his hands and groaned. "Go on back, child."

Lela dropped to her knees and lovingly smoothed his hair back from his forehead. She laid her cheek next to his and then left him there in his thoughts. Letting herself out, Lela slowly made her way back to Blakemore House.

Chapter Sixteen

How shall we sing the Lord's song in a strange land?

PSALM 137:4

The heavy rainfall of late November had swollen the river out of its banks. Even now, as the month of December wore on, the stepping stones of Parson's crossing were still submerged in angry, swirling, high water. Parson and Praiseworthy made several dangerous and difficult attempts to reach the far bank and, half drowned, were at last washed ashore downstream. The two soggy, spent refugees sought out Weems' store and were greeted with hospitality and readily taken in by Weems and his hounds. Though they were cramped, they enjoyed their stay, helping out and making frequent visits with Weems to the Blakemore's house.

The Advent of Christmas, 1867, was promising in all of nature's winter loveliness. Light, clean snow fell gently each day for the first two weeks of December, with the gray skies promising more to come. The nights, however, were cold and clear. The myriad stars shone out of a deep blue heaven, reflecting off the white-blanketed earth.

Emmy sat at the dining room table composing her first letter home. It was almost midnight, and she was dressed in her nightclothes and ready for bed. She had been restless and thoughtful, and had come downstairs an hour before with paper and pen and her oil lamp. Some warmth was in the coals left in the fireplace, but she shivered nonetheless, not only from the cold, but also from the mingled joy and sadness within her heart. Larken and E. had written several letters over the months, but she had procrastinated. Tears flowed down her cheeks, and she wiped them away with the frilly cuffs of her sleeves to avoid smudging her writing. She missed her mother and father and Billy and Chloe. Would she see Uncle Marcel or Fetch again? She laid down her pen and, putting her hands to her mouth, sobbed quietly. She had not written before because she dared not think of home. Even her prayers for them had been forced from habit.

As the mantle clock chimed twelve, Emmy smoothed out the paper, dipped the pen in the inkpot, and began to write.

"Dear Ones, How can it be eight months since we left

civilization? Time has both drug on and flown past. Lela has been living with us for almost two months. I am sure Larken has written you about our dear new friend. She is a delightful, precocious, eleven-year-old orphan girl, and is now such a rich part of us that, were she to leave, my heart would break. I know Larken's would. Dear Uncle Billy, how I wish you could see your son at work. You'd be so proud of him; I am. We've had boarders almost every day since we opened for business. It's lucrative and I feel sure we will be free from debt someday. I don't know how long that will be, but we are learning patience, which brings us peace as this Christmas draws near. We send you our love and hope you are all well as we are. Emmy. 15 December 1867. Blakemore House, Post Office Tree, Utah Territory."

"P.S. Mama, on Christmas Eve, Aunt E., Ivy, and I will wear our more formal dresses that you bought for us and think of you all."

Emmy read what she had written, folded the papers lovingly, and tucked them in the envelope. There was quietude within her.

All the while, Larken had watched her from the stairs. When she stood and took up the lamp, its light shone on her beautiful, serenely calm face. He held his breath, lest his joy at the very sight of her escape him. As Emmy approached the stairs, Larken slipped down the hall and disappeared into his bedroom.

⊹⟪⟨⟨⟨⟨⟨⟨⟨⟨⟨⟨⟨⟨⟨⟨⟨⟨⟩⟩⟩⟩⊹

Parson and Weems arrived early in the afternoon on Christmas Eve, bearing bundles of candles, juniper boughs, and the tree. Praiseworthy's Christmas bells jingled from the cord tied around her neck. She nipped at the bells as she leapt up the front porch and into the house, seemingly delighted and annoyed at the noise of the bells.

Weems had closed his store at noon, having received this most sought-after invitation to come along with Parson and join in the festivities. He was dressed for the occasion in a fine orange-and-green tweed suit, matching overcoat, and black string tie.

Parson wore his clerical collar and black cassock under a flowing magenta woolen cape. Spreading it out in courtly fashion, he bowed to greet the ladies and extend the glad tidings of the season. Lela squealed with excitement as Parson swept her up under the folds of his cloak and whirled her around.

The goose and the venison and the wild turkey, which Parson and Weems had delivered the day before, roasted in their pans, mixed in with radishes, onions, and dried herbs. Larken and Runner joined Parson and Weems to festoon the doorways with the evergreen branches. In and out of the kitchen and dining room, and through the hall into the parlor, they all flew in their preparations, bumping into each other, laughing and joking. Aunt E. and Lela cut ginger squares and placed them on sugar cookies, while Emmy arranged the bowls of cinnamon, licorice, and peppermint sticks. Ivy directed them all from her kitchen to stir the pots, steam the green beans, and dice the turnips, beets, pumpkin, and yellow and white potatoes.

When the dishes were placed and the table was set, the ladies retired upstairs to change into the fancy dresses Alice had bought for them before they left Ponchatoula. Runner and Larken were already attired in their formal casino best. Ivy instructed the men to build a grand fire and bring in more firewood, for a heavy snow was falling. They were further instructed to place and light the candles as it got dark.

Aunt E. was the first to descend. She entered the parlor as elegantly as a Boston debutante. She wore black velvet with lace ruffles at her throat. Her red hair was powdered with henna, swept up and held in place with a black velvet bow. She took her place at the piano and began the caroling.

Larken opened a bottle of port as Ivy entered the parlor singing, and they joined her in song. Runner held his breath at the beauty of his wife. She wore a wine-colored woolen dress with a pink satin sash at her tiny waist.

Lela skipped in with bouncing curls, held back from her temples with lavender ribbons and pink silk rosebuds. She wore her lavender birthday dress and lavender beads. The hem of her skirt was held up at intervals by more rosebuds, revealing a ruffled, pink taffeta petticoat. The child wore white silk stockings and pink kid slippers.

Emmy paused halfway down the stairs. The candles were lit in abundance on the mantle, the sideboard, and the piano. The evergreen tree stood in the far corner of the parlor, with a dozen lit tapers illuminating its dark branches.

Leaning over the banister, Emmy saw that six candles were placed in the center of the dining table. She thought, *Isn't it odd; this might be the most glorious Christmas I've ever known.* Emmy joined them in singing, radiant and happy. She wore a soft-blue woolen dress, plain and clinging to her slender but well-formed body. Her auburn curls were held back at the nape of her neck by a blue satin ribbon. Larken took her hand and led her toward the mantle, never taking his eyes from hers.

Lela giggled with joy as she watched Larken offer his arm to Emmy. Runner took Ivy's hand. The two couples led the way, as they walked arm in arm into the dining room. Parson escorted Aunt E. and Weems gallantly offered Lela his arm.

When all was made ready, the group stood at the table awaiting the blessing. Raising his arms above his head in prayer, Parson thanked the Almighty for their food and for this night and for family. He took a candle from the table and ceremoniously held it high. All eyes were fixed on its flame as Parson ill-quoted: "A light for the Gentles and the glory of thy people as well."

Lela glanced up and saw tears on Weems' old red cheeks. Praiseworthy broke up the solemnity of the occasion with a ferocious scratching and Christmas bell jingling.

With hearty appetites, they ate their Christmas dinner. There was little conversation, except for extensive praise to the cooks, until all was cleared away and the men sat back smoking their cigars.

"Been ever' bit of fifteen years since I had such a fine Christmas dinner with such a close family group." Parson spoke in earnest as he scratched Praiseworthy's ears and fed her scraps.

Parson now seemed like a lifelong friend to E. and she asked him without feeling intrusive. "Where were you then?"

Parson grinned at E. in reply. "The prison at Rapid City."

E. smiled incredulously. "And this reminds you of that?"

Lela interrupted with surprise. "I didn't know you ever done time."

Parson relit his dead cigar before he answered their questioning stares. "Didn't really. Naw, I was sent as chaplain up there fer about two months. It was the Easter after when the fallin' out happened down at Prescott."

Lela continued her questioning. "Anybody ever come after you over that?"

Parson shook his head thoughtfully. "Naw, thought they might. But the preacher I shot, he'd jist killed a man the week before."

Larken stood up to open the kitchen door and let in a bit of fresh air. He spoke to Parson over his shoulder. "The preacher you shot had just killed a man?"

Parson waited to answer until Larken took his seat once more. "Weren't nothin', really. But the folks down there was right addled jist the same. He, the preacher, was at the river baptisn' the sheriff's brother when he clean forgot the words. Held him under thinkin', then he said 'em, an' by the time he pulled the man up, he'd drowned. Could've happened to anybody."

"Well, I got to go. Horace Haggar died an' I told Ma Haggar I'd bless his grave. Got to go over early tomorrow.

Good-bye, an' may the Lord bless you on this fine birthday of His."

All stood up at Parson's farewell gesture and hugged each other, saying their good-byes and well wishes for a merry Christmas. Larken walked with Parson into the front hall ahead of the others. He motioned toward the door and spoke in a low voice as Parson retrieved his cloak from the coat rack. "Let me see you out."

They stood on the porch breathing in the fresh and icy air of the cold night. The snow had stopped, and quiet and calm permeated the earth and the heavens. Overhead, the clouds chased each other in rapid course, dimming and revealing the stars. Parson stooped down and removed the rope collar and bell from Praiseworthy's neck, urging her out for a frolic while he and Larken talked. Weems and Runner would come around with the wagon at any moment.

Parson already knew what Larken had on his mind, and he hurriedly addressed it. "You're wantin' to know if I heard anything 'bout Pinky and Vic?"

"Yeah. Pinky and his boys went up to Brown's Park for a couple of days and I haven't heard from Vic." Larken told Parson what he probably already knew. Not wanting to worry his family, he needed to share his concerns with someone he could trust outside of Blakemore House.

Parson did not wish to conjure up trouble needlessly, so he replied, "Me either." With leery optimism, he added, "Might be they made their peace. Mighty quiet with all them gone. Well, Merry Christmas, Larken." Parson whistled for Praiseworthy as Weems' wagon pulled up in front.

Larken called back. "Merry Christmas, Parson." As he started into the house, he spied a small package set to one side of the front door. It was for Lela. He found her sitting under the Christmas tree with Emmy and handed her the tiny present.

Lela turned her face up to Larken with a surprised smile and questioned coquettishly. "Who's this from?"

Larken answered her honestly, a bit bewildered. "I don't know; it just says 'Lela' on it."

They assembled around her, Runner just returned from the barn and E. and Ivy from the kitchen. Lela pulled from the tissue an exquisite miniature cameo necklace and, speechless with wonder, stood up and handed it to Larken. She backed up to him, lifting the curls off her neck so he could fasten the clasp.

Lela sighed with utter joy. "Is this from you?"

"No, I just found it at the door." Larken's voice held the tone of regret that he felt, wishing that the gift had been his to her.

Emmy heard his disappointment and quickly suggested, "Maybe it's from your daddy."

Lela smiled faintly, looking sideways at Larken. "I bet it is. It's the most beautiful thing I ever had."

Runner lifted the cameo from her little chest to admire it. "It's on the most beautiful girl in the Roost." He patted her cheek and she hugged him in reply.

Ivy drew Lela to her and kissed her forehead and, reaching for Runner's hand, spoke to Lela and to Runner. "Come on, Runner, let's try out that bed-warmer you gave me."

Runner took the bed-warmer from the fireplace, and he and Ivy went up the stairs, calling back "Good-night" and "Merry Christmas."

Aunt E. stretched and yawned. "This has been quite a day." She put her arm around Lela's waist, moving her toward the stairs. "You ready for bed, Lela?"

Lela gently removed Aunt E.'s arm and turned to Emmy and hugged her. "You all made me such a pretty Christmas, like I never had before."

Larken knelt down beside her, and she hugged him while touching her cameo and whispered in his ear. "Thank you. I love you, Larken."

Larken held her tightly for a moment. "I love you, too, baby." He handed her over to Aunt E.

Larken moved throughout the house, licking his fingers to pinch out the candles. When he returned to the parlor,

Emmy waved him away from the tree. She sat cross-legged in front of it, nurturing its last few moments of splendor. The candles burned dangerously, low but Larken allowed her a little more time. He added a log and stoked the fire, for the room had grown chilly.

Emmy sighed in her reverie. "It's not like any Christmas we've had." She hugged herself, shivering, and got up and took one of the chairs by the blazing warmth of the fireplace.

Larken stood before the Christmas tree himself, taking in its loveliness. "Hell of a tree, though." He uttered his final gratitude to the tree, as one by one he extinguished its candles.

Larken sat in the chair across from Emmy and lit a cigar with a burning twig. Satisfied it was lit, he blew several puffs and tossed the twig into the fire. The house was quiet, but both of them could hear E.'s voice overhead singing to Lela their old familiar Welsh lullaby.

"You made us a beautiful Christmas, Larken." Emmy smiled at him, offering her love.

Larken received her gift and returned her smile. His heartbeat pounded within his bosom. Overcome with her inviting gesture, he was speechless; he lowered his eyes and stared at the gold ring on his little finger. They sat in silence. The clock ticked away the minutes, then paused and began its eleven o'clock chiming. Emmy's head lay back and her eyes were closed when Larken gently touched her arm and placed his ring in her palm.

He squeezed her small hand in his and whispered. "Merry Christmas, Emmy."

Emmy sat up. "I can't take this. It's all you have that was your mother's." Emmy tried to give back the ring as she spoke, but Larken moved out of her reach.

Larken was afraid the spell was broken. He thought, *I want Emmy on her terms. I know her so well, but can't seem to hold her affection long enough for it to amount to anything.*

However, this night he would keep trying. "She would have wanted you to have it. Back then the family thought we'd marry. Our fathers' agreed to our betrothal on the night you were born."

Emmy fingered the cherished keepsake in her hand and replied pensively. "So did we, grow up thinking we would marry."

In a flash of irritation at her reply, Larken spoke off-handedly. "Anyway, you don't have to wear it." He reconsidered and added softly, "I just want you to have it."

Emmy looked at the ring, taking into her heart the loving sacrifice of Larken's gift to her. She put it on her wedding finger; it fit perfectly. There was no question now in her mind that it was meant to be hers. Reaching up, she pulled Larken's face down to hers and kissed his cheek. Then she pulled back and smiled at him thoughtfully.

When she spoke, it was with regret. "I wish I had something to give to you."

Larken lifted her from the chair and engulfed her in his strong arms. He spoke to her with the tenderness of their childhood. "Every day since you were born, you've given me Christmas."

Emmy stayed secure in Larken's embrace for a moment or two. Then she wiggled free and giggled girlishly. Smiling at him she took her leave, calling back as she ascended the stairs. "Good night, Larken."

Larken looked up after her as she disappeared into the shadows. He was giddy with anticipation but bewildered at how to proceed. He shouted loud enough to awaken the sleeping household. "Good night, Em."

Upstairs Emmy took her time undressing. She hung up her blue dress carefully and pressed her petticoat into the trunk, deliberately folding it. Sitting at her dressing table, Emmy brushed her hair, mused, and turned the gold ring on her finger. She held up her hand to the mirror to enjoy the ring's reflection. She glanced several times at the wall separating Larken's bedroom from hers.

In his own room, Larken took off his shirt and put on a robe. He poured water into the basin and rinsed his face, looking at himself in his shaving mirror. Listening, hardly daring to breathe, he quietly tiptoed to Emmy's bedroom wall. He listened but heard nothing.

Emmy put on her robe, looking toward Larken's bedroom. She slipped noiselessly across the room and put her ear against the wooden wall. She heard nothing.

Larken sat in his chair, facing away from the wall to Emmy's bedroom. He turned his oil lamp down low and sat in the shadows, thinking and listening. He thought he heard a stir in her room and, turning up the lamp, he once more crept over and put his ear to the wall.

Emmy sat at her dressing table, once again brushing her hair. "Why am I so nervous? It's as if we'd just met." She spoke out loud to herself. "Larken seems different somehow."

She glanced toward his room and, summoning her courage, threw her hairbrush against the wall. She sat still as stone and listened.

There was a discreet knock at her door. Emmy sat marooned and her voice was hoarse as she quietly inquired. "Who is it?"

He whispered. "Larken."

Emmy replied breathlessly. "Come in."

Larken stuck his head around the door, looking at Emmy and questioning the noise that offered him this intrusion. "I thought I heard something." He entered her room, securely shutting the door behind him.

Emmy did not turn around to face him, but stared at Larken's handsome reflection in her mirror. She smiled as she apologized. "Oh Larken, I'm sorry I woke you; I dropped my brush."

Larken spied her hairbrush lying on the floor against the far wall. He picked it up and brought it over to her. Keeping a straight face, seemingly innocent to her prank, he laughed to himself. *You darling little vixen. You didn't drop the brush; you threw it!*

He stood behind her, taking in the luscious countenance of her in the mirror, and passionately replied. "I was up."

Emmy fidgeted with white silk ribbons at the throat of her wrapper, nervously babbling. "I can never go right to sleep after a party or a holiday."

"You never could. I'll sit with you till you feel sleepy." Larken placed his hands on her shoulders as he spoke. He could feel her tension, so he gently massaged her neck.

Emmy closed her eyes. She enjoyed the warmth of his wonderful hands and let him continue. She purred and murmured sweetly. "You used to do that a lot when we were growing up. I mean, sit with me."

Larken perched on the side of her bed, facing her at the dressing table. He smiled as he reminded her. "Runner would bring word that Miss Emmy couldn't sleep, and

I'd get up and run through the orchard to your house and sit till all hours."

Emmy laughed as she confessed to Larken. "Did you know that I used to send him just because I wanted to see you?"

Larken nodded his head, with a hint of a smile. "It was good, those days growing up with you. I remember the day you were born. I said you would be mine, named you after Aunt E."

Emmy sighed. "We got on so well back then. Why do we argue so now?"

Larken stood up behind her once again. She stared back at his reflection in the mirror, awaiting his explanation. "We're too much alike. Pride maybe. I don't know."

There was an awkward pause. Larken held her mirrored gaze firmly in his. "I promised to keep our relationship out of my bed. Lately, it's harder to keep that promise, but I will."

Emmy replied so quickly that it took him by surprise. "But Larken, this is not your bed." Her hand trembled.

Larken was both thrilled and weakened by what she suggested. He put his hands on her shoulders; now they were supple and inviting. He caressed her shining hair for a few moments. Emmy took his hand and coaxed him to sit beside her on the bench, turning her face to him. She touched his cheek and he kissed both of hers; finding her mouth, he passionately devoured her. Emmy made a small gasp for breath. She was shaking with ecstasy.

Larken smiled at her innocence. He gathered her up in his arms and laid her on the bed. Removing his robe, he slowly let himself down onto her, powerfully kissing her, engulfing her inviting, open little mouth.

"Larken, I feel dizzy." She panted, her breasts heaving with excitement.

"Just wait." Larken smiled down at her.

"You mean it gets worse?" Emmy gasped with wonder.

"Better. Much better." Larken whispered as he took Emmy to be his wife.

The following morning, Christmas day, Larken let himself quietly and quickly out of Emmy's bedroom. He was tying his robe sash and didn't see Runner coming down the hall. Runner didn't hide his exaggerated look of surprise, for he couldn't help but notice Larken's tired and disheveled state. Larken rolled his eyes in anticipation of the ribbing he was about to endure.

"You just shut up," he defended at Runner's broad and knowing smile.

Runner, still grinning, threw his hands out with innocence. "I didn't say a thing."

Larken growled. "I know what you're thinking; we think alike."

"Then, like me, you must be wondering why it took you so long to find the right room." Runner carried on, shaking with laughter.

Larken pushed past Runner and started down the stairs. "Just shut up. I'm going down for breakfast. I'm starving."

"I bet you are!" Runner called down as Larken reached the hall.

Larken poked his head around the banister."Shut up!"

They could both hear Emmy humming sweetly in her room. Runner sat at the top of the stairs, laughing boisterously. Pointing at Larken with one finger and motioning toward Emmy's room with the other hand, he was bent double and howling.

Larken grinned up at his friend. "I said shut up, damnit."

Chapter Seventeen

News from a foreign country came
As if my treasure and my wealth lay there.

Thomas Traherne

fter Christmas Larken and Runner stocked up at Weems' store for much-needed supplies because Pinky and his gang had returned to Blakemore House. They managed with those supplies during the next three weeks of bleak, icy weather, when the road was almost impassable by wagon. Finally, on an unusually mild day in January, Larken and Runner returned to Weems' store for fresh supplies.

Weems rounded up all their purchases, totaling the cost in his ledger. He smiled at Larken with approval. "Think this is everything?"

Runner eyed the sack of flour cautiously. "I was just looking the flour over for weevils."

Weems pushed Runner aside and poked his boney

finger into the flour and stirred it around. Satisfied, he wiped the white dust on his shirt, speaking all the while to Larken nonchalantly. "Seen a man says he knows you."

Larken jerked his head toward Weems. "An Indian?"

Weems heard apprehension in Larken's voice. He tied up the remaining sack of flour and took his time replying, shaking his head as he recalled his unpleasant encounter. "Naw, looked like dirty lard. Don't worry, he can't git in the Roost."

After Weems flung the sack over his shoulder and headed outside to the wagon, Runner whispered an aside to Larken. "Bates."

Larken nodded with agreed suspicion, putting his finger to his mouth to hush Runner as Weems reentered the store, talking to himself loud enough for Larken and Runner to hear. "Bounty hunter, I s'pect."

After further thought, Weems spoke directly to Larken. "Better stay clear of the entrances. Heard Pinky an' his boys was back from Brown's Park, stayin' at your place."

"Yeah," Larken replied absentmindedly. His attention was fixed on Parson, who had entered the store a few moments earlier. He seemed somewhat agitated.

Parson looked at Larken as if to say something to him, but stopped short of utterance, changing his mind when Weems' hidden form rose into view from behind the counter and he greeted him. "Parson."

"Weems, say, I got a cloudin' up in my head. Get me some spirit of camphor, would you?" Parson kept his eyes on Larken, holding his attention as he spoke to Weems.

At the sound of Parson's voice, the lazy hound dogs sauntered past them and out the door in search of their compadre, Praiseworthy.

Weems motioned to a room at the rear of the store, where he kept notions and potions. "It's in the back in a pile." He replied to Parson as he greeted several men entering the store.

"I could find it," Larken offered as Parson followed along, motioning for Runner.

As soon as they were out of Weems' and his customer's hearing and safely in the back room, Parson turned to Larken and whispered. "Git out there quick as you kin. Vic sent me. Don't go past the house where Pinky'll see you. Mr. Runner, you take these here things back to the house an' tell 'em Larken went to Post Office Tree. Here, Larken, here's a letter; I got it to buy you some time." Parson wheezed in a low and anxious voice.

Larken steadied Parson's shaking shoulder. "What is it? Is Vic all right?"

Parson's fear turned to anger at the impossible situation, and he growled his anguished reply. "Jist git over there an' don't let on to Pinky."

Larken sighed in disgust. "Then they're still at it. This is their damn fight, not mine."

Parson retorted, "Not mine either, but you learn to do what you're told when you got a gun at your neck."

Larken hurried back into the front room of the store and brushed past Weems and his customers as he hurried out. Weems peered into the back room and stared at Runner and Parson, inquisitive. "Where's he off to?"

Runner covered for Parson with a cool reply to Weems. "The women will jerk a knot in him if he doesn't check for mail."

Weems cackled falsetto. "Women kin be right positive." He reached for a bottle standing in plain view and added suspiciously, "Here's your camphor, Parson."

"It'll do me good. Thank ya, Weems. See ya, Runner." Parson called out to them, as he whistled for Praiseworthy and took his leave.

Runner stood on the front porch while Weems totaled the bill. He casually handed Weems some money as he watched Larken's far-off figure head toward the hide-out caves on horseback. Parson stood on the other side of Runner's wagon. He, too, watched Larken's progress, with his hand shading his eyes from the sun.

Both Parson and Runner noted with concern the large

number of boxes of ammunition being loaded into the wagon of the men who had previously entered the store, a gang unknown to Runner and seemingly ignored by Parson. Runner said to himself. *Parson came prepared. He brought Larken that horse. I don't feel so well; can pure fear cause me this much misery in my chest?* And Runner rubbed his heart.

Larken rode in and out amid the canyon walls, always returning to his place of entry. He was lost and confused. *Surely*, he thought, *one of Vic's men will show up to lead me in*. He tried another approach and found he was right back at the entrance again. Halting his horse, he just sat there and waited and muttered over and over. "Damnit."

After about ten minutes, Larken spied one of Vic's men standing up to the right on a high butte. As he approached the man, he recognized Bobby, his first acquaintance from the Roost. He was silently flailing his arms, motioning. Larken rode his horse to the bottom of the butte and dismounted. Bobby, who had descended, took the reins of his horse and directed Larken to duck down and enter the mouth of the cave. Once inside, Larken stood up to full height, while adjusting his eyes to the eerie gray darkness. Slick, rounding a boulder with a lighted torch, showed him the way and led him further and deeper into the cave.

They entered a large hall that was brilliantly lit by

a dozen or so torches stuck into natural fissures in the walls. A good-sized fire burned in the center of the cave-room, alleviating the dampness. Larken noted the bedrolls and other paraphernalia: pots, pans, and axes, saddles and horse blankets, all neatly arranged along the floor to the far left of his point of entry. Hooks were miraculously fastened to the walls and high ceiling. Larken wondered how. The hooks held suspended bridles, braids of onions, dried green, red, and yellow peppers, and other foodstuff. Boxes of ammunition were safely placed far from the fire, opened and ready.

In the center of the room, to the right of the fire, Big Vic sat on a campstool behind a rough makeshift table. Maps were spread all over in front of him, along with several metal cash boxes that shone and blindingly reflected the firelight and torches. One box lay open, as Vic counted coins and placed them in orderly stacks. Big Vic stood up and rounded the large table. Without greeting and wasting no time, he spoke hurriedly and ordered Larken with ominous warning in his voice.

"Get Pinky and the boys out of your house. Now!" Vic took a torch and ushered Larken back along the cave corridor toward the entrance.

"Why? Why now and not a month ago?" Larken shouted out at Vic, breathlessly trying to keep up with Big Vic's long strides and his torchlight which, when Vic rounded a turn, left Larken stumbling in pitch dark.

On the way back out Vic picked up a box of ammunition.

Big Vic reserved his reply until they reached the cave opening. With the bit of light graciously shining in from the outside world, they could now see. Finally, Vic replied to Larken as he extinguished the torch.

"It's not just me they're robbing. Now, they're holding up every outfit in the Roost. I won't come after him as long as he is with you, but others might. He's got to be stopped, but not at the expense of your lives and Lela's."

Larken threw out his hands in hopeless dismay. "They've been at our house for months. I've asked him to go and he won't do it. What reason would I use?"

Big Vic was angry, and he spoke his final say to Larken, berating him with a warning threat. "It might help your creativity to realize that your lives depend on it." Vic put his hand on Larken's shoulder and softened a little. "Larken, if anyone can talk Pinky out of that house it's you. You've been a good friend to me, Larken. Don't fail me now. Good-bye." He squarely thrust the box of ammo in Larken's gut and said, "Oh, and, load your damn gun for a change."

Vic called back into the cave. "Slick!"

Slick emerged from the darkness behind Larken and

ushered him out the entrance. There Bobby handed him the reins to his horse. The three men disappeared inside the cave and Larken mounted his horse. He had been dismissed.

Larken left the canyon wall behind and headed for the Post Office Tree road. He rode slowly and anxiously, not knowing what to do or how to handle this impressive assignment of Vic's. He gathered from Vic's insistence that he had little time to spare; nevertheless, he dismounted. Letting his horse graze freely, Larken sat under a shade tree, kicking at rocks and thinking out loud. *You've spent your life smart-assing your way out of everything. Now you dry up?* Mimicking Big Vic he said to himself. *Be creative. Your lives depend on it. Threatened by the best and I've got nothing.*

Larken picked up two limestone rocks and mindlessly beat them together. White powder crumbled on his hands.

"God help me, I feel sick." Larken stared down at his powdered white hands. The idea hit him! He frantically rubbed the chalky rock dust on his face and neck and the back of his hands, laughing out loud. *It is a crazy thought, but it just might work. Thank you, God.* He looked into the blinding sun that was setting over the nearby ridge of mountains and smiled broadly.

Larken retrieved his horse and filled his pockets and the saddlebags with the white powdery rocks. Swinging up into the saddle he chuckled to himself. *Larken, you clever bastard, how could I have ever doubted you?* He rode off toward Blakemore House with high purpose, titillated at the sham he was about to perform.

It was nearly dark when Larken arrived home. The others were nervously serving dinner to Pinky, Jim, Mute, and Choirboy. They were busy, scurrying about with their eyes fixed on the front door and their ears alert for the sound of Larken's horse.

E. was pouring coffee when she heard Larken's footsteps on the porch. She overfilled Pinky's cup. In reply to his curse, she handed him the pot and hurried for the front hall. Emmy and Ivy caught up with E. from the kitchen; Lela and Runner were already there and tried to catch Larken as he stumbled through the door and fell in a heap on the floor at their feet.

"What's the matter?" Lela cried with alarm.

Larken pulled her down to hear his whisper, and Runner knelt beside him. "Follow my lead. We're in trouble." Larken's low voice seemed strong and reassuring.

"Larken, what is it?" Emmy's scream brought Pinky from the dinner table. He still carried the coffeepot, which he thrust with irritation back into E.'s hand.

Larken cast his eyes on Ivy and held her attention deliberately, as he spoke to her but for all to hear. "I've got a fever and my throat's closing up. I can hardly breathe."

Ivy wiped Larken's ghostly ashen face with her dish-towel and removed chalk dust. Catching on, she quickly smoothed dust from Larken's neck and re-dusted the wiped spot, making it look like she was just patting his skin to feel the fever. "It's diphtheria," she solemnly pronounced.

Pinky exclaimed with horror, "People die from that, don't they?"

Ivy looked at Pinky with a sad and pitiful glance and, patting his shoulder reassuringly, comforted him. "Not *every* time."

Pinky stood transfixed with his mouth wide open at the pallor of Larken's face. "I don't want to get it." He whined and an infantile sob escaped him.

"Then get away from him." Aunt E. spoke to Pinky as he backed into the dining room.

Runner waved Pinky on with his hand and added, "As far away as you can."

Pinky's boys were camped on the kitchen porch, for they had heard and had vacated the contaminated house. Pinky found them and ordered them out the back door. "You boys git our gear. We're gittin' outta here!"

The men stayed put, refusing to obey for fear of reentering the house. Pinky kicked open the back door, shaking his fists and cursing them.

Lela called to them from inside with the sweet voice of a rescuing angel. "Mr. Pinky, I got your stuff all packed out here on the front porch."

She joined them and led the way around the corner to the front of the house. Choirboy started to cry and Pinky slapped him, then pushed Mute out of his way down the back-porch steps.

Jim explained to Lela. "Choirboy's pa, he died of that."

Lela led Choirboy by the hand as Runner emerged from the barn with the gang's horses, which he helped them saddle quickly. Lela extended her hand up to Pinky as he made ready to ride off. She gestured toward the interior of the house as she spoke to him. "It looks bad. Y'all better git. I'll miss you, Mr. Pinky."

With the gang pounding off down the road, Larken sat up on the floor of the front hall. He was pleased with the performance of his family, now gathered around him. He grinned at them, the peak of health now restored, as he explained.

"Pinky and his men have been robbing all the gangs in the Roost. Vic says one of them will finally come after Pinky, and he didn't want him here when it happened."

E. sighed with joyful relief. "I was tired of them anyway."

Emmy hugged Larken and kissed him on his chalky mouth. She pursed her lips and pouted with her own little sigh. "I will miss their money."

Runner stood by Ivy, laughing about Larken's skillfully executed and victorious charade. The seriousness of their predicament and the danger it afforded had oppressed him. The burden was removed from Runner's heart, and he breathed with more ease as he spoke for them all. "Dying rich isn't nearly so good as living poor."

Several days later, after an icy spell of weather had broken, Larken ventured out on horseback near one of the Roost's entrances. Weems' casual mention of Bates days earlier made Larken curious, though still heedful of the danger Bates posed. As Larken approached the guard sitting on his rocky vantage point he bellowed out to him.

The guard, having heard about the diphtheria scare, shied away as Larken came closer, so Larken called out to reassure him. "I'm much better. I'm not sick anymore. Anything come for me or my family?" It still struck Larken as funny that every piece of their mail was read and OK'd by these men. *But, hey, for the safety of the Roost it's worth it.*

The guard raised two fingers and, shuffling through his saddlebag, replied to Larken. "Two letters."

As the guard handed the opened letters to Larken he wondered, *How hard would it be for Bates to make his way into the Roost. This guard would not be someone I would want to mess with, but Bates is pretty persistent.* The guard continued speaking with the smug air of his own importance. "Your family back home is doin' good, an' you done paid back a good bit of what you took from a hotel back East."

Chapter Eighteen

. . . doubly dying, shall go down to the vile dust from whence he sprung, unwept, unhonored and unsung.

SIR WALTER SCOTT

Emmy and Lela, wrapped in warm woolen shawls recently sent from Louisiana, rocked and chatted on the front porch as they peeled potatoes and popped the naked results into a large pan between their chairs. They tossed the peelings over the rail into the front yard, to the delight of a pair of mule deer that had wandered close during the winter and become pets. It was a breezy, sunny morning in early March. The winter's weather had been moderate, and the approaching spring was announced with wild sprouts of yellow daffodils bowing in the warm gusts of wind. Tiny, purple, wild crocus flowers were snuggled in the tufts of green grass, as the valley awoke and whispered mild hints of new birth.

Emmy spoke to Lela about her mother, Alice, and how

different she and her mother were. Lela patted Emmy's hand when she saw a mist of tears in Emmy's eyes. The two laughed as Emmy explained that her mother had sent them only brown items of clothing since they left the colorfully clad, civilized world of Ponchatoula.

"How funny that all the items of clothing that mother sent are brown," Emmy said, indicating her woolen shawl. "My mother is always so practical in her gifts. Her recipes that she sent have been so helpful to me. Before, I never had an interest in cooking or mother's recipes. I know you will enjoy the fried potatoes and onions we will have for dinner tonight."

"What's it like to have a mother?" Lela asked.

Emmy thought for a minute and then smiled. "Having a mother is a little like you having Parson. You don't always like what they tell you, but you are always certain that it is the truth."

Emmy continued, "I never thought Mother approved of me, but now I see that she has always just wanted what was right for me. My mother has always done what was right and supportive for her family, for her husband."

They lapsed into a pleasant and comfortable silence. As Emmy's mind wandered, her thoughts turned to May McInally, and she wished that her mother, Alice, could know May. She now realized what she had admired in

May was what she had seen in her mother all her life. She leaned back in her chair, put her head back and smiled, still holding the half-peeled spud. When Lela saw Emmy's contented expression, she too smiled.

Lela put her potatoes down, leaned over, and hugged Emmy joyfully.

"Ain't it good to be glad in your memories, Miss Emmy?"

Emmy smiled again and said, "So good," and hugged Lela back.

Several mountain goats rounded the corner of the house to share the potato peelings that Emmy and Lela had been throwing from the porch for the mule deer. Lela and Emmy chuckled at the sight of them and watched the deer, with their necks stretched high and aloof, trot off, leaving the remaining potato peelings to the rude, pushy goats. Blakemore House attracted not only the peculiar in humankind but also the shy, dumb creatures that found this place a refuge.

A horseman approached around the bend in the road. When Lela recognized that it was Big Vic, she raced down the steps to meet him as he dismounted in front of the house. Vic set his horse free to roam, and Lela grabbed him around the legs and hugged him, her tight little arms greeting him with her heart and body's expression of relief and affection. Big Vic took Lela's hand and spoke to both Lela and Emmy in a pleasant but distant salutation, avoiding any contact with their questioning eyes.

"Pretty morning, ladies."

Emmy, noticing the frown on Lela's brow, replied. "It is at that. The best days look like spring but feel like winter. How have you been?"

Emmy stood in front of Vic and forced him to look at her, her piercing green eyes evaluating the set of his jaw and the look of concern that he tried to mask with a grin and nonchalance.

Big Vic could not avoid Emmy's beautiful green eyes nor the vivid blue of Lela's eyes blinking in the sunlight. Lela shaded her eyes with her hand in order to maintain her relentless stare.

He answered them truthfully. "I have been very well. I have good news concerning the disagreement between Pinky and myself."

Emmy looked away, satisfied. "I'm so glad." She spoke with obvious relief. E. stood in the doorway and heard Vic's news, as did Ivy, who had come onto the porch to retrieve the peeled potatoes for the boiling pot.

Vic cleared his throat and continued. "There'll be a gathering concerning this, here at Blakemore House, at dawn tomorrow. And since this is Roost business, I'd appreciate it if you womenfolk stayed out of sight and kept the child with you."

"All right." Emmy answered for them all.

Big Vic mounted his horse and rode off with a wave of his hand.

Several moments of silence passed. Even the noisy crows on the hill hushed their cawing, and the wee feathered ones paused in their chirping and peeping. No cattle lowed nor horse whinnied.

Dark storm clouds chased away the sun, and thunder rumbled through the valley and echoed off the cliffs and hills. All of the women shivered and drew their shawls closer. Lela stared at the ground and kicked a rock with the toe of her new boot, until she scuffed off a piece of the leather. As the wind blew the leather bit away, a part of Lela's heart chipped off as well.

She had something to say, but Lela kept it to herself. Fear, grief, and anger warred within her. No one heard her, for the wind was howling and the rain began to fall in large drops. She sobbed, "I knows what's up!"

Emmy watched Lela closely as they moved inside out of the rain. She had never before seen the girl so withdrawn and unapproachable. Emmy confided her concerns to the other women but, though they tried, they could get no conversation out of Lela, or even a reply to their reserved advances. As the day passed, they stayed near her and round about her as she helped with the chores in silence.

The women all obeyed Big Vic's order to remain inside

the house. From time to time, the women glanced through the windows toward the rear of the house, as groups of men gathered and set up small camps here and there in the yard.

⊹⊱✿⊰⊹

The next morning Emmy awakened just before dawn. Larken had not come to their bed that night, nor had he entered the house at any time to answer her questions and assuage her confusion and worry. She was put out with him, but not angry; she was afraid. Emmy dressed hurriedly as the dark night gave way to early light.

Yesterday's storm had blown through. A brief but pounding rain, followed by a cold north wind, had dropped the temperature. The house felt damp and lifeless.

Emmy found Lela on her knees, with her small hands folded in prayer and rested on the upstairs windowsill that overlooked the backyard. Though dawn provided enough light to see directly below, Lela's eyes strained as she peered further into the yard at the oak tree and the men gathering there.

Emmy stood silently behind Lela, and both saw Larken and Runner greet Big Vic by the near side of the old tree. Vic spoke to the men, but his words could not be heard inside the house. The men were orderly, and their murmuring ceased when Vic addressed them. Bobby and Slick carried a large bundle from the direction of the barn but were quickly hidden in the shadow of the tree.

Emmy burst forth in delight and made room for Ivy and Aunt E. to see. The two sleepily looked out the window, while Emmy continued with guarded exuberance. "A piñata! They're going to celebrate their friendship. Wonder what's inside. I'll get a stick for them to beat the piñata."

Lela stopped her with a gasp, turning to Emmy in disbelief at her ignorance. Emmy had no idea of the horror taking place below. She grasped Emmy's hands firmly, hurting her, and sobbed. "I'd hold off on that stick, Miss Emmy."

Pinky's lynching took place in a matter of seconds. A rope was thrown over the largest branch of the oak, and Pinky, with a noose around his neck and his head uncovered, took his last glimpse of the world. His eyes met Larken's where he stood at the rear of the crowd, held back by Runner. Larken broke loose from Runner's restraint, yelling and running toward the tree. He was too late. Above Larken's head, Pinky's bound body swung and twirled like a scarecrow in the north wind. Immediate whoops and hollering erupted, and shots were fired in the air.

Runner caught up with Larken as he approached Big Vic, shouting at his friend above the raucous noise and gunfire. "Hold tight, Larken, hold tight."

Larken heard Runner, but his voice shook as he cried out at Vic over the uproarious celebration. "Emmy said you worked things out with Pinky!"

Big Vic pointed to the corpse, now cut loose and sprawled on the ground. "And so I have."

Runner continued to hold onto Larken, but Larken didn't seem to mind his friend's steady grip; he did not resist but rather leaned on Runner for support. He lowered his voice to rationalize the craziness out with Vic.

"Working things out doesn't mean hanging people. You negotiate, you compromise, you reason."

Bobby and Slick, their dirty work done, interrupted them to speak aside to Vic. Runner and Larken, propping up each other at this point, waited patiently until Vic turned back to them and spoke, motioning to Bobby. "Bobby, tell Mr. Blakemore."

Bobby, looking hard and long at Larken, spoke slowly, deliberately, and dramatically. "Pinky was coming after you and your family and the girl."

"What?" Larken questioned, but instinctively he believed Bobby.

Bobby continued, very pleased with his role in the conversation and gratified that Big Vic had, by this gesture, promoted him to equal status. "He was gonna cash in on your set-up."

Larken looked at the dead man on the ground, feeling less sorry for him by the minute. "He was going to kill us? All of us?"

Slick, thinking of Aunt E. most especially, made the convincing remark. "Yes, sir, by now you'd all be dead."

Larken had only one question for them. "Why?"

Big Vic, shaking his head, had only one answer for Larken. "Money."

Larken and Runner stood silent, relieved and grateful, yet shaken and bewildered.

Bobby ventured to speak to Larken confidentially. "Don't ya see, Mr. Blakemore? This is definitely the wrong gatherin' fer your cocky attitude 'bout murderin'."

Runner looked up to the upstairs bedroom window to see his Ivy staring down at the tree, her face whiter than a black woman's face ever should be. Next to her, Emmy's eyes were wide with astonishment, and then suddenly her hand clasped over her mouth, and she vanished from the window.

As Runner moved toward the house he said hurriedly, "I'm goin' in to check on the women."

Larken, still in a daze, watched Runner go in the house, but quickly turned a blank face back to Vic. Big Vic went on to further explain to Larken. "Some people cannot be reasoned with, Larken. Sadly, Pinky, like his father, was one of those people. His death will save lives, like yours."

Larken nodded his head in understanding assent, as he watched six men hoist Pinky's body to their shoulders and carry him away. Despite the horror of the hanging, he was glad to be rid of Pinky and the chilly threat of the gang's presence at Blakemore House. It crossed Larken's mind that the early morning sun was already warming up the north wind. He wanted deliverance from the whole rotten, decaying mess.

Larken turned to Big Vic with one last question. "Why here, at my house?"

A wide grin spread across Big Vic's craggy face. "Everybody in Robber's Roost likes to come to Blakemore House. It's always so festive."

Larken returned Vic's humor with a weak smile.

A window from the upstairs bedroom of the house slammed open with a loud thud. Hysterical sobs could be heard from within. Runner, who had left Larken only moments earlier, leaned out of one window, beckoning and calling for help.

Larken, Vic, Bobby, and Slick rushed forth to assist. They found Runner hovering over his Ivy. She sat with her back to the wall, eyes glazed and staring.

Aunt E. was out cold on the bed and Slick, gallantly removing his hat, immediately took charge to fan her. He took his bandana from his neck and, dipping it in the washbasin, gently mopped her brow and whispered endearments.

In one corner, Lela held Emmy by the hair, as she vomited repeatedly into the chamber pot. Lela released one hand from her charge as Emmy came up for air. Pointing her finger at Vic, Lela regarded Vic and Larken with disgust.

"I could've told him these women wasn't up for no hangin'. Not yet, anyhow." Lela closed her eyes and sighed. "Wonder is it 'a eye fer a eye' or 'vengeance is fine', said the Lord?" Lela shrugged her shoulders and opened her eyes, patting Emmy on the back. "I'll ask Parson; he'll know."

<hr />

The roads to Fort Laramie were crowded from both the eastern and the western approaches on this particular day in April of 1868. Wagon trains packed the Fort's streets as adventurers, prospectors, and humanity in general headed west in search of open land, gold, or excitement— whatever made a man forsake the security of what he knew and hazard the unknown.

Captain Harris rode into town about midday, guiding his hoof-sore horse in and out of the confusion of mules and cattle and wagons and noise. Pigs squealed above the shouts of bossy wagon masters, and hawkers bargained last-chance offers at scandalous prices.

Harris dismounted in front of the Fort's office and handed over the reins of his horse, with explicit instructions for the animal's care, to the young corporal, who stared at Harris in disbelief. Harris' uniform was dingy and his hair, long and unkempt, was streaked with gray. His face was raw, burned, and unusually lined for a man not yet forty.

Forgetting his lower rank, the corporal shouted to his superior. "You were gone so long I thought you weren't coming back, sir."

Captain Harris' impatience boiled over when he spied captain's stripes on the corporal's sleeve. He gripped the stripes to wrench them free and exploded in anger at the audacity of the young opportunist's premature assumption.

"Thought I was dead and you'd take charge of my men, did you?"

The corporal replied in his own defense, trying to stand up as tall as his short stature would allow. "Just trying to show some responsibility, sir."

Harris kept his hold a moment longer and then released the corporal in disgust, issuing his final order with a threat. "Yeah, well, I am back and I am not dead, corporal. Get rid of those captain's bars or I'll rip them off and paste them to the roof of your mouth—going up from the south end."

"Yes, sir." The young soldier stood straight and saluted his officer with genuine respect. He turned on military heel and, opening doors for Captain Harris, advanced ahead to announce his arrival to Colonel Fenton.

Colonel Fenton's office door was wide open, as were the colonel's arms, to receive in grateful embrace the captain, his friend. The two men moved apart and stood at attention for a while, taking in the relief of the unexpected meeting again. Dismissing the young corporal, Colonel Fenton shut the door and offered Captain Harris a chair. Harris sat in silence as the colonel foraged for cigars and whiskey.

Harris thought about the young ambitious corporal. He was not sorry he had dressed down the young man. He remembered his early days in the cavalry and his need of a cut down to size by his superior's directives. And it was good for the corporal to see the esteem and affection shared by men of high rank.

Colonel Fenton began their conversation with apology, as he handed the captain his whiskey and lit his cigar. "Months and not a word, Tom."

Harris accepted the colonel's explanation with a nod, as he offered his own. "I didn't dare wire. I couldn't tell who I could trust."

"What do you know?" Fenton asked as he stood up,

facing the open window. He watched his cigar puffs vanish blue into the sunlight. He saw that Tom Harris had faced a bad time, and he was in no hurry, now that he had his friend safely seated across from him.

Tom commenced his report to the colonel. "Vic and Pinky's gang split up. Pinky's dead. There are other gangs, but none too powerful. Biggest bunch left the Roost altogether. Overheard Weems in Moab; he's the only supplier for the Roost. I heard him say he was cutting his usual order by half. Said he figured there were less than forty men left."

Colonel Fenton refilled their glasses, and Captain Harris stood to receive the toast. "Then it's time to sober up and go to the Roost, together."

Harris replied to the order. "Looks like it."

The glasses clinked and the two men swallowed the remains in one gulp. Colonel Fenton dashed his glass against the wall, as did Captain Harris. They saluted each other with resolve.

There was a sheepish knock at the door, and the colonel allowed the inquisitive corporal admittance. The corporal came in and saluted. He was glad for the improved moods of his ranking officers, especially after his dressing down. But he realized quickly he would be responsible for cleaning up this celebratory mess of glass debris.

Chapter Nineteen

Out of the day and night a joy has taken flight;
Fresh spring, and summer, and winter hoar,
Move my faint heart with grief, but with delight
No more, oh never more.

PERCY BYSSHE SHELLEY

The inhabitants of Blakemore House went about the daily duties in the weeks that followed the hanging, submerged in thought, in solemn sublimity, with grateful hearts for their safety. Time only added to the awareness of the narrow escape from what would have been their certain death. There was less frivolity and joking among them and more abundant and sensitive attendance to each other.

Larken recalled with thoughtful deliberation the events of his life: the most precious gift of Emmy as his childhood playmate, his little charge who followed him everywhere. She was his damsel and he was her knight. He loved her so these days as his wife. He continued in his happy role as her protector, but her gift to him was his soul's completion, a wonderful oneness, filling up unto overflowing the burden of the awful emptiness that had made him hollow, metallic, unmanly.

It was interesting to him in his moments of reflection that his thoughts leaped from the early days to the recent and the present. All their extended travels, their expensive indulgences, and those things which he once considered vital to living were now a blur of indifference, time wasted.

Aunt E., Billy, Ivy, Runner, all of them, had indulged him and been ever present at his summoning. He now wanted to shout them away from serving him. He wished to take charge and see to them, as repayment for all the years of his selfish immaturity.

Runner and Ivy churned butter on the back porch on an extremely hot day in late April. Their laughter reached Larken near the woodshed. He was chopping the wood that would probably feed the last fires of the season except for their cooking. Parson had advised them a few days before that there would be at least one more cold snap in April, and probably one in May, before summer suns removed the morning and evening chills.

Larken wielded his axe, enjoying the flexing of his newly developed strong arm and shoulder muscles. Emmy spoke of them with admiration and called him handsome. He thought it somewhat odd that she noticed mostly his hands and his muscles. Larken grinned when he heard Ivy from the porch squeal with delight; Runner continued after all these years to court and flirt with her.

Larken rested his axe as a thought came over him. Overwhelmed, he sat down on one of the unhewed logs and spoke aloud for his private hearing only. "Oh God, forgive me. Runner has carried my load for me all my life. He has taken my blame, saved my skin, gone before me, protected my rear, and covered my weakness. He has been like an elder brother. I owe him so much and will never take him for granted again."

Interest in staying at Blakemore House waned after the "Hanging Party." Outlaws were ruthless and wily; they were also unanimously superstitious. In the weeks that followed, only one group of guests stayed at Blakemore House, and their stay was short.

Thankfully, they had made enough money before the dreadful hanging to send some payment back home. The time for rest restored and calmed everyone's nerves. They set to planting their garden, and the ancient, blessed labor refreshed them.

Aunt E. and Emmy approached the hen house to gather eggs. Emmy set a basket beside one row of early spring peas, which she intended to pick on her return. She smiled at Larken as she walked past. She and E. filled the baskets full of eggs in contemplative silence. Emmy stopped by the garden to gather early peas, and let E. carry the eggs inside the house.

Emmy's feelings continued to engulf her as she watched Larken stack the wood out of the corner of her eye. When he glanced her way, she turned her head away for the love of him. *How can I begin to understand how much I respect, honor, and adore this man? Could anyone be so much in love as I am?* Larken glanced over at Emmy once again, and this time her thoughts were communicated to him through the sweet silence of her smile.

Chores completed, Larken and Emmy walked hand in hand to the back porch and sat on the steps in the shade. E. brought them mugs of Ivy's cold buttermilk and joined the two.

Runner, pole in hand, excused himself past them down the back steps. "Ivy's resting and I'm gonna catch us some fish to go with the peas for dinner. Keep an eye on Ivy's cornbread that's baking, 'cause she's liable to fall asleep. I'll hold up at the river until Lela returns from visiting Parson and walk back with her."

Those days of spring were carefree for the six happy dwellers at Blakemore House and their frequent visitors, Parson and Praiseworthy. Weems had made only one stop in the past weeks. Runner and Larken were able to carry the easy wagon-load of supplies, which was needed only now and then. Weems informed them, when asked, that he had not seen hide nor hair of Big Vic's gang or any of the other gangs for quite awhile. Weems' mood was bad that day, most likely due to his reduced revenue.

Early in the morning on a day that promised to be hot, Larken set out for Post Office Tree, accompanied by Emmy and Lela. They hadn't heard from the family in Louisiana in several weeks and thus figured a letter might be awaiting them. They were not disappointed, but Larken made the girls wait until they got home to read the news. Runner had told Larken he would wait for them to get home before going to Weems' store for some chew, not wanting to leave Ivy and Aunt E. alone while everyone was gone.

On the way back Lela insisted that she and Emmy help Larken unharness the mules, so when they arrived back at the house he drove into the barnyard area. The mules secured and fed, they walked arm in arm to the front of the house by way of the upper pasture. Finally Larken produced the letter from inside his shirt and read to them a portion, some very good news.

". . . and with the last money you sent, you are without debt in Louisiana. I'm proud of you, son. And I know your sweet Mama would be, too. There is more debt left, but you may at least return to your home without fear of the authorities. I felt certain that someday you would find a way to harness all the talents that the Good Lord gave you and you sure have. Before long you will have made good on all your debts. I miss you. Your loving father, Billy. Fairlake Farm. Tangipahoa Parish. Louisiana."

Emmy hoorayed with joy and congratulated Larken, kissing him over and over passionately. Lela looked on tickled, girlishly blushing and giggling. As they approached the house with their wonderful news, Lela repeated over and over. "Fairlake Farm, Fairlake Farm. Sounds like Paradise itself."

Coming into view of the front porch, Larken held back Emmy and Lela in alarm as he spoke his misgivings.

"Wasn't Runner going to Weems? Surely he would have seen us return to the barn, or at least noticed our walk through the pasture. He could see us at any time from the house. His horse is tied to the front-porch post, and look, there's Ivy's sewing lying on the grass."

Emmy's heart raced with alarm and she shouted at Larken. "They were out of chew. He was leaving right after we got back."

The three of them raced around the eerie quietness of the upstairs and downstairs of the house, frantically calling for Runner, and then feebly whimpering and pathetically calling for E. and Ivy. Lela looked out the kitchen window and pointed. "Look there."

They found them out in the yard under the oak. Ivy rocked back and forth, holding Runner's lifeless body to her breast, crying and crooning and giving him to Jesus. Aunt E. stroked Runner's head and sobbed.

Emmy and Lela knelt down and held each other and began to cry. Larken stood still as stone and stared at the remains of his most trusted friend.

Ivy raised her hand to hush them, for she had Runner's last words to share with them. "He said, 'Ivy, I'm going for some chew for me and E. You want some rock candy?' And I said, 'Yes, lots.' He asked Miss E. if she wanted anything else. She told him to bring her an extra hundred years to live, and he asked if he and I could spend those years together."

Ivy's usually strong voice cracked, and it became high and childlike as she continued, her tears splashing down her cheeks and splattering onto Runner's calm and peaceful face. "Then he looked at me kind of queerly. He said, 'Ivy, I'm not going to make it to Weems' place.' He smiled at me sweetly and told me, 'Honey, I will be seeing you again, soon.'"

Ivy gently wiped her tears from Runner's face and, sighing heavily, she whispered, "and then he died. It must have been his heart, just gave out."

Larken, choking back sobs of anguish, gently removed Runner's body from Ivy's embrace. Lifting him up into his arms, Larken carried him, slowly walking with him and talking with him, weeping and hugging him all the way to the house.

Chapter Twenty

Not mindless of the growing years of care and loss and pain,
My eyes are wet with thankfulness for blessings that remain.

JOHN GREENLEAF WHITTIER

Runner's mourners bore their grief deeply and privately, protecting the individual sorrow of each other. Ivy, godly woman that she was, became just more so, sweetly meditating and humming her hymns, staying busy with her chores, and maintaining precise order in the daily routine. It was at night that she took her vigil. She went to Runner's grave on the slope of the hill, to the east of the house, and told him good night. She bundled her small body, wrapped and protected against the windstorms and downpours of the season. She laid fresh flowers gathered during the day and raised her lantern high to show them to Runner and for light enough that she might read his epitaph. Ivy reasoned rightly, and the others silently agreed, that the constantly repeated ritual worked its way through her denial of Runner's physical absence from her. She read aloud to herself and to him the inscription etched on his modest stone:

RUNNER BLAKEMORE
BELOVED BROTHER-FRIEND-HUSBAND
SEPTEMBER 15, 1816–APRIL 24, 1868

Parson's predicted cold snap arrived with a violent storm on an early May evening and plummeted the temperature with howling winds out of the north. Larken stoked the fire with added logs from the front porch. From his vantage point, he could see the crest of the hill and make out Ivy's little form in the flashes of lightning, her body and lantern swaying in the gusts.

In the living room, Emmy continued her recitation from Emily Bronte's *Wuthering Heights*, a cherished novel she had first read when traveling to England all those months ago. She raised her voice above the tumult outside. She sat as close to the warmth of the fire as she dared, sticking one foot toward the fire and then the other, then stretching them both forward to toast her icy toes.

"She stands out there every night, no matter the weather." Larken interrupted Emmy's reading as he again fed the fire.

Emmy closed her book and folded her feet under her

blue flannel wrapper, staring into the crackling blaze. She shivered from the cold and from the sadness in her heart— for poor lost Catherine and Heathcliff on the moors, and Runner in the grave, and dear, brave Ivy.

"They were married almost thirty-two years. Says she feels close to him at night." Emmy gazed lovingly at Larken as she spoke; he knelt by her and kissed the tears from her cheeks. He glanced into the hall as E. descended the stairs and knew it was time to call Ivy in.

Aunt E. encouraged sweetly from the kitchen door, her contralto voice carrying aptly aloft in the wind. "Ivy, honey, tell him good night for me and come on in."

Larken and Emmy heard E. stifle a sob and, in but a minute, shut the back door securely as Ivy returned. Aunt E. walked with Ivy, her arm around her, through the hall and gently up the stairs to the empty bed.

"I fixed you a warm bath. There's a chill out tonight." Larken and Emmy sat hushed and listened intently to E.'s nurturing.

"He wouldn't want you fussing over me." Ivy's voice floated childlike down the stairs.

Larken and Emmy smiled at E.'s reply. "He's up there watching over us." Ivy chuckled as she spoke. "And laughing at us, most likely."

Larken pulled Emmy with him to the bottom of the

stairs and called up to Ivy in all seriousness. "Ivy, is he watching over Emmy, Lela, and me?"

"He is, and he likes what he sees." Ivy looked down on Emmy and Larken and spoke with convincing faith.

Larken took Emmy into his arms to feel her warmth, to hold her close, and to heal their broken hearts. They clung to each other for a while and then Emmy pulled away and whispered, "I'll check to see if Lela is in bed and covered up."

Blakemore House rested in the quiet of the night. Larken and Emmy sat together on the sofa in front of the fire's last dying embers. Their thoughts had intertwined these past months of their finally consummated marriage. The sparring and bickering continued at times, but now their remarks were playful, with hints of mirth and satisfaction. The sting was gone.

Emmy read the concern on Larken's face as he shared his brooding thoughts with her. "Pinky's been buried for weeks, but I don't think we're through with him yet."

Emmy was glad the gangs were no longer under her roof. Her pecuniary desires waned and her confidence grew, secure in the long-desired demonstrative affections of her husband. Emmy stretched her arms and legs and grunted with satisfaction. Her fingers fell to ruffle the hair on the back of Larken's head, slithering down the nape of his neck with an enticing invitation. When she detected the concentrated bother on his brow, she became serious.

"Lela says Vic and the boys haven't worked for months. Listen to me, feeling sorry for a murdering thief because he isn't murdering or thieving! Strangely in all of this Vic is such a man of conviction. Sometimes that life is thrust upon you and you have no recourse. I would have never known that had I never met Big Vic."

Larken took Emmy's hand from around his neck and gripped her fingers tightly in his rough fist. He mustered a faint smile and uttered a halfhearted tease. "You're pathetic."

Emmy sat up and stared defensively into Larken's dark eyes. "Around here, in this place, you begin to get right and wrong confused."

Larken nodded with affirmation and added sarcastically. "I'll write the rules down so you may refer to them."

Emmy had her back up at Larken's high-handedness. "You're so mighty and righteous. You sure take their thieving money happily enough."

Larken dropped his eyes and patted Emmy's knee affectionately. He spoke to her with honest resignation. "Honey, it's the only way to get us out of here."

Emmy sighed and covered Larken's hand with hers and pressed his knee. "Well, it makes me feel *dreadful*." She spoke with pitiful surrender, hanging her head.

"I feel bad about it, too." Standing up, Larken added the last log to the embers. It was late, and their predicament would not be solved with or without sleep. Yet he felt the need to retire on a better note.

Emmy pouted. "You feel bad but not *dreadful.*"

Larken scooped her up in his arms and rolled with her onto the floor, sitting them both upright in front of the fire. "I feel dreadful," he placated.

Emmy laughed at their foolish bickering. Determined to get in the last word, she giggled and poked Larken playfully. "You said *bad.*"

"I *meant* dreadful." Larken let her win.

Pulling Emmy into his lap, he continued to voice his concern. "Look, if Vic and Pinky's gangs go at it again, I hope they aren't here to put us in the middle."

Emmy frowned and gasped with horror. "That'd be terrible."

Both sat silent for a while, deliberating their plight. Larken whispered inaudibly, "It'd be absolutely *dreadful.*"

He could feel Emmy's heart pounding in fear. He held her fast against his chest, with no intention of letting her go now or of allowing anyone or anything to harm her in the future.

Emmy sensed Larken's avowed protection. "You have to keep that from happening." She spoke to him softly, while tears filled her eyes. She knew how sorely Larken grieved for Runner and how desperately alone he felt without him. He alone carried the awful responsibility for her, Aunt E., Ivy, and Lela. He was left to see to four women.

Larken released Emmy and stood before the mantle facing her. Thrusting his arms forward, palms up in supplication, he begged of her and God as he spoke.

"How? Right or wrong, who's to say?"

Emmy responded with all of her strength and a bit of irony. "You are . . . Remember, you know the rules!"

Larken laughed with her. Emmy could not see his face as they climbed the stairs together. Resting her head against his shoulder, she was well aware that he was worrying enough for both of them. When they climbed into their bed that night and all was dark, Emmy abhorred the burden Larken was carrying, for he turned his face to the wall and refused her earlier invitation.

Bates sat alone at a back table in the saloon at Moab. He was acutely excited, for he felt that, on this day and in this place, luck would favor him. He even moderated the drinking to keep his senses alert: a keen eye and a sensitive ear. The hairs on his neck bristled in anticipation.

Bates' passion was so great that he drooled; he wiped the saliva with his coat sleeve.

The Moab saloon was packed, even so early on this May afternoon. A biting cold spell and icy rains had driven the men indoors. Bates furtively watched each group of men and poured only his second whiskey from the bottle he had purchased well over an hour ago. The gulp of liquor warmed and fortified his patience.

Jobe, the bartender, rolled another cask of beer from the back room. He waved and said "howdy" to three men, who entered and stood stamping icy mud from their boots.

"Boys, I see you got the word."

Bates strained forward, cupping his ear to hear these strangers that had just walked in over the raucous jeering of the men and the tinny piano.

"Yeah," Jim replied to Jobe.

Taking his place behind the bar, Jobe continued to shout above the din as he poured their usual drinks for the three men. "Business always picks up when the sheriff's off on posse."

"Who're they after?" Choirboy asked. The pretty-faced boy interested Bates. He felt sure these three could lead him to Blakemore. *This one sure has an attitude, though. That's good.*

"They're after what's left of the Haggar brothers for a

train job they pulled a week back." The bartender spoke with obvious pride in his information.

The pretty boy continued. "Parson'll feel sorry to hear it."

The third man stood with his back to the bar and eyed the room fixedly. Bates thought that he had never seen a meaner looking critter, this one part Indian and blank faced.

The man who had spoken first, Jim, looked full-blood.

"Pour Mute another one. He gits the prickly hairs when we're outta the Roost."

Lightning bolts of recognition shot through Bates at the mention of the Roost. Leaving his table, he sauntered unobtrusively to the far end of the bar, nearest the saloon's entrance.

Jobe wiped glasses and, filling rounds two and three for Jim, Choirboy and Mute, continued his conversation with the two vocal men of the threesome. Mute never moved from his scrutiny, his drinks handed to him carefully one after another.

"Jim, you boys been stayin' at the roomin' house?" Jobe inquired. He had told what he knew and was itching for information.

"Naw," Choirboy answered loudly, full of whiskey. "Hadn't been there since Pinky was kilt."

Jobe wandered Bates' way, serving other customers, while Bates nursed his drink. The bartender had seen all kinds, but he hesitated at the ugly snarl of this brute and quickly returned to the conversation with Choirboy and Jim. Jobe looked over his shoulder once more at the yellow-eyed man at the end of the bar. He could have sworn the man hissed.

Addressing Jim, Jobe continued. "Never met the man what runs it. Heard about him, though."

Jim nodded. "Fancy sort, seventeen thousand."

"I heard. Brought his family." Jobe offered the hearsay to pump them further.

"Yeah." Choirboy hiccupped.

"Parson all right?" Jobe asked this knowing he'd get a rouse if the idle gossip was correct.

He was rewarded with a violent outburst from Jim. "Son of a bitch sided with Vic over Pinky."

Jobe delved with vigor. "Son of a bitch. Heard Vic had a stash."

Jim nodded. "He does."

Jobe felt free to go on, and directed his next statement with a calculated punch. "I 'spect the good Parson knows where it's at."

Jobe, the bartender and information center, had become a troublemaker. He was not such a bad sort, but his inquisitive nature was planting a deadly seed.

Choirboy wasn't drunk enough to lose his smarts, and he spoke up to Jobe to show he had him figured. "You jist be wantin' us to git it so we spend it here."

Jobe shrugged the innuendo aside. "I'm a business-man."

Jim smirked, mean and sarcastic. "See ya, Jobe. We're goin' to 'pray' with the Parson."

Jim led the way out, followed by Choirboy. Mute remained in fixed position. Bates kept his head down but spoke loudly enough, with intensity and venom. "I hate Vic, I hate Parson, an' I hate Blakemore."

As the men stopped in their tracks, Mute turned his head for the first time to face Bates with his blank stare. Bates shuddered just slightly at the look of Mute's mean-ness. His voice cracked a bit. "Don't want me no piece of no stash. Retribution's all."

Jim spied the scalp in Bates' belt. He was repulsed, yet impressed. He asked with authority for the three, "You be wantin' in the Roost?"

Choirboy interrupted, grinning. "Jist to kill them three but fer no money?"

Jobe's flushed face paled with fear and shame, as Bates addressed him with the final remark. "Jist want enough to come back an' pay this businessman a call," pointing at Jobe.

Thinking it over for a moment, Jim stepped aside and made a place for Bates between himself and Choirboy. He gestured with his arm as he ordered, "Then, come on."

The three filed toward the door, and Mute backed out behind them, keeping a vacant stare on Jobe, who, with a shaking hand, gulped down a shot glass of whiskey.

Chapter Twenty-One

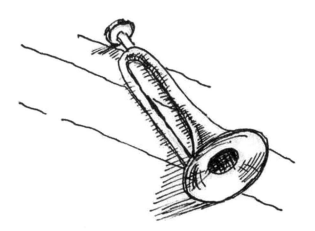

No coward soul is mine; no trembler in the
world's storm-troubled spheres; I see
heaven's glories shine and faith shines
equal, arming me from fear.

EMILY BRONTE

Within a week following the cold spell, sunshine
flooded the Roost, pale and gentle at first, and
then vibrant and warming, flourishing spring
into the heat of summer with budding and sprouting.
The foliage greened within days and yellow deerclover,
milkweed, and garish slickrock paintbrushes crowded out
foxglove and purple sage. It was as if a season was skipped
in summer's impatience to take over. The days were sultry
and close, with hardly a breeze of relief. With woolens and
flannels packed away, flower-sack sunbonnets, calico, and
denim were brought out and quickly mended, washed,
and ironed.

Emmy and Larken sat in the main room of Blakemore
House, drinking their third and fourth cups of morning

coffee. The windows were raised to their highest and propped up with slats; the front and back doors, with newly fashioned screen doors in place, were open night and day for any circulating breeze. E. folded laundry on the dining table while calling back and forth to Emmy, who sat perched on the front-porch window ledge, mending the strings on her bonnet. Most of her hair was tied into a knot on the top of her head, and the curls stringing down onto her neck and temples were wet with perspiration.

Larken set down his coffee and swatted at flies and a couple of wasps with a dishtowel. Even the little intruding insects were confused by the odd and abrupt change in the weather.

Lela sang in the kitchen, happily absorbed in filling a basket with carefully selected provisions for Parson. She spoke a cheerful good morning to E. in passing and stopped in the hall to poke fun at Larken and Emmy. An errant wasp landed on top of Emmy's head. She sat stiffly still and squealed as Larken charged and stalked it with sharp, popping snaps of the towel.

"Parson's still ailin' with some aches and pains after that cold snap, so I'm takin' him breakfast." Lela called back to them as she scurried out the door and down the front steps. She had purpose in her errand. She carried a real concern for leaving Parson alone, while she enjoyed the luxury and companionship of her new family. Runner's sudden death made her sorely aware of loss. She hurried on her way before anyone could detain her.

Inside, Emmy kicked the dead wasp with her toe and smiled with admiration at her valiant hero. Larken took her hand, and they strolled arm in arm to the front porch to watch Lela's progress.

"She has so far to go to get to his shack." Emmy spoke to Larken out of their protective love for the most precious child.

"You stop her. I tried yesterday, and she said, 'If ye does it to the least of my brothels, ye might jist as well have did it fer me.' Parson said.'"

A sudden puff of wind blew up Emmy's skirt and petticoat, and dust from the road filled their eyes and nostrils. She sneezed and buried her face on Larken's chest. Holding her to him, Larken cherished the moment and the touch of her. He entwined a limp wisp of her hair around his fingers, forever marveling that this golden, auburn-crowned beauty was his very own.

He whispered to Emmy passionately. "There's a storm coming. After breakfast I need you to help me spot for leaks in the attic."

Emmy responded with a sigh of desire and, nodding her head while snuffling on his bosom, she wiped her nose on his blouse, just over his pounding heart.

Emmy pulled back and looked up at Larken. "Kiss me, sir, so I may start my day."

Larken kissed her long and hard. He took her beautiful face into his strong hands and held his eyes to hers with adoration. "You are very good, Mrs. Blakemore."

Emmy coaxed him. "Yes, I am. Everyone says so." And Larken kissed her again, more passionately than before.

———

Late that same afternoon, a column of cavalry filed through the narrow gorge near one of the secretly guarded entrances to the Roost. A billowing dust storm sent stinging sand through the canyon, nearly blinding the men and spooking the horses. Menacing yellow-black clouds hovered in the narrow aperture above their heads.

Colonel Fenton led the line, with Captain Harris riding close on the heels of his horse. The corporal brought up the rear. Fenton raised his hand, shouting loud to Harris to halt the advance. He choked from the sand in his lungs and tied his bandanna to cover his mouth and nose. He issued orders through Harris to the men.

"We'll camp here till tomorrow. Our odds are better in daylight."

Captain Harris reminded his colonel. "So are theirs."

Fenton and Harris exchanged looks of apprehension. In charge, and therefore making the decisions, Fenton replied. "I can't march forty men into a blind situation."

Captain Harris stood tall in his stirrups and bellowed the command to the corporal. "Encamp the men."

Lela ran as fast as she could against the wind, pulling a horse that carried an unconscious Parson lying across its back, an anxious Praiseworthy at its heels. Her crying screams flew back in her face in the pelting rain and deafening claps of thunder. She hoped the hard rain gave them cover so no one could see she was taking him to safety. At Blakemore House, she quickly tied the horse to the front hitching post. Taking the steps in one bound, she burst into the front hallway, yelling at the top of her lungs with great urgency. "Larken, Larken!"

Ivy and E. ran from the kitchen and caught her exhausted, trembling small body in their arms.

Lela pointed outside as she collapsed against them. "It's Parson!"

Emmy, hearing the commotion, appeared at the top of the stairway. "Emmy." Lela wailed breathlessly. "Hurry. We got to help him. It's Parson out front."

Emmy rushed to Lela, hugged her reassuringly, and told her, "Larken's out back. Go get him. We'll go out to Parson."

Lela flew out the back door and found Larken high on a ladder leaned against the roof. He was hammering tarpaulin, hanging for dear life onto the swaying ladder. He shouted down to her, "Lela, get out of the wind."

She held the ladder firmly by the bottom rungs, mustering what little strength she had left in her skinny, strong arms. When Larken reached the ground, she let go. Tears and rain poured down her face as she looked to Larken for rescue. "Larken, it's Parson! Come quick. Pinky's men, they got to him."

E., Ivy, and Emmy struggled to drag Parson's unconscious body through the hall. Praiseworthy hampered their progress, straddling Parson's limp body as she growled and snapped at their hands. Lela called the dog into her arms and sat on the floor with her, hugging the animal's soggy form to her chest, rocking and sobbing, while the bewildered dog groaned. Praiseworthy's silky black coat was kinky and matted with dried blood.

The women laid Parson on the sofa and Larken knelt beside him, repeatedly and gently calling his name and patting his cheek.

Ivy whispered to Larken. "He can't hear you."

Then she turned to E. and took charge. "Miss E., get my sewing basket. Emmy, get a lantern. It's too dark in here to work on him."

Praiseworthy stretched out on the floor. She was exhausted from whatever part she had played in defending against the tragic attack on her master. The hushed voices ministering to Parson calmed the dog; she eyed them cautiously but was content for the moment. Lela patted Praiseworthy's head, reassuring her. She quietly commanded the dog to stay and crawled away to Parson's side.

Caressing Parson's limp hand for a few moments, she took it up and squeezed it between hers, begging and imploring God to send her strength into him. She spoke to Ivy with pleading eyes. "Will he die?"

"Larken, get Parson some whiskey." Ivy issued her directive and then turned to Lela.

She answered the child with compassionate honesty. "I don't know, baby. Help me get his shirt off."

Ivy poured whiskey over the bruises and abrasions, and dabbed Parson's swollen lips. She pried open his clenched teeth with her fingers, and squeezed droplets of the liquor from her doused handkerchief into his mouth.

When Lela saw that Parson's wounds were not fatal, she cried uncontrollable tears of relief. Larken coaxed Lela aside and sat with her in his lap. She laid her head back against his shoulder, as delayed sobs and sighs shook her little body. With Larken's arms encircling her, the trembling eased and then ceased; she began relating to them what she had discovered when she reached Parson's cabin.

"When I got there, he was jist layin' on the floor with blood everywhere. Praiseworthy, she was crumpled in a heap in the corner. I thought she was dead fer sure when I seen her. No tellin' what that darlin' dog did fer Parson's life. Parson was jist strong 'nough to pull hisself up on his horse."

Now that Lela was calm, Larken prodded for more information. "But he said it was Pinky's boys that did this?"

Ivy, E., and Emmy worked together, tearing cloth into bandages. They soaked the strips in aloe balm and applied them to Parson's wounds. Lela watched them closely and was comforted that Parson was being given the very best care.

Lela asked Ivy quietly, "Can I have some of that cloth to bandage Praiseworthy's head? Not all that blood is Parson's."

"Here, darlin'." Ivy patted her hand as she handed her one of the strips for a bandage.

Relieved, she looked up at Larken and continued. "He said Mute, Jim, an' Choirboy. They's a loyal bunch, Pinky's boys. He told me, 'I weren't so loyal; they beat me till I told 'em where Vic was.' Said there was a man there he didn't even know. He said had the eyes of a rattlesnake."

The three women looked up from their patient and glanced at Larken with apprehension. He exclaimed for them all. "Bates! They have a lot of time on me."

Lela, unaware of the cause of their concern, continued. "Parson, he told 'em the wrong cave. But they'll find 'em."

She began to cry again. "Said he was jist like Judas, turnin' on a friend. He ain't a Judas, Larken, he's good. It's jist they beat him."

Lela pulled at Larken's sleeve and he hugged her close. "He is good, Lela. Ivy knows what to do."

Lela sat up straight on Larken's knee. She wiped her eyes with the hem of her dress, and reached her hand up and turned Larken's face to hers. "Worryin' is the devil's work. Parson said."

Larken admired Lela's strength and Parson's sound, if unorthodox, instruction. He nodded agreement. "That's right, Lela. Where is Vic?"

Lela frowned. "I'm scared for Mr. Vic, but I'm scared fer you, too. Them men, they'll kill you jist like they tried Parson."

Emmy stood before them adamant. She pointed a finger at Lela, her voice raised with fearful admonition. "She knows these men, Larken. If Pinky's boys catch you warning Vic, they won't think twice about killing you."

Larken gave Lela his chair and paced the length of the parlor. When he finally spoke, he declared his intention.

"I can't just let them find Vic and shoot him, can I?" Larken anticipated Emmy's concern, but he begged her understanding.

"Yes!" Emmy screamed at Larken. "These men expect to die that way. When Vic killed Pinky, he knew Jim, Mute, and Choirboy might try to get him back. Don't you remember that hanging?"

"Yes!" Larken turned on her defiantly. "Don't you? I can't sit here knowing the same thing might be happening and not intervene. Who's to stop them from coming after us again?"

Parson moaned, and Emmy's voice dropped to a whisper. "How far can your arrogance take you, Larken? Do you really think you will be the one to bring peace and harmony to this place?"

Larken threw out his hands in despair. "This God-forsaken hole in the earth will end up being a grave for us all if I don't do something. Lela," he implored, "you see that I have to go, don't you?"

"Yes," Lela agreed with Larken. Her sad, resigned, small voice quivered.

"Yes?" Emmy spoke sharply and turned on Lela with fearful anger. "How can you send him out there?"

Lela unflinchingly stood her ground with Emmy, speaking bravely to them all. "Larken's a man an' they does what they has to. They're up at Two-Hole Cave."

Ivy crooned her "Balm in Gilead" plaintively. Lela bent over Parson, kissing his forehead, whispering to him.

Emmy had gone too far with Larken and it wasn't working. She retorted in exasperation. "Where in the hell is Gilead?"

"Jeremiah 8:22. Parson said." Lela answered sweetly and Parson moaned, opened his eyes, and looked into hers. Praiseworthy sat beside them, slapping the bare wooden floor with her long, ample tail. The whites of her wolf eyes and her exposed teeth showed forth through her bandaged head, and she showered them all with affection.

It was mid-afternoon and yet chilly and damp in the house. Larken lowered the windows and built a small fire. He took his gun and bullets from the sideboard drawer and raised the gun's barrel like a telescope. Satisfied, he tucked the gun into his coat. Seeing Emmy and Lela's scared frowns, without uttering a word he walked by them and out the front door.

Emmy stared after him into the empty space that his presence had occupied only a minute ago. The room was deathly still with fear. The mantle clock ticked and chimed the half hour.

The four women breathed heavily, knowing that they were now totally alone, without male protection. Parson was too hurt to be of any help if they needed it. Even Parson's groans subsided and he slept. Praiseworthy raised her head alertly, as dogs will at silence.

Lela sneezed. Her face was flushed and her body trembled with chill. "Lela, come sit by the fire; you are wet and frozen through." Emmy's gentle voice sounded motherly to Lela and, seating the child by the warmth of the fire, she dashed hurriedly upstairs to fetch dry clothing and a quilt.

E. stood from her squatting place beside Parson and rubbed her back. "How is he?" She asked Ivy with concern but with a glimmer of hope.

Ivy reassured her with a nod to Parson's even breathing. "There's more to do, but for now we wait and see. Would you make us all some tea, Miss E.?"

Larken rode out against a howling wind. He pulled his hat down tightly over his ears and huddled low under his slicker, hugging his horse's neck. Although it was not yet dusk, it was dark as night. He cautiously made his way in the direction of the Roost's caves, blinded by the blowing rain. His horse slipped in the muddy ruts and shied to keep its footing.

Larken did not feel the least bit brave. Contradictory thoughts plagued him. He and Emmy had always been self-serving. Maybe she was right. He should have listened to her. Lela said a man has to do what he has to. None of this made any sense.

He was afraid. Larken spoke aloud to himself, trying to dispel his fear and aloneness. "I am riding to save a man from another man who stole his stolen money from him. God, why am I doing this?" His horse bolted at a crack of thunder and nearly unseated him.

When Larken finally reached the canyon, for over an hour he rode in and out of recesses in the wall, trying to find Two-Hole Cave. Each time he thought he had arrived, he was in the wrong place. The rain stopped, affording him some vision. He strained his eyes to see across the canyon to the adjacent wall.

Larken dismounted and led his frightened animal. All was quiet but for the horse's hoof clops. He stopped to listen, and then with anger and frustration shouted. "Damnit." His "damnit" echoed in the night up and down the canyon walls.

While Larken wandered, looking for the cave but lost in the storm, back at Blakemore House, Parson rallied and ranted. He lay back on pillows with his legs stretched out on the sofa and quoted scripture. "Yea, though I walk through the valley of the shadow of death."

Gloom and concern hung over them as they imagined what Larken might be facing; Parson did his best to comfort them, extolling the mighty ways of the Lord. Lela stayed close to Parson's side, holding his hand. She nodded her head with rapt affirmation in response to his petitions and gratitudes.

The women stayed busy to calm their nerves. Emmy brought in more firewood and carefully laid and poked it. E. and Ivy brought in a tray of roasted apples, sweet potatoes, and warm milk.

Emmy squatted on the hearth with her back to the fire. It was wonderful about Parson, now cozy and restored to them. But their gathering was incomplete. When she looked at Ivy without Runner, and now maybe her without Larken, the grief in her heart was unbearable. Her tear-filled eyes scanned the room that they had made together, lovely and hospitable, and then with horror she saw the bullets on the sideboard. She shrieked. "Damnit."

Parson swung his sore, swollen legs to the floor at her outburst. Emmy pointed a shaking finger, and they saw what she saw. Larken was out there unarmed.

"Damnit!"

Larken mounted his horse once again and rode into yet another gap in the canyon wall, and, at last, there it was in front of his face, the entrance to Vic's hideout. He got off and tied his horse. As he entered the mouth of the cave, he checked his gun and patted it firmly. When he reached into his jacket pockets for the bullets and found them empty, he swore. "Damnit!"

"Who's that?"

Larken heard Big Vic's gruff voice call out, and raised his hands in surrender to Bobby and Slick's pointed guns. Smiling sheepishly, in relief they lowered the weapons when they recognized it was Larken.

Vic and Larken shook hands, and Bobby and Slick rolled a barrel near the lighted torches in the center of the cave for Larken to be seated. Vic offered Larken a tin cup of whiskey and a cigar, obviously glad for the visit, but quizzical.

Larken downed the whiskey gratefully but waved away the cigar and the offer of a seat. He felt he had precious little time.

"Vic, there's trouble. Pinky's boys are on their way to fight it out with you. I'm prepared to help, if you can spare some bullets."

"Blakemore! Damnit! You've never got bullets when you need them."

It seemed to Larken that the large and astute outlaw already anticipated a showdown. It no longer concerned Larken that he admired the man who hanged Pinky. Brave or cowardly, with good reason or idiocy, by his presence in Two-Hole Cave, Larken had joined with Vic and his boys. He heard the horses' hooves pawing and noses snorting back deeper in the cavern, indicating a stable further in and most probably a second way to the outside.

Vic's face softened and he smiled at Larken. "We've got all the guns we need. And ours are loaded. Slick, get'em some bullets for the ride home! Where are they now?"

"I don't know." Larken shook his head at Vic with emphasis and nodded to Bobby's offer for more whiskey. "But Pinky's boys beat Parson half to death trying to find out where you were."

Vic swore to himself. "God help Parson."

He hoisted his saddle, as did Slick and Bobby, and motioned to Larken to follow them. They rounded a corner at the far end of the cave, where another torch shed light on the horses. Vic mumbled to himself as the three men worked in silence, bridling and saddling the horses.

Larken couldn't make out all Vic muttered to himself, but he picked up a little: "I thought of leaving, but I was too weak to leave it all behind."

Returning to the business at hand, Big Vic spoke directly to Larken. "That's Jim, Mute, and Choirboy against us three."

"No!" Larken warned, wishing that Vic knew the menacing Bates as he did. "There's another man, Bates. He's after me, but it sounds like he's in with them."

"That's all right. Bobby and Slick and I can take four." Vic grinned at his men, and they replied with broad smiles.

Vic ushered Larken out of the others' earshot, toward the cave entrance. "You've been a good friend, Larken. Now go."

"I'm ready to help." Larken turned abruptly as he spoke, almost blinded by the flashing metal of Vic's gun aimed at his heart.

With apology, Big Vic lowered his gun. "This is not your fight."

Larken protested, "But Bates . . ."

Vic held up his hand to shut Larken up. The two men stood silently eyeing each other. Vic looked over his shoulder once or twice, verifying their privacy. He hesitated. Larken saw the set of that craggy jaw working Vic's temples in thought. Some momentous decision was taking place.

When Big Vic spoke at last, it was in painful confidence,

as if Larken was his only friend. "You will not intrude. There is more important work for you. Six feet west of the stump at the back of your garden, there is a box buried. See to it after I'm gone."

Larken whispered. "You don't know you'll die here."

Vic raised his voice in normal, and seemingly indifferent, conversation as Bobby and Slick joined them. "No, and if I don't, I trust you will keep my personal matters to yourself. Leave now so you can be of real use."

Bobby shrugged his shoulders, accustomed to Big Vic's highfalutin repartee. He was now in charge, for Vic had withdrawn to the back of the cave. Bobby stretched his height full-length with importance.

"Go back by the top of the ridge. Thank you, Mr. Blakemore. Makin' your acquaintance has been awful entertainin'."

Larken did as he was told. He was trusted with an errand of confidence. He left and untied and mounted his horse. The rain was still pouring down, and the darkness was solid. He looked for the mouth of the cave but couldn't see a thing. The outlaws had extinguished their torches for protection and left Larken in pitch black.

A friendly voice called out of the void. It was Slick's. "Give my regards to Miss E."

Larken smiled at the thought of E., charming the men

from Paris to Baltimore, down to this God-forsaken hell hole.

The abruptness of the shout that rang out and the simultaneous illumination of the canyon walls in lightning stunned Larken with deadly fear.

It was unmistakably Jim's voice. "Vic, you gonna die bloody!"

The shooting began. Larken prayed, *God go with them, Slick, Bobby and, especially Vic.* Larken felt sick at the carnage he was leaving behind, but he thought, *I'm such a lousy shot, maybe Vic's right; I'm more help back with the women. Oh, Emmy, I just want to make it out of this alive.*

Lightning struck once more and illuminated the canyon. As quickly as it was light it was now dark again. *I must be losing my mind. I could swear I saw an Indian on the ridge above me.* Larken strained to see through the darkness and waited for another bolt of light. And when the lightning came he looked, but there was no one there. The hairs on Larken's neck bristled, for he had an eerie feeling he was being watched. He vigorously kicked his horse and sped off down the trail, mindful of the slippery mud and the loosened rocks.

Close to the cave where Vic and his men faced their enemies, Harris and Fenton sat huddled in a tent, as orderlies unsuccessfully tried to peg down and secure the canvas flaps against the howling wind and sheets of blowing rain. The heads of the two officer-friends nodded now and then, as each man tried to stay awake and made feeble attempts at conversation. The shots from the Roost pierced through the noisy gale, startling Harris and Fenton to attention. One of the young noncoms poked his wet head inside the tent with a questioning look; Harris answered his undisciplined intrusion with respect.

"Sounds like they're bettering the odds for us."

Larken returned to Blakemore House unscathed. He quickly relieved the fears of the women and, amidst their joyful hugs and interrupting questions, related to them the night's events at Two-Hole Cave. He did what he could to encourage Parson by assuring him of Vic's optimism over the showdown with Pinky's men. Larken kept the secret of that which was buried at the back of the garden to himself. Parson called on the Lord, imploring Vic's safety, and respectfully thanked and gratefully praised the Almighty.

Emmy clung to Larken as he walked toward the

kitchen, out of the hearing of the others. She was so happy to have him back.

"Parson told me not to worry. Oh Larken, you're all right!"

Larken kissed Emmy repeatedly. They stood at the back door comforting each other in their acknowledged oneness and need for each other.

"Then Parson's going to pull through?"

Emmy brushed his ear with a kiss, answering softly. "Ivy thinks so."

Larken guided Emmy to the tool niche, where he silently retrieved a shovel. "What's that for?" She pointed at the shovel.

Larken put his finger to her lips and bade her stay there; he slipped quickly out into the night.

The storm's fury had subsided to a drizzle with a gentle, chilly breeze. Larken was grateful that the rain had loosened the earth. In no time, he located the stump Vic had described and started digging; with little time or effort, he struck metal. He easily lifted the gray rectangular box from its hiding place. Wiping off the blobs of reddish mud, he encased it in his arms and hoisted it onto his shoulder as he stole stealthily to the kitchen porch.

Emmy had not budged from her vigil. She strained her eyes to see and opened the door at Larken's approach.

Mystified, she whispered breathlessly, "Whose is that?"

Believing his wife was honorably allowed to know the secret, Larken revealed all. "It belongs to Big Vic. I think it is a box of his papers. He asked me to see to them."

Larken's curiosity was contagious, and Emmy trembled as she knelt down; Larken cautiously lowered his find to the floor. She gasped. "Then Vic's . . ."

Larken shushed Emmy once again. "I don't know. I wanted to stay and help. He wouldn't let me, but I would have."

Larken's thrill over the contents of the box was clouded with dismay, and a bit of shame crept into his reply to her.

Emmy sensed the conflict in her husband's emotions. "I know you would." In loyal confidence she reached for his hand as she spoke. Larken lifted her upright and held her to him for a moment. He was so very grateful for her trust.

His misgivings were almost dispelled and he sighed as he replied. "It's enough that I know. Light the lantern."

Larken squatted over the box and noiselessly pried open the lid. Emmy held the light aloft to reveal the contents. A sheet of paper lay on top, and the bold printed letters startled them both: It read simply, "Larken Blakemore."

It was hard to believe Big Vic had made the significant decision to place into Larken's hands his life and, as further revealed, his fortune. They wondered when Vic had decided.

Larken heard movement in the main room and the low murmur of E. and Ivy's conversation. He stood up and gingerly peered into the parlor. Lela was resting against Parson on the sofa. It seemed that the two were asleep. He shut the kitchen door.

In fact, Parson was sleeping, and Aunt E. and Ivy sat by the fire. They meant to remain there through the night to be close by Parson if needed. They were settled comfortably under their gaily colored caftans and nodded off now and then, exhausted and relieved of any immediate emergency.

Lela, however, was not asleep and was roused when Larken shut the kitchen door. She was not a nosy child, but something in Larken's demeanor puzzled her. She was eased in her concern for Parson, but not convinced that Larken had told them all he knew of Big Vic. Lela crept into the dark dining room and laid her ear to the door of the kitchen.

Emmy and Larken's voices rose above their previous cautious whispers as they beheld the stacks of legal U.S. government notes, totaling thousands of dollars in currency. Then Larken opened the letter attached to the paper addressed to him. His hands shook as he read to Emmy.

"My name is Victor Brock. All that I own is listed in these papers and has been put in the name of my daughter,

Lela Victoria Brock. I was in Fort Worth on New Year's Eve, 1856. Her mother was beautiful, and I loved her very much. Lela was very small when her mother died. I had Parson take care of her, trusting that she would learn from him and take after her dear mother. Parson has kept my secret, but you may tell Lela the truth when you think it is wise. I thank you for your kindness to myself and to my daughter. Victor Brock. Robber's Roost, 1868."

Tears splashed down Emmy's cheeks. "There's a fortune here. This will take care of Lela for years." The joy inside her overflowed for Lela's sake, as she reverently laid the stacks of money back into the treasure box.

Larken murmured in shock and disbelief. "It would also pay us out of here."

Lela heard every word. She crouched, stunned and immobile, just outside the door. Deep within her she knew it was Vic; she dared not hope it was Vic. She did not question his secrecy for a moment and loved all the more both Vic and Parson for their alliance on her behalf. Then, too, she had come to respect, almost worship, Larken. A lump in her throat burst into tears of anguish and worry. *Was the danger to Vic's life so certain? And what had Larken meant by "Pay us out of here?" Did Larken mean to take all of them to a better place or was his intent to take advantage of her and betray Vic's trust?* The joyful revelation had come at last:

who she was and to whom she belonged. But fear for her father's safety and confusion wrenched Lela's heart.

Having been trained by Parson, it was Lela's way to face facts, both good and bad, squarely, head on. She rubbed and restored feeling to her cramped legs and stood up carefully, leaning against the wall for support. Her small hand shook as she slowly reached for the kitchen doorknob.

Lela jumped when, suddenly, Praiseworthy growled a warning and lunged toward the front door, barking ferociously at the sound of running horses, laughter, and hoopla yelling. There were three loud thumps, and then the noise faded away, leaving a horrific silence.

Larken and Emmy bumped Lela aside as they burst through the kitchen door into the hall and out to the porch. Three bloody bodies lay strewn on the steps. Two of them were mutilated, and one of the two was scalped. The third man was not yet a corpse. His faint groan pierced the deadly stillness.

Lela shoved past the others and knelt beside him. Vic was covered in blood from head to toe. He shivered from loss of blood, and she removed her wrapper and laid it across his chest.

Big Vic opened his eyes and spoke to her weakly. "You're my girl, Lela."

"I know, an' I'm glad you're my daddy." Lela hugged

her little body against his large form, using caution but willing her life into him.

Vic rallied at her words and touched Lela's locket. A moment's smile flickered, as he whispered to her. "It's her hair you take after."

"My mama's." Lela sighed and unashamedly kissed her daddy's cheeks and swollen lips.

Big Vic's body stiffened with quivering spasms and a gurgling cough. Lela grabbed his shirt and shook him, wailing loud and strong. "You can't die! I spent my whole life wantin' my daddy!"

Bobby and Slick were beyond help, so Larken and the women covered them with blankets and left them. Parson stood over them and cursed and prayed, and Praiseworthy sat between their lifeless shrouds and howled.

It took them all but for Parson, who was too weakened from his beating, to carry the massive Victor Brock into the house. They made a pallet for him in front of the fire, for his frame was too large for the sofa.

Larken issued his orders. "Ivy, bring your basket! Emmy, get whiskey!" The ladies were already feverishly at work, stripping and bandaging and cleaning Vic's wounds.

Big Vic opened his eyes briefly and issued his own order. "Port, if you have it."

One large, choking swallow relaxed him and he slept.

Lela stood by him, sobbing. Ivy pulled her away into the arms of Aunt E. to console her, while Emmy and Ivy repaired Vic's broken body.

Later that night, Larken stood on the front porch smoking a cigar and staring at the covered remains of his first friends in the Roost. He took two swigs from a bottle of whiskey and, raising the bottle high, poured all that was left over their dead forms and saluted them.

Larken's office was made into an infirmary for Vic and Parson. By the early morning of the following day, Vic rallied enough to be moved and to advise Larken that Pinky's boys assumed that Bobby, Slick, and Vic were all dead. It was due to their arrogant and sadistic enjoyment of bestial brutality that Vic survived. If they had left the three victims back at the caves, Vic would have bled to death. It was a miracle that they stopped their slaughter when they came to him. Vic said he recalled vaguely hearing a bugle blare before he passed out.

That afternoon Larken dug three graves next to Runner's in the field east of the house. He carried out Bobby and Slick's bodies first. The third he carried out and buried was a ruse: Aunt E.'s dressmaker dummy wrapped in blankets just like the other two. Big Vic stayed out of sight in the house. If Vic was presumed dead, then Pinky's men would think that Blakemore House was theirs' for the taking. Praiseworthy wanted to stay with Parson to guard and protect them until the others returned from the gravesites.

A blowing wind carried their voices into the hills above to any listening ears. Larken, Ivy, Emmy, and Aunt E., a solemn entourage, followed Lela and Parson. After gathering at the gravesite, Parson expounded a glowing eulogy over the presumed remains of Big Vic. Growing stronger by the minute in the staged drama, Parson's voice rang strong and true, echoing his usual eloquence.

"Oh Lord, you kin see we're here to lay Bobby Gary, Slick Lindon, and Victor Brock to rest. Now Bobby, Slick, and Vic, they done died a quick enough death. They was killed 'cause they hung a man what stole from them that which they had stoled. 'Vengeance is mine, saith the Lord,' but Pinky's boys, they was too quick to do it fer you. So we give you Bobby Gary, Slick Lindon, and Victor Brock, you havin' made them an' all. If you accept them into your heavenly kingdom, your angels will surely sing, 'cause they had some good in them down under. If you don't take them, then to hell with them, 'cause there's nothin' them or us kin do about it now. Amen."

Aunt E. strewed a few wild flowers over Slick's mound and, shedding an earnest tear or two, she dabbed her cheeks with her scented handkerchief and sighed. "There goes the last of my ardent admirers."

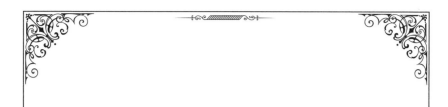

Chapter Twenty-Two

The day is done, and the darkness falls, from the wings of night,
as a feather is wafted downward, from an eagle in his flight.

HENRY WADSWORTH LONGFELLOW

arken cached Vic's fortune under the bed he shared with Emmy. He didn't feel at all original, but surmised that the obvious might be the best ploy to dumbfound Pinky's not-too-bright boys. His upper hand was that Jim and his gang continued to stupidly outsmart themselves. *Hadn't they fallen, months ago, for his fatal-illness ruse?* Larken was reminded that his wits were his mightiest weapon. He knew the gang was watching and would make a move any day for Vic's money. He prayed for Vic's recovery, not only for Vic's sake, but also for his own hide; he was the lone defender of the women. Parson was barely on his feet and still a little queer in the head. He was a bit of a nuisance, with his bright ideas of vengeance. He kept badgering Larken, stating that the

Lord was on their side, and was positively peeved with Larken's sick, halfhearted nods of enthusiasm.

Emmy's nerves were shattered, and she resorted to her childish tantrums when she discovered the treasure beneath their mattress. She envisioned what Jim and the boys would do to her in that bed and refused to sleep there. Larken's rebuttal shocked her sullen and speechless.

"It won't matter whether you're in this bed or on the parlor floor when they come after us."

Ivy did all she could for Big Vic, who still wandered in and out of consciousness for several days, with Lela and Parson hovering around him. Ivy put E. in charge of the bandaging and washing of Vic's wounds and returned to the kitchen to make up her bean soups and herbal broth "vitalizers." She sang her prayers sweetly, as if all was peaceful and normal. The melodious tones of her soul's cantatas wafted through the window and door into the tiny voice boxes of the birds and echoed through the hills behind Blakemore House. Ivy's singing, however, did not relieve the apprehension in the house.

Aunt E. nursed Big Vic with ardent determination and intuitive feminine care. She never once pushed aside Lela or Parson, or even Praiseworthy, but soothed the humans with a fairly optimistic smile and the dog with an assuring caress.

Parson shuffled through the wrinkled pages of his Bible, offering verse after verse of consolation and trust.

"Pray hard, girl. He's worth saving. He couldn't let nobody know you was his. They might've hurt you to git to him." Parson held Lela close to his side as he spoke to her and pointed his gnarled finger at their scripture lessons. Leaning her head back into the crook of Parson's arm, Lela looked up into his dear face and treasured the goodness that he taught her.

She put her hand over his on the page and pressed it and held it there while she affirmed what he taught her. "He done right. I forgive him."

Parson chuckled with the pleasure of a teacher's efforts, acclaimed by a bright pupil. "Of course you do. No sense in temptin' hell, darlin'."

Larken was touched and amused. As he listened to them, he wondered at their intimate simplicity. *Which was the elder or the younger of the two? Maybe Parson and Lela were ageless, like eternity.*

Larken had enough fret inside him for them all and was tired and bent with worry. He left Parson and Lela with their "Attitudes" and started outside for a while, to stretch his aching body and clear his befuddled brain. He passed Ivy and Emmy in the kitchen on his way out back. He was glad to see that Ivy had Emmy employed chopping garden leeks for her pungent, bubbling brew.

He marveled at Ivy's courage. With her strong faith, she had given Runner up to heaven. His own bereavement was selfish, a deep and scary chasm inside his gut. Without Runner, no wise discernment warded off Larken's hasty impulses with brotherly protection, no one assumed blame and feigned responsibility on Larken's guilty behalf. He felt let down and abandoned, his silly weaknesses uncovered, exposed and obvious.

Deep in thought, Larken wandered far past the garden, but stayed within hearing distance of Ivy's newly selected hymn from her vast repertoire, "Marching to Zion." *Of all things*, Larken thought. *What a lark*. His dark mood vanished. He laughed out loud with renewed vigor, cavorting in capricious circles and then straightening into rigid pose, keeping military time, ever forward to the beautiful City of God.

Larken smelled the Indian's presence before he saw him. Sickened, fearful nausea choked his swallowing. This was the inevitable dreaded showdown; the Indian had chosen the time and the place. Larken was the one the Indian wanted. He was to pay the price alone. Larken, worn out with the re-occurring nightmare and shame, was almost relieved that the day had finally arrived.

The phantom vision of a mounted Indian that night in

the lightning flash at Two-Hole Cave gave him prophetic warning, and he had mentally prepared his defense on the grounds of mistaken judgment. He prayed that he was dealing with a reasonable man. The Indians were reputed to serve justice and demand truth.

Larken kept his back to the Indian, humbly and fearfully avoiding what he knew would be a scornful and accusing countenance. He prepared to confront him momentarily, if he lived long enough to turn around. He hastened to voice his long-rehearsed appeal but was struck dumb before he commenced, halted by a powerful unearthly warning. Larken, heeding the uncanny voice, turned around and faced his adversary. He raised his hands heavenward in surrender, invocation, and affirmation. *The single eye of The Great Spirit sees and knows all.* Then he lowered his arms slowly and began his apology.

"I'm sorry about that other man, your friend. I shot him because I thought he hurt the women and my wife." Larken improvised with much grunting and gesturing, and then paused for an evaluation of his performance; but the red man's face remained stoic.

With everything to lose, he continued in a shaky, high-pitched voice. "Please understand how much I regret the death of your friend."

"Brother." The Indian spoke with a disarming fixed

stare on Larken. It seemed he had no eyelids, for they were held taut. The lids never wavered nor blinked, though the sun was fiercely blinding this time of day.

Larken's shameful regret overruled his fear, and he respectfully lowered his eyes and removed his hat in reply. "Oh God, he was your brother."

The Indian raised his left hand and spoke but one word. "Honor."

Larken could not move, even though he knew what was coming when the Indian approached him: some sort of ritualistic satisfaction, a duel for honor's sake. He recalled Lela's misquoting. "Vengeance is fine." At this moment, and in the predicament in which he found himself, she was, sadly, quite correct.

Using his teeth and his free hand, the Indian bound their right wrists together with an intricately beaded, leather strap. He produced a knife from his belt and offered it into Larken's left hand. Circling around and grunting, he thrust his knife at Larken with experienced accuracy.

Larken jumped back twice, to be missed by a fraction, but the third swipe cut through his blouse. Stammering in fright at the sight of his own blood oozing from a slight wound in his chest, he stood still in obstinate anger and refused to further parley.

Shaking, Larken shouted at the Indian, almost deafening him in their close proximity. "Oh, I see. We keep at this until one of us is dead. I've heard of this Indian bit. It's stupid, and it doesn't make sense. And I can't see what will be accomplished by it. And I'm completely inept with knives!"

Unaware that the drawing of his blood had satisfied the Indian's law of retaliation and that the challenge was over, Larken screamed into the Indian's ear. "And I'm no Indian."

His opponent, no longer guarded, protected his deafened ear with the free hand that held his knife, and Larken agilely knocked the upraised hand, sending the Indian's knife sprawling in the dirt. He quickly cut the strap and grabbed hold of the Indian's wrist, turning him around and pressing the knife to the Indian's throat.

Larken panted for breath and, in the closeness of their bodies, was respectfully impressed with the Indian's courageous calm and stoic resolve. His grip held firm while Larken contemplated his next move. Larken was amazed that he had the advantage. *What was he to do with this man who had stalked him for months? He had no grievance against him.* Larken released his captive and threw the knife into the mud.

The Indian's stone face contorted into a frown of utter surprise. His eyes questioned.

Extraordinary, those pupils, observed Larken. *Agates*

encircled with amber. "To answer your question, my friend
. . . honor."

Larken turned his back on the Indian and walked away.
Still fearful that the man might jump him, Larken looked
once over his shoulder. The Indian had vanished.

Larken headed slowly back toward the house, his spirit
lifted with relief and his body racked with exhaustion.
Parson had been watching and waited for him, crouched
down in the shadow of the kitchen steps. He handed over
Larken's gun, assuming it was loaded.

Parson cautioned Larken to squat down in the dark
area. Nodding his head toward the house, he whispered a
warning as he finished loading his own gun. "I'm not the
only one done seen you dancin' with the injun. When you
took off I followed you a bit, and I seen them congregatin'
up there behind that rock. Your injun friend interrupted
their earlier plans fer you. 'Cause, you see, now that they
think Vic's dead, you're the one they're after. Ya know, that
set-to with the injun jist might have saved you. I know fer
sure, it gave me the precious time I needed. I done moved
Vic an' barricaded them all in the dinin' room an' kitchen.
The Lord, he does work in strange ways, but mightily, an'
don't you ferget that. Emmy, she's been worried 'bout you.
That's her peepin' through the window."

Larken raised his head to look up, but Parson shoved

him down.

"Mr. Blakemore, I believe you got our money." Jim shouted out at Larken from the top of the ridge.

"It was Vic's." Larken shouted back. There was dead silence for a moment or two. Nervous as he was, Larken smiled at the thought of the idiots in conference behind the rock. *Jim didn't have much to work with, being the only brain in the crazy bunch.*

As if no time had elapsed, Jim continued. "And we was with him when he took it; it's ours now. Throw it out to me an' you an' your family jist might git outta here still breathin'.'"

"You can lose that notion right now. That money is Lela's." Larken had barely uttered her name when, to his and Parson's horror, they saw Lela standing spread-legged and defiant at the edge of the back-porch steps. Everybody's "little darling" stood tall, looking tough and mean.

She addressed Larken loud and clear, for all to hear. "I don't know what you done with my money, Larken, but you're gonna have to kill them an' me to keep it."

Parson kept his eyes unflinchingly on the men on the hill above. Whatever was discussed in the vicinity, he was not distracted; he concentrated his gun on the rock. He made a quick and important observation. "They have the frightful advantage of firin' down on us but, praise God, the sun's in their eyes."

Larken was dumbfounded at Lela's disloyalty. Chagrined, he whispered to her from the shadows beside and below her. "Lela, you can't think . . ."

She turned her head slightly to him. For only a moment Larken saw a pleading in her glance, though her lips were pressed tight and determined.

Lela shouted loudly once more in a fit of fury. "Mr. Blakemore an' everybody, I think whatever I want to. I heard you makin' plans to git yourself outta debt with my money. I only known you a while. I known these men all my life!"

Larken clutched Parson's arm for an answer, but Parson jerked away and would not avert his eyes from the hill. He did, however, respond to Larken's consternation. "She always done her own thinkin'."

The first shot fired from the top of the hill ricocheted off the rain barrel in front of Larken. The errant bullet creased Parson at the nape of his neck, but exposed Choirboy long enough for Parson to return fire, killing him instantly. From below and from above, all eyes watched the kid's body first crumple and then roll off the rock, breaking branches and stirring loose dirt in its descent into the gully at the base of the hill.

Jim and Mute squatted on the rim of the ledge, looking down. Jim yelled angry obscenities and, taking aim at

Larken, shot the gun out of his hand. Lela scurried into the yard to retrieve the gun, disregarding the screams of warning from the women inside the house. Praiseworthy's muffled barking emanated from the cupboard, where she was locked out of harm's way. Her sharp claws scratched frantically and dug deep into the wood of the door, loosening it at the hinges. She knew she had to get to her master.

The half-breed, Mute, stood in plain view, gaunt and suicidal, wailing primal high-pitched intonations over the death of Choirboy. With two-fisted barrels blazing, he fired wildly into the air, without regard, and then at them indiscriminately. Shots barely missed Lela, who lay pinned down on the ground. Parson crawled to her under fire and, straddling her prone form on his knees, took aim and killed Mute.

Jim swore. "Preacher, I thought I finished you off days ago."

Jim's last shot found its mark. Parson was dead.

The earth stood still. Lela screamed. She wept openly and looked longingly at Parson, engraving his countenance, even sweet in death, into her memory. She then removed her hat and covered his pallid face. Out of the silence came a splintering of wood, a thud and then the sorrowful whining of Praiseworthy as she broke free from the cupboard and bounded out the kitchen door and down the steps. The black fur on her back still bristled for attack, but she collapsed onto Parson's body with a terrible howl. And then all that was heard was the katydids chattering and a dickey bird singing its prophetic song from within the cool sanctuary of the oak tree.

Jim kicked pebbles aside with his boots as he walked, cocky and bemused, down the hill and into the yard. Vic's money was his; no one was left to demand a share.

Lela sat still, watching and thinking. She retrieved Larken's gun from under Parson's lifeless body and stealthily examined it. She couldn't fathom why it was empty, for to her knowledge Larken had never fired a shot. But, then, Larken's guns were always empty. She turned the thought over in her mind. *Maybe that's why he ain't dead.*

Parson said on her last birthday that she had reached the wisest age. He explained that she was still in her heavenly innocence, but teachable. Parson couldn't have gone far. His spirit, now free, remained with her. She squeezed her eyes shut to receive his instruction. When she opened them, Lela saw her daddy out of the corner of her eye. Just inside the back door, he was leaning on Emmy but he was on his feet.

Jim's gun was trained on Larken.

Lela stood up and waved her hand over Parson's body, as she spoke to Larken. "You caused all this. My daddy's dead 'cause of you. Parson, too."

"Mr. Jim!" Lela pouted her lips as usual to get her way and pointed her own gun at Larken. Jim was fascinated and totally taken in by her persuasive charm.

"Yeah." Jim drawled in response. He thought, *I might jist take her along with the money.*

Lela flipped her curls with her free hand and, back to business, issued her order to Jim. "Put yer gun down. He's mine to kill."

Damn, thought Jim. *She'll be somethin' else when she's full blown.* And Jim did as Lela requested; he lowered his gun and nodded to her. Lela knelt to the ground, allowing Big Vic to shoot over her head, and Jim fell dead.

Sobbing, Lela ran to Larken and her daddy, to comfort and to be comforted. "Now, who's gonna pray over Parson?"

Vic held Lela to him as she clung to his unsteady leg. He lifted her chestnut curls in his fingers and strung them out, appraising the exquisite color of each individual strand.

"You will. He taught you well enough."

Lela left Vic to Emmy and E. Ivy insisted he must rest. Lela returned to Larken, who knelt beside Parson; she, too, knelt down and took Larken's hand in hers. Larken was so sorry, but also so grateful. He had played no part in any way in the day's fateful drama. He could not boast of his wits. Larken recalled Parson's last advice to him. And

Parson had told him never to forget it. *How did it go? The Lord does work in strange ways, but mightily. Yes indeed,* Larken thought, *mightily.*

Attempting to lighten Lela's load with a bit of teasing, Larken prodded her with gentle sarcasm. "For a minute, I thought you were going to do me in."

Lela looked away from Larken toward the corner of the house. She seemed surprised for a moment. Her body stiffened, her lips trembled, and her eyes widened with fear. He didn't think his remark that caustic.

Then Larken heard the old, hatefully sinister, familiar voice. The nasal intonation registered forked tongues and tails in Larken's imagination.

Bates literally hissed when he spoke. "I thought the same thing, Mr. Blakemore."

Larken saw the women gathered at the dining room window. The fright on Emmy's face was unforgettable. Larken looked down at his unloaded gun lying next to Parson and thought, *Damnit.*

Larken spoke with utmost disgust. "You beast, you son of a bitch!" When Larken looked up to confront Bates, he was gone.

Lela whipped her head around and nudged Larken. Bates now stood at the dining room corner of the house, just outside the window and below the cowering women, who had shrunk back into the darkness to avoid detection by the monster. That side of the house positioned Bates above Larken; the yard sloped a bit, with the house poised on the side of the hill.

Bates smiled down at Larken and continued his earlier taunting. "Thought the girl would do my job. It'll be a good bounty what with you and that injun. Thought you'd killed him, huh? You jist winged him; I did him in and took a prize fer myself." To their disgust, Bates shook one of the two scalps on his belt. The other was Bobby's.

The women returned to the window, resigned to stand fast, whatever befell Larken and Lela, and they heard Bates' final remarks.

The projectile whirred with a whistle through the air. With an explosive thud it ceased its flight, imbedded in Bates' skull right between his eyes. His blood splattered the dining room windowpane. Lela screamed in uncontrollable hysterics.

Bates lay dead, with a brightly feathered tomahawk sticking out of the bridge of his nose. The look in his startled eyes was horrendous. The death was too ghastly even for Bates.

The Indian crossed the pasture and entered by the garden. He paused for a moment before Larken and bowed. They looked into each other's eyes unflinchingly, and the

Indian uttered the word that was now the bond between them. "Honor." He removed his brother's scalp from Bates' belt and handed Bobby's to Larken. Then he was gone.

Aunt E. went back inside the house to care for Vic and to explain to him what had happened. Emmy and Ivy went into the yard to console Lela. Emmy rocked and soothed Lela on the porch. They had to tether poor Praisewor-thy to a tree in the front yard until all the bodies were attended, especially Parson's. The dog knew; she barked and howled. Her silky black muzzle was matted the color of dung, streaked with her tears, and the whites of her eyes were wild and bloodshot.

A bugle blared as the United States Cavalry rode in per-fect column onto the Blakemore property. Fenton halted his men, and he and Harris dismounted and approached a very angry Larken.

"This, gentlemen, is exactly why the name of the U.S. Cavalry is what it is. Your timing stinks!"

The officers ignored Larken's lack of hospitality; they eyed with suspicion the carnage strewn about.

Captain Harris eyed Larken in disbelief. "Did you kill these men?"

Lela elbowed and squeezed in between them. "He sure did, an' there's more bodies up the hill. An' buried over there's two more."

Larken placed his hand on her shoulder. "Don't help me, honey." He spoke aside to Fenton and Harris. "If you'd gotten here . . ."

Lela, consumed with her wise savvy of the bent of the law, interrupted. "Larken, them dead men . . ." Larken caught her drift.

Captain Harris scratched his forehead, trying to recall and, remembering, recognized Larken's name. Poking a finger into Larken's chest, he thumped with his thumb. "Blakemore." He announced it as if Larken needed to be told his own name.

"My God," said Colonel Fenton. "It is Larken Blakemore. I guess the Point knew you'd turn bad. What'd you make it? A month?"

"Almost two, Fenton." Larken grinned. He had been through too much lately to mind a little bit of character assassination. Besides, at this juncture of his life some of his best friends were questionable.

"And now you're a murderer. Hard to imagine that after you were thrown out some of the cadets thought you'd never amount to anything." Harris resorted to sarcasm, but it was his way of probing. He was a good officer, but lacked the polished upbringing of the colonel.

"No, sir, he ain't no murderer." Lela spoke respectfully, as Parson had taught her. Respect led to one's advantage.

CHAPTER TWENTY-TWO

Parson said.

Colonel Fenton was charmed by the child. "But you just said there were more bodies."

"He's a hero. He's jist protectin' us." Lela didn't like the slurs these men had made at Larken, so she emphasized "hero."

Vic hadn't heard his name mentioned yet but still he nervously searched in his mind for a hiding place. *It has to be down here. I'm not able to climb the stairs.* He, Victor Brock, a man of action, was without recourse. He could neither run nor hide, but he could listen. What he heard swelled his big chest with pride. It was his daughter, Lela, outsmarting the U.S. Cavalry.

"Look." She dramatized, as she stoically lifted Jim's lifeless head by the hair. "This pretty one here's Jimmy Calahan; he's wanted in three states an' two territories. Papers on him come up to six-thousand five-hundred dollars."

Lela glanced at Larken momentarily, and he urged her on with a slight nod. "This here's Mute Starcloud. Total on him is nearly four thousand."

Colonel Fenton stepped over one body after another, taking head count while calculating bounty.

Aunt E. and Ivy eased down the back steps and stood huddled together, their eyes wide with horror but ever stalwart and alert.

Larken whispered to them. "We have a gold mine in dead bodies here."

Aloud, for the benefit of the Colonel and the Captain, Larken called out, "Good girl, Lela."

Lela continued her morbid introductions. Colonel Fenton scanned the yard with eyes aghast at the slaughter and murmured to himself. "I've seen wanted papers on all these men." Turning back to Lela, the Colonel removed his hat respectfully and inquired, "What about a man called Victor Brock?"

A buzzing insect covered the sound of Lela's momentary gasp for air; at the same time, Colonel Fenton came upon the sprawled body of Bates with a red-and-black-feathered tomahawk stuck in the forehead of his unidentifiable face. Fenton grimaced at the blood and gore.

"Nice touch, Blakemore. Was he a particular favorite?"

Lela stepped between Larken and Colonel Fenton. Her voice rose high and shrill and her little body trembled.

"God in heaven," moaned Larken. "The child has lost Parson, and now all of this death reeks about her."

Lela hollered, "Parson was right about cavalry men. They isn't very smart."

Captain Harris rebuked her possible discourtesy to his colonel. "What are you talking about?"

Lela flashed her eyes at Captain Harris and pointed

toward Bates' body. "Why, sir," she said, "this here's Victor Brock. I heard his papers good for ten thousand by hisself. That's 'cause he was the smartest, finest, cleverest, hold-up man in the history of the train and cavalry. But now he's a angel an' gonna be sweet an' honorable, jist like somebody's daddy would be, there in Heaven jist like God wants him to be."

Lela looked proud and rocked back and forth on the heels of her boots and laughed. Fenton and Harris looked put in their place and very uncomfortable. Seeing their chagrin, Aunt E. brought sherry to the officers; of course, decorum demanded that she serve the colonel first. He sat on the bench under the oak tree, and Lela perched upon Captain Harris' knee next to the colonel. Her infectious giggle continued at the end of her discourse and caused Fenton and Harris to laugh with her.

Lela was aware of Larken's inability to lie or, really, to even sidestep the truth. She loved this beauty of Larken's spirit and covered for him. (Lela was forever asking forgiveness for her fibs.)

Vic was listening from behind the kitchen door. He laughed quietly to himself. *Lord, that child's entertaining. Parson, you old rascal, you did yourself one helluva job. As for me, I know your reward will be great.*

Vic felt relaxed and strong. E. was a capable nurse.

Her very presence calmed him, and her strong and independent coaxing set into motion the early stages of his healing. She was lovely to see and, even when his eyes were shut, he detected her nearness through the delicate lavender scent of her. He steadied himself on his cane. *Believe I'll give those stairs a try.*

Outside, Colonel Fenton's head ached from the relentless sun and the liquor. It was time to tidy up the mess and take his tired men home to the Fort. He instructed Harris to call in the orderlies to see to the multiple burials. Fenton understood that one body, in the gully at the foot of the hill, was that of a young boy. The women indicated that some of the bodies went one place and some another. Whatever they wanted was fine.

Harris removed Lela's hat from Parson's face. "And this one?"

The child's face blanched white with grief. Harris was immediately sorry for the girl's obvious affliction, and then he noticed the clerical collar. He hadn't meant to be indelicate, especially not with Lela and especially not with a preacher.

"His paper run out the end of last year. He wasn't wanted fer nothin' too big. Cavalry payroll holdup was all."

Fenton and Harris exchanged looks of irritation at Lela's impudent disregard for authority. Lela stared at the body at her feet while she spoke. Slowly she turned her head away and, looking up at both officers, fixed a penetrating grief on their hearts, one that, try as they might, would never leave either Fenton or Harris.

Colonel Fenton glanced into the sky above her head with a thought tugging at his heart. *She has the face of a child, but those eyes have seen too much.* Fenton summoned his corporal, who was never far from his side. "Go with the girl and add all this up. We'll check it out when we get back to the Fort."

Left to themselves, the three West Point men shook hands. Fenton spoke to Larken. "I'll need an address where the government can send you what you're due."

Larken did not hesitate. "First City Bank of New Orleans."

Colonel Fenton raised his eyebrows and pursed his lips, obviously impressed.

Captain Harris shook Larken's hand once again, this time with admiration. "We all came to do what you seem to have done single-handedly, Larken."

"Well, Tom, I'm a helluva guy!" Larken grinned.

Chapter Twenty-Three

Sweet are the uses of adversity, finds tongues in trees,
books, in the running brooks, sermons in stones, and good
in everything.

WILLIAM SHAKESPEARE,
As You Like It

The family knelt in its usual gathering place, the small sacred spot east of the house. They frequented this silent corner of their world more often as the day neared for their final departure from the Roost. Back in April, Larken had reverently cleared the earth and rocks from under a grove of evergreen cedars to lay for Runner a cool place to sleep. In May he added the bodies of Slick and Bobby and then, finally, Parson.

That fateful spring, it seemed as if every species of tiny, defenseless bird built a nest in the safety of the rough acrid branches. The noisy chirps and the shrill whistles enlivened the grove during the day. At sundown, the birds sang sweet songs of praise, and when they tucked their heads in stillness, the mourning moans of the family were heard in the grove.

Blakemore House was a place of the past, a prison and a reform school for this time of maturing for Larken, Emmy, and even Aunt E. and Ivy. Its inhabitants no longer needed or heeded it; they were finally freed and impatient to go home. Since Providence had provided for Larken mightily, he made extravagant arrangements with Weems, giving back to him the house and all the contents. No single item was coveted by any one of them; they shut the house down and out of their thoughts. They packed only the most needed provisions, leaving ample space in the wagons for five adults, one child, and a dog.

The morning was clear and already hot on a day in the third week of June 1868. The wagons were loaded and the mules hitched.

Ivy and E. sat in the refreshing shade by Runner's grave. Lela held Praiseworthy in her arms, next to Parson's grave. Teary but brave, she ran her hand over the fresh earth.

Vic, leaning on his cane, rested his back against the tree trunk above Lela. As always, he cleared his throat before he spoke. Lela, cherishing this habit of his, looked up at him respectfully. Vic's rugged face was drawn with sadness, but his eyes were clear and earnest. He stretched his free arm out toward Parson's dirt-covered, crumbled mound.

His voice was stronger than it had been in weeks. Ivy and E. turned their heads toward him. Larken and Emmy, who had arrived to hurry them along, instead stood hushed as the big man spoke.

"I've never known another human, nor think I ever will, who so fulfilled his calling."

Larken hammered four crude little crosses, pounding them securely into the earth. Runner's stone carried the only formal identification, but it gave the year for them all. Larken had carefully burned the names on the crossbars: Bobby Gary, Slick Lindon, and Parson. When Larken asked for a full name for Parson, Vic replied simply, "That's how I knew him."

Larken stood back to survey his work and laughed. "Can you all just imagine these four rising up together on Resurrection morning! I'm damned envious. I want to be with them."

Ivy stood up and, nodding her head, smiled at Larken. "We ready to go?"

Larken put his arm around her thin, small body and gently whispered. "Yeah."

"Come on, Miss E." Ivy reached for her friend and pulled E. to her feet.

E. looked sadly at Ivy. "How can you leave him behind?"

Larken embraced them. "Since you three were born, you've been side by side. Then Emmy and I joined you. He's in our hearts. You can't leave behind someone you love."

E.'s and Ivy's tears flowed in unison, as the two women started up the hill arm in arm. "Our darling, Runner," E. sobbed.

Larken and Emmy helped Lela walk Vic slowly toward the wagons. They paused halfway for Vic to rest and looked back at the graves in the distance.

"You know, Larken," Lela addressed him while smiling impishly at Emmy. "If it hadn't been Parson or Big Vic what fathered me, I'd wanted it to be you."

Vic and Larken smiled at Lela. "Come on, Vic," Larken persuaded. "This leave-taking is drawing out, and we've got to make tracks before dark tonight." Larken leaned Vic's weight against his side. "That Lela's got us both hog-tied."

Emmy waited for Lela while she took her last, long look at Parson's grave. Lela had released Praiseworthy and there the dog lay, a black-and-white blanket sprawled over Parson.

Emmy attempted to console the forlorn child. "Oh Lela, honey, we know it's hard to leave all you've ever known and all the ones you love."

Lela interrupted Emmy. "I'm all right. You don't grieve fer them that's went on, 'cause they stay in your heart,"

Larken said.

Lela pointed down the hill at Praiseworthy. "It's her that worries me most. Course, lately she's taken a likin' to my daddy." Lela's whistle brought the dog bounding toward her. Flipping her pigtails over her shoulders, she headed for the wagons; Praiseworthy trotted along beside her.

Emmy sat fanning on the front seat of the first wagon. She wore as few clothes as needed to be decent and protected from the sun. *Not Aunt E.*, Emmy mused. *She's all dolled up and smelling sweet for Mr. Brock. He seems taken with her, like all the other men she's ever met. E. acts different than I've ever seen her. You know what they say about men and their nurses. That Ivy's a sly one, for all her hymn singing. I wonder if she sent E. to tend Vic on purpose. I'll never know; she won't boast for sure, and she's so tight-lipped.*

Emmy wondered why the others were taking so long, but she wouldn't turn around. She didn't want to look at Blakemore House anymore, now that her sights were pointed home. She smoothed her thin, once blue, now gray, calico dress over her hips and down her thighs, and tucked the hem up between her knees. She grunted with disgust. *I'm already perspiring and it's still early morning.* Emmy reflected, *Mother packed this dress for traveling over a year ago.*

Emmy had not received word from home since just after Easter. At that time Uncle Marcel was still living, but mostly bed-ridden. Her mother insisted that he continued to be "bright as a berry." Emmy sighed. *Poor Fetch*. Her heart ached for him. Larken had written them immediately after Runner died.

"Larken," Emmy mused, "I wonder if we'll be able to manage some manner of privacy on our way home. What with all the killing and burying, we've not . . ."

Larken hopped on the seat beside her and startled her. "We're ready to pull out," he announced with relief. "What were you saying?"

Emmy blushed. "Oh, nothing."

"Then you take the left mule's reins and hold tight," Larken ordered. "I'll check them all out just once more, and be ready to go. Aunt E. and Ivy are already flustered with their mules. I'll be right back."

Emmy felt the rocking and pulled on the reins of the left mule when Larken hoisted Lela and Praiseworthy into the rear of the wagon. Soon enough, both heads popped out the front at her. The hairy one's long pink tongue slurped her cheek, and the human child's strangling hugs shortened her breath. For the sake of their joyful exuberance, Emmy endured without complaint.

Larken made a few adjustments and reassured Ivy and

E. He stood at the back of their wagon and shared part of a departing cigar with Big Vic. The two took their last look at Blakemore House.

"You know, Vic, I performed my first honest day's work in this place." Vic was amused at Larken's irony. Larken looked him over. "You all right? You look somewhat piqued to me."

Larken gave Vic his turn on the cigar. One puff and Vic replied, "I'm fine." He took another puff and gave the cigar back to Larken. There was a moment's hesitation between them, and then Vic cleared his throat. "You're giving me a second chance."

Larken gestured toward Vic with the cigar, but Vic shook his head "no." Larken threw the cigar on the ground and snubbed it out with his boot heel. He gestured toward the front wagon in reply. "Naw, Lela's the one who gave you the second chance."

Vic nodded. "That she did."

Larken stuck his head through the back flap of the wagon. "Wowee! Someone has fixed you an eider-down beauty fit to ride all the way to Louisiana in royal comfort. I'll bet it was that dear little aunt of ours."

Victor Brock laughed out loud for the first time in weeks. "You win that bet."

"Now," said Larken, "just one more point of business.

CHAPTER TWENTY-THREE

Mr. Brock, sir, how am I going to hoist you up and onto your fancy bed?"

"Mr. Blakemore, sir, just cup your two hands, give me a foot up, and throw me in. It won't kill me; nothing else has."

After getting Vic settled, Larken went back to the other wagon and climbed up beside Emmy in a jovial mood. He grabbed the reins of the right mule and hallooed the wagons forward.

Dangling her legs out of the backend, Lela watched E. and Ivy's confused mules stagger one way and then the other, enjoying the banter. She spied a man at the side of the road and hollered. "See that man? He's bearded an' wearin' a sheet. Why, that ain't no man. It's Maw Haggar come to wave bye." Lela waved back and Praiseworthy barked.

No one else observed what Lela had seen. Larken and Emmy saw no one at the side of the road when the front of the wagon rolled by. E. and Ivy were too busy with their mules, and Vic was stretched out, hanging on for his life.

"Larken," Lela called up front to him. "You reckon Weems might give our house to Maw an' her boys? Maw's always had a hankerin' fer it, seein' how it joins onto her property. Hey, whatcha bet they call it Haggar House? I know Maw's been missin' Parson somethin' awful. Whatcha think?"

"I think you're right, Lela." Larken felt bad humoring

her, but he had his hands full with two wagons and four mules. He kept leaning out and looking back at E. and Ivy; he was concerned about Vic's discomfort inside the rollicking wagon. Besides, all Parson and Lela's talk about the Haggars had given him the creeps. He saw no sign of any one of them in the entire year in the Roost. He saw only their cows and the damaged fences torn down by the Haggar cattle. Lela claimed, as had Parson, that Maw and her boys were there the day they moved the furniture into Blakemore House. From Lela's description of Maw, Larken thought he couldn't miss her, unless he mistook her for a man and overlooked her. When he asked Weems about them, Weems looked at Larken as if he'd gone daft.

Emmy giggled with happiness. "I can't wait to get back home."

Larken kissed her on the cheek once, and then again, and then three times for good luck.

Emmy twittered all the more, bursting out with sheer joy. Lela's giggles erupted inside the wagon, and Praiseworthy barked and chased her tail. The wagon rocked and swayed and made the mules jumpy, so Larken curtailed their frivolity.

"You started it by kissing me," Emmy reminded him.

"Then, Mrs. Blakemore, the next time I feel the urge you must rebuff me. Yes, I want to get home and pay our debts. Fairlake Farm. I never thought it would sound so good."

Larken was in full accord with their unbridled outbursts. Considering what they had all been through, the eruptions were like an engine letting off steam to avoid an explosion.

Lela peeked through the opening, poised and compliant. She heard Larken's mention of Fairlake Farm, and her longing little heart pounded just at the name. In her mind's eye it must be the loveliest place on earth.

"Can me an' daddy come too?"

"Of course," Emmy answered. "Your daddy will need time to get better."

Lela scurried and hopped down out of the back of the wagon, closely followed by the big dog. They dodged E. and Ivy's mules and, darting around back, Lela scampered up into Big Vic's pallet. Praiseworthy followed to share the good news.

"We're invited to their family's place. Fairlake Farm!"

The pain in Vic's body took hold once more and he lay tired, spent with the exertion of the day. He tried to hide his misery from Lela, greeting his adored daughter and his old friend's "best friend" with glad welcome. He patted their hot little heads as he replied to Lela's breathless good news.

"Sounds respectable."

Aunt E. would much rather nurse her patient than fight with the mule. She didn't want to interfere with Lela and Praiseworthy's visit to Vic, but it concerned her. *Total rest is his cure. Besides, my hands are full of stubborn mule. Emmy ought to be here helping Ivy, and I should be back with Vic. But she just sits up there gazing at Larken. He could handle both their mules by himself.*

The wagon veered dangerously to the left, frightening Ivy. "Pull harder, E."

"I'm trying." E. scowled and glared at Ivy. E. was hot. Beads of perspiration streaked her painted cheeks, and her riding habit itched her.

"You'd better try harder or we'll zigzag all the way home. Poor thing," Ivy commiserated. "E.'s all out of sorts."

Aunt E. turned back to Lela and Vic in the wagon, and her mule pulled to the left again. "Lela, darling, hug your daddy and then take Praiseworthy and yourself back to the other wagon. The patient needs his rest."

Vic liked being looked after by E.

Lela's sweet "Yes, ma'am" as she hugged Vic's neck tickled Ivy. Ivy thought, *They make a right nice little family though Vic and E. will indulge her more like a granddaughter!*

Out loud Ivy said, "E. stop pulling so hard. Your mule's

gonna head back to the house if you keep pullin' like that."

"Pull. Don't pull. I don't know how to steer these things," E. quipped.

"Those things are mules. God's creatures, and you need to steer yours straight."

Larken listened to their bickering with amusement. For sure, E. was not born to this. He could make different arrangements and put Emmy with Ivy. One glance at Emmy's glaring green eyes convinced Larken that she had read his mind. He dropped the idea as foolish thinking for the hell he'd have to pay.

The mules clumped along in blessed silence with a reprieve, for finally not a word could be heard from the second wagon. A breeze blew over them, fluttering the wagon cover. It blew dust, but any stir of air offered some relief in the morning's stifling heat. A hawk screamed in its flight above them, and Haggar cattle lowed in a pasture nearby.

"How are they doing?" Larken lowered his voice to Emmy.

She looked back inside the wagon. "Praiseworthy's asleep, and Lela's rebraiding her hair and humming and daydreaming."

Larken motioned behind them. "I meant the ladies and their mules." Emmy leaned out. "Fine enough. By the time we get home, they will have gotten it right."

Aunt E. pulled tighter on the reins, and her mule cooperated with Ivy's, veering back into line behind Larken's and Emmy's wagon. The challenge was met. E. and Ivy smiled at each other and their progress.

With this arduous task accomplished, E. addressed the important, not too distant future. "Later, I want to go to Savannah. The Season will be starting soon."

Hearing E. and stirred with her own enthusiasm, Emmy called back. "Let's go to New York and have some new clothes made."

"Oooh!" Ivy piped. "I would love a new frock."

A cheerful voice from inside the wagon behind E. and Ivy interjected his own input into the discussion. Vic's voice seemed stronger than earlier that morning.

"We'll go to Savannah, too, Lela. You have lots of family waiting to meet you."

E. turned away from her mule-driving and peeked in on Vic. He returned her smile.

E. sat at her post behind the mule, flushed and silent in her delicious thoughts. *Savannah. Family. Lela's growing fast into a young lady. Vic will need to carry with them some female know-how.*

While E. mused, Lela squealed her response to Vic's suggestion. "You told 'em 'bout me?"

Lela wasn't just any ordinary kid. Vic meant it when he

answered her. "Honey, they are going to eat you up."

Aunt E. called out to Larken. "Stop at Weems' place on the way out. I'm almost out of chew, and I can't be expected to make this hellacious trip without chew."

Larken was not the least bit surprised when Ivy added, "I'd love some rock candy, too." Hadn't the order for chew always been followed with an order for rock candy? In the past it had been chew for two. Now Aunt E. must chew alone. The thought saddened Larken.

"This dust is enough to choke a body. Better get some brandy, too, Larken."

Emmy's request is right on cue, third down in the ordering. Funny thing, she always blames thirst and dust to justify her need for brandy. Larken answered. "I was going to make a short stop at Weems' even before you asked. Weems has a map for me, I'm sure you're all relieved to hear, showing the route we take once we're past Moab."

"It's important to keep Vic out of sight or hearing; Weems has a big mouth," Larken added. "I'm asking you, Aunt E., to stay with Vic. We're nearing Weems' place. We'll halt and let you climb in with him. Emmy, you hop up there with Ivy."

When Emmy grimaced, Larken patted her bottom and set her on the ground. He pledged to her, "It's a short haul and a one-time deal."

The stop at Weems' place was brief. Weems' red face colored purple, and he was effusive with praise for Larken's and his family's generosity in the gift of Blakemore House. He was so grateful that Larken felt that Blakemore House and its contents assured Weems' abundant security for life.

Maybe Lela was right. Larken now considered it highly possible that the Haggars were involved. For sure, cattle rustling was lucrative. *This is Colonel Fenton's problem, not mine.*

Weems' tiny eyes moistened with tears of remorse over the recent deaths, and he promised proper tombstones free of charge. Larken waved away the offer as unnecessary and too costly, a little alarmed at the idea of Weems poking around and uncovering Aunt E.'s dressmaker dummy in Vic's bogus unmarked grave.

Weems eyed them closely as they said their good-byes and walked with them into the front yard of his store. "Where's the charming Miss E.?" His little eyes darted furtively from one of them to the other.

Emmy paled, but Lela smacked Weems' puffy cheek with a loud and juicy kiss.

"Miss E., she's laid up in the back of the wagon with a sick headache. I'll sure tell her you sent your regards."

In the wagon, E. and Vic covered their mouths to stifle their laughter. Vic whispered to E. "Please don't be offended, but I'm the sick headache you're laid up with."

⚜

They rode south through the canyon of the Roost before noon. The sun beat down upon them mercilessly. But they were free. Free to go and free of debt. They rode silently, submerged in their longings and in their gratitudes.

Larken could not see one part of Emmy. She was shrouded under every available cloth and hat she could find. When she spoke, it was muffled. He grew tired of asking her to repeat, and she tired of repeating. Any exertion was trying on the disposition in this heat.

Emmy finally unfolded the bandanna from her lips and, looking mummy-like, offered her first coherent observation. "Geez, this sun's hot!"

Larken leaned his head back, with his face bared toward heaven. "Oh God above, not all the way back too!"

Emmy fumed. "Well, it is hot."

Larken ignored her. Aunt E. and Ivy were back in the midst of their mule dispute, and Larken determined to ignore them as well.

Emmy ventured yet another original thought. "It is just so dusty. I hate dust." She punched Larken with her mittened fist, rounded like a boxer's glove. "Don't you?"

Larken noted that her wrapped hands reinforced her

grip on the reins. At least she was better at this than the other two.

Emmy covered her mouth and muttered from under the cloths. "You do, but you don't want to talk about it?"

Larken spoke to himself or to anyone close enough to care. "I'm in the middle of nowhere with all these bitching women!" Then he arose and stood up in the wagon trough, shouting. "Runner, where are you?"

The echoing reverberation skipped like a fire bolt, bouncing here and then there off the boulders. It was an incredible phenomenon. Larken actually looked up to see if he could catch sight of his almost human echo, and that was when he saw the Indian.

His stance was amazing to behold, an imprint in Larken's mind for the rest of his life. He stood by the side of his paint horse, at attention in reverent pose, his feathered lance stretched arms' length skyward. It was an honorable tribute. Larken was glad that the Indian found him standing with equal respect, and he returned in reply a military salute.

Larken watched the red man mount his horse as they traveled past him, a movement quick and graceful, without effort. His tawny skin and raven-black hair radiated in the burning sun, as did the chalk-white mane, swishing tail, and brown, black, and ecru hide of his marvelous stallion.

The Indian's severe and somber stone face broke into a

broad grin; he threw back his head and laughed out loud.

Larken immediately saw the source of humor: Ivy and E.'s zigzagging mules. The Indian rode down the hill quickly and over to their wagon, still laughing; halting them, he made a momentary adjustment to Aunt E.'s mule's harness. He backed his horse and nodded, and they drew into precise file behind Larken. They all cheered and thanked him.

The Indian followed them to the canyon entrance. Lela waved until she could see him no longer.

In Memoriam:

As this book went to press,
the inspiration for Praiseworthy, Muncie, joined
Parson in their Heavenly Roost.

27 March 2008
Dallas, Texas